W9-DIJ-588

World of Hurt

Also by Richard Rosen

Novels
Saturday Night Dead
Fadeaway
Strike Three You're Dead

Nonfiction
Psychobabble
Me and My Friends, We No Longer Profess Any Graces

Humor
Not Available in Any Store

World of Hurt

A HARVEY BLISSBERG MYSTERY

RICHARD ROSEN

WALKER AND COMPANY
NEW YORK

First published in the United States of America in 1994 by
Walker Publishing Company, Inc.

Published simultaneously in Canada by Thomas Allen & Son Canada,
Limited, Markham, Ontario

Library of Congress Cataloging-in-Publication Data
Rosen, Richard Dean
World of hurt / Richard Rosen.
p.   cm.
ISBN 0-8027-3251-8
I. Title.
PS3568.O774W64   1994
813'.54—dc20   94-11253
CIP

Quoted material on pages 203–5 used by permission of: Tremlow S. W., Gabbard G. O., Sexual Exploitation
in Professional Relationships, ed. Glen O. Gabbard. Washington, D.C., American Psychiatric Press,
1989, pp. 71–87; the Division of Scientific Publications, The Menninger Clinic; and the
American Psychiatric Association.

BOOK DESIGN BY CLAIRE NAYLON VACCARO

Printed in the United States of America

2 4 6 8 10 9 7 5 3 1

For Lucy and Isabel

Acknowledgments

I'd like to thank some of the people whose help, advice, and expertise are reflected in the pages of this novel. That many of these people are good and, in some cases, lifelong friends makes me feel especially blessed. For their help on real estate issues, David Smith, Alan Orlowsky, Edward Orlowsky, Robert Rosen, and Joanne Kennedy; on legal issues, James Friedman, Mary Lawless, Robert Crosby, and David Thomas; on psychiatric issues, Arthur Zitrin, Irwin Hirsch, James Mulry, and Rachel Ritchie; on issues of criminal law enforcement, Special Agent Vincent Sullivan; on environmental issues, John Chamberlin and Michael Orloff; for her skills as a party planner, Jane Hicks; and for their generous editorial, spiritual, and practical support along the way, James Atlas, David Bloom, Veronica Bowden, Lincoln Caplan, Charles Dawe, Tom Friedman, George Gibson, Gail Hochman, Robert Lescher, Stephen Molton, Michael Seidman, Stephen Schiff, Paul Solman, Philip Snyder, my parents, and, as always, Mac.

Suburban Chicago

1

TALL ROADSIDE SIGNS advertising everything from formal wear to Vienna Red Hots couldn't contradict the great flatness of what the local disc jockey on the radio in the Lincoln Town Car rental referred to as "the Chicagoland area."

It had been farmland forty years before, but now the litter of American culture lined the old county road parallel to the expressway that took Harvey Blissberg toward Garden Hills: German car dealerships, windowless surf 'n' turf restaurants, spanking new strip malls, low glassy corporate headquarters. Here and there among the new structures, like destitute relatives lurking at a family picnic, was a seedy bowling alley with defunct neon or a Soft-Serve drive-in with tattered photographs of huge sundaes taped in the canted windows.

Harvey stifled a yawn—with unnecessary politeness, since he was alone in the car—and tried to imagine the hotel room that lay ahead in the midwestern dusk. It was after eight and still not dark enough for headlights. He glanced at the directions he had scrawled on a Post-it stuck to his dash—"1½ mi past Scrub-A-Dub car wash on right"—and rubbed his temples.

The pain in his brain was due mostly to this plain. He had come here, he was convinced, against his better judgment. It was now only three days since he had picked up the phone in Cambridge to hear a voice say: "There are four Golden State Warrior jerseys hanging in the Oakland Coliseum. Whose are they?"

"Hello, Norm," he had said wearily, "how are you?" When Harvey was still in the majors, his brother, Norman, professor of English at Northwestern University in Evanston, Illinois, tormented him with late-night calls relating one obscure baseball statistic or another he had computed in his spare moments. Norm knew more about Harvey's numbers than Harvey did. Now that Harvey had retired to become an investigator—no jersey hanging in the rafters, just the pension—Norm like to punish him with sports trivia.

"C'mon. You'll never get all four."

"Rick Barry," Harvey said.

"That one's obvious." Norm sniffed.

"Nate Thurmond."

"Two," Norm said. "But that's all you're going to get."

"Al Attles."

"I was wrong. I'm impressed. But you'll never get the fourth. Even Harold Nash over in sociology couldn't cough up the fourth."

"Tom Meschery."

His brother was silent for a moment. "I'm stunned."

"Norm, you forget you're dealing with a professional."

"Yeah, well, anyway, listen, speaking of professional status, I've got a problem here that could use your, uh, attention. Is there any chance you can drop what you're doing and come out here?"

"Excuse me?"

"Something happened about six weeks ago. A friend of mine"—he cleared his throat—"was, uh, murdered. Up in Garden Hills. You know, that's a suburb north of here."

The abrupt transition from sports trivia to homicide left Harvey disoriented. "A friend of yours? Murdered? My God, Norm. Why didn't you tell me about this before?"

"I guess we haven't talked in that long."

"Can't be." But it was. They had never gone this long without a phone call. Harvey felt a stab of abandonment. For the past year he had felt himself drifting quietly away from the world he once knew. One college friend of his was dead at thirty-eight from a virus that ate his heart; another was gone with cancer. The elements were dispersing. "I'm sorry, Norm," he said. "Who was it?"

"A fellow who was part of my regular basketball game at the Y in Winnetka for the last three years. His name was Larry Peplow. A real estate agent."

"What happened?"

"He was shot once in the head near some luxury housing development in Garden Hills. But look—I think the local cops are in way over their heads. It's the first homicide there in something like a decade. These North Shore cops—you know, they do a lot better when it comes to parade routes."

"You know something the cops don't?"

"Not really. Larry and I were buddies on the court. I rarely saw him outside the Y. But, listen, he was this charming, bright guy." As if murder victims who were charming and bright deserved a higher-quality investigation. "You know what it's like, Harv, these locker-room relationships."

"Yeah."

"There was a bond. Besides, Larry was the only guy who'd look for me on the fast break."

"He must've been a good friend, Norm, to pass *you* the ball on the fast break." Harvey couldn't pass up the cheap joke at his older brother's expense, but Norm wasn't listening.

"It's weird, Harv, that you can see a guy two, three times a week for years and, you know, not even know if he was married. Which it turns out he wasn't."

"I assume you've talked to the cops—"

"Women have to know every damn thing about you, but all guys have to do is share a few dirty jokes in the locker room and we're blood brothers."

"Norm, did you talk to the cops?"

"Yeah, sure, a few of us went up there for questioning. But *they* told *us* stuff. Not much, though. He was pretty reclusive. He was forty-four, lived alone in a rented house in Coleridge, one of those fat suburbs up on Lake Michigan, just east of Garden Hills. Where he was killed. He's got a mother living in upstate New York somewhere. Let's see, he came to the Midwest from Maine four years ago and worked at a real estate agency in Coleridge."

"That's it?"

"That's it. I called the detective a few days ago to see how the investigation was going. Fellow named Walter Dombrowski. He said not to get our hopes up."

"Meaning what? That it was a senseless, random murder?"

"I don't think so. Anyway, robbery wasn't the motive. His wallet wasn't touched. Apparently, the only thing missing was the back of his head."

"He was shot from the front?"

"In the face. Can you imagine? What a fucking way to go."

"No sign of struggle."

"I don't think so, but I don't know for a fact."

"So it was someone he knew?"

"I don't know. You'd have to ask Dombrowski about it."

"Ask Dombrowski? Wait a second. I didn't say yes to this."

"Well, you're asking all these questions, Harv."

"You want me to drop everything and fly out there and look into this? Some guy, it turns out, you didn't know all that well?"

"For chrissakes, Harv, I played ball with him for three years! You can't just let a guy take a bullet between the eyes in a wheat field somewhere and say, 'Okay, that's done, got to get on with my life.' Besides, we took up a collection for you."

"Who did?"

"Some of the guys who played with Larry."

"I can't take money from my own brother."

"Don't worry, I didn't kick in any dough. I'm offering you free room and board for as long as you're out here. Linda redid the attic into a guest room. Of course, I don't know how you feel about tartan bedspreads."

"Look, Norm, I'm not saying yes, but if I did this, I couldn't stay with you and Linda. I'd need a place of my own. Some crummy motel in the area."

"You and your *nostalgie de la boue*. There *are* no crummy motels up there. You're talking about a string of suburbs where a BMW's an impulse purchase. Look, Harv, as to the actual numbers we're talking about—I don't know what your rates are—"

"Don't worry about that."

There was a pause during which Harvey knew that the deed had been done.

"Thanks, Harv. It means a lot. Maybe you could bring Mickey."

"Can't. She's busy producing a documentary for public television about gender and competition."

"She does like to tackle the big projects, doesn't she?"

"None bigger than me."

" 'I,' Harv. It's 'I,' not 'me.' "

"Thank you, Norm."

"Don't mention it. Are you guys ever going to get married or what?"

"And let matrimony ruin a good relationship? When the passion's gone, Norm, that's when we'll make it official by getting hitched."

"It's still that good, huh?"

"That good? Are you kidding? At night sometimes we just sit around looking deeply into each other's adoring eyes and wondering if two people ever felt this kind of love before." It was a relief to be joking.

"You're a lying sack of shit."

"Well, at least the part about sitting around at night is true." In the last year he and Mickey had landed somehow in adulthood. And all they had to show for it, he thought at times, was a couple of aging Siamese cats.

"Anyway," Norm said, "you know what Kierkegaard said. He said that marriage marks the passage from the aesthetic stage to the ethical. Of course, that's not an exact quote."

"No problem, it's close enough," Harvey said. At moments like this, Harvey liked to recall that he had once been able to hit ninety-five-mile-per-hour fastballs over four hundred feet.

Now, in the fading June light, he passed another mall and resisted the urge to pull in. His dazed, aimless, compulsive wandering in discount stores had been one of the symptoms that drove him three months before to Dr. Ellyn Walker in Lexington, Massachusetts. It was as if he would suddenly wake up and find himself going through the men's clearance racks at T.J. Maxx with the distinct impression that he was avoiding his life. He rarely bought anything. Once Dr. Walker had asked him what he was looking for; when he conceded that Caldor or Kmart probably didn't stock it, she had said, "But whatever it is, you'd like to get it at a discount." He drove on, grimly; the mere thought of him, an ex-jock, in therapy still shamed him a little.

The empty lobby of the North Shore Suites Hotel was covered with new periwinkle carpeting and sprinkled with scalloped tub chairs in pale peach. It was not crummy at all, yet its very newness was pleasantly tawdry. The desk clerk, a young blond woman in a French braid and identified as Shari by a plastic plate pinned to her breast, called up his reservation on the screen and spoke without raising her eyes from the humming terminal. Harvey took advantage of this to study her soft, wide Scandinavian features.

"I see you have an open-ended reservation. Do you know yet how long you'll be with us?" "Long" came out "lawng."

"No."

"I'll put you in room four-thirty-four for four nights, but I'll have to move you if you're staying longer."

"Fine."

She looked up with a smile. "Whom are you with?"

"I'm self-employed."

Harvey recited the address of the stucco house in Cambridge that he and Mickey shared and where he lived, he sometimes felt, like an undereducated interloper among all the glib professors, management consultants, and public television producers.

"Sign here." She slid the registration card under his nose, adding, "Nice shirt."

Harvey glanced down at his Hawaiian shirt covered with palm fronds and repetitious purple sunsets. "Thank you." In the time it took him to scrawl his name, he experienced a detailed sexual fantasy involving himself, Shari, and a complimentary bottle of shampoo. Lately he had been suffering not just the usual reflexive urges but desires as specific as the taste for a delicacy.

Without the slightest indication of having participated in Harvey's reverie, she held up a coded white card and explained to him how it worked. "Welcome to the North Shore," she said.

"North Shore?" he said, returning the desk pen to its plastic base. "This implies water."

"Lake Michigan's about two miles east of here."

"Let me ask you a question."

He could see her tense a little. "Sure," she said. It sounded like "Shar."

"Are you familiar with a housing development around here called Rimwood Estates?"

"No, I haven't heard of it."

"It's right here in Garden Hills."

"There've got to be a thousand new developments around here. I live in one myself. Lakeview Acres."

"You can see Lake Michigan from it?"

"No, but there's a small man-made lake on the property."

"That's the lake that inspired the name Lakeview Acres?"

"Are you making fun of where I live?" she asked.

"I wouldn't dream of it. I was just curious."

"You're very inquisitive."

Was this a rebuke or a come-on? "Well, you seem like a friendly person."

"I hope you're not confusing my midwestern openness with something more."

Rebuke, he thought, and backpedaled. "You misunderstand my intentions."

"Anyway"—she held up her left hand—"I'm wearing a wedding band."

In truth, he was relieved. A few months of psychotherapy had shortened his leash, not that he had strayed in years. "I have," he said, leaning down for his bags, "a high regard for the sanctity of marriage."

"So you don't need, like, an ulterior motive to ask this many questions?"

"It's part of my job."

"What are you, a market researcher?"

"In a manner of speaking. I'm researching who might've murdered a man a few weeks ago at Rimwood Estates."

Her green eyes widened. "Oh, I read about that. What does that make you, a detective?"

"Yeah, but that's our little secret, Shari. Anonymity is essential to my work."

"In that case, I hope you've brought another shirt to wear. Room four-thirty-four. Enjoy your stay."

In his room he pulled the heavy curtains aside and looked out over Edens Expressway. It was almost dark now, but the identical rooftops of a residential development were visible through breaks in the lush trees. He unpacked, marked his new territory by taking a leak in the *faux* marble bathroom, and admired the complimentary bottles of shampoo, conditioner, and hand lotion arranged on the glass shelf.

Then he went to the bed to call Lieutenant Walter Dombrowski, chief of homicide for the Garden Hills Police Department.

"Lieutenant, this is Harvey Blissberg."

"Yes sir."

"I spoke to you from Cambridge yesterday."

"Yes sir."

"I'm in Garden Hills right now."

"Congratulations."

"Any breakthroughs in the Peplow case since we talked?" Maybe they'd collared someone and he could turn right around and fly back to Boston.

"No sir."

"Well, as I said to you yesterday, Lieutenant, I'll do my best not to get in your way."

"That would be appreciated."

"Are we still on for tomorrow morning?"

"I've had to rearrange my schedule a little. I can't see you till noon."

"I see. All right. And I can take a peek at the case file?"

"It can be arranged."

Harvey reached for the hotel notepad and cocked his pen. "Lieutenant, maybe you can give me the name of Peplow's former employer. Now that I've got some free time in the morning, I thought I might start with him."

"Her. Virginia Schmauss. Schmauss and Weevens Realty in Coleridge."

"And that's where Peplow worked the last four years?"

"Yes sir."

"Thank you. I have one more question."

"What's that?"

"I'm over here at the North Shore Suites Hotel."

"Fine establishment."

"And I was wondering if you could recommend a good place for a late dinner."

"What do you like to eat?"

"I'm partial to seafood."

"Then here's what you want to do, son. Get on Edens Expressway going north, get off at Sky View Road and go west about four miles—you got that?—and just past the light at Sawyer you'll see a restaurant on the left. Clarence's, it's called. Go in there and order yourself a piece of Lake Superior whitefish."

Harvey wondered why he had been demoted from "sir" to "son." It made the cop's earlier deference suspect. "What if I ordered something else?"

"You're not going to order something else, son. You're going to order the whitefish. Lake Superior whitefish. With a nice baked potato. You tell Clarence that Walter sent you."

"Will do."

"And the bread pudding is excellent. I'll call Clarence and make a reservation for you. And another thing, son."

Harvey was sure he was going to recommend an appetizer.

"When you're on Sky View going west, you're going to pass Behnke's Nursery on the left. Just a few hundred feet past it, on the right, you'll see a brick gate. That's the entrance to Rimwood Estates. In the field west of the houses, that's where Laurence Peplow was killed."

"Oh."

"But I don't want you to stop in there tonight, son."

"Why's that?"

"Why's that? Because Clarence's closes its doors at nine. It's now eight-thirty-five. If you don't drag butt you've got just about enough time to make it."

2

THE NEXT MORNING, Harvey could see the money in Cole-
ridge's business district. It was parked in the diagonal spaces in front
of the two-story Tudor-style storefronts: Mercedes, BMWs, Jaguars,
Porsches, Olds Cutlasses, Buick Regals, Saabs, Infinitis. Harvey
wondered if they impounded lesser vehicles at the town line. Schmauss
& Weevens Realty occupied its own prime one-story brick building
two blocks off the main thoroughfare. Harvey had to wait in the fern-
cluttered vestibule only a moment before Virginia Schmauss appeared
before him, moving silently in a shirtwaist silk dress, shaking a dozen
bracelets down her wrist to announce her presence. It was obvious she
had made a profession out of being formidable.

"Mr. Blissberg," she said.

"How do you do?" he said, rising to take her well-kept hand with
its red fingernails as thick and curved as pistachio shells. Her frosted
hair gave the impression of being freshly polyurethaned. She was sixty
going on immortal.

"Come in, come in, come in." With a game show hostess's
gesture, she swept Harvey ahead of her through an office filled with
desks at which middle-aged women were already, at nine in the
morning, working the phones.

When they were seated in her private office she said, "So you're a private detective."

"That's right."

"Well, I suppose those jokers over in Garden Hills need all the help they can get. Who brought *you* into this thing?"

"My brother. He played basketball with Peplow." "My brother" made it sound so trivial—not an actual job but a family favor. He changed the subject by gesturing toward the agents through the office's interior window and saying, "Doesn't look like the recession's hurt your business one bit."

She sighed elaborately. "Mr. Blissberg, you're a detective. People must lie to you all the time, so you'll understand. There's a phrase in this business: 'Buyers are liars.' The vast majority of people looking for a house simply don't know what it is that they want. Haven't a clue. They tell you they're looking for a three-bedroom Tudor, and after you've shown them a few, they decide it's really a colonial they want, as long as there's a powder room. You show them a colonial with a powder room, but now they say the most important thing is a kitchen with a sight line to the living area so Mom can keep an eye on the children while she's cooking dinner. That's when it occurs to them that a more open split-level would better serve their needs. And some couples, it turns out, don't really want a new house at all. They're just looking for one as a substitute for a new and improved marital relationship. Do you understand the psychology of that?"

"Yes," Harvey said. He often wondered if there was a sign on his forehead that read: "Talk as long as you want. Don't feel any pressure to get to the point."

"So the fact is that we look a lot busier than we are. Now," she continued in an impressive, throaty voice, "when they start out, most agents are frustrated by this behavior. Looking at it from a cost-benefit point of view, agents waste an enormous amount of time with clients. But when you understand that this is a service business—you're catering to the complex psychological needs of the client, and only incidentally sometimes to actual real estate needs—*then* you are ready to be an effective agent. People don't just buy houses. They buy feelings. And they buy the agent as well. Understand, I'm not saying a good agent can sell someone a house they don't want. I'm saying that a bad agent can prevent someone from buying a house they do want."

Schmauss paused to feel her dome of hair. "Now Larry wasn't in the least bit surprised to discover to what extent clients, especially in affluent suburbs, use the house-buying process to act out deeper issues." Harvey relaxed at the mention, finally, of Peplow. "He understood intuitively he was selling *people,* not property. He loved the phrase 'Buyers are liars' because he understood human nature. Why? Because he had a terrific advantage over most people in this business. What was that? He had been a psychotherapist. You knew that, of course."

"No, I didn't." Had Norm forgotten this detail or had he, incredibly, not known it? Harvey suddenly felt the weight of all he didn't know.

"Oh, yes. Larry had been a shrink of some sort back east. I remember quite clearly Larry sitting in the chair where you are now. It was maybe a year after he started here and he was doing very well. We were just talking and I told him how pleased I was with his performance, and he told me, he said, 'I was a psychotherapist for many years'—I hadn't known this before—'which means,' he said, 'that I was in the business of dealing with people's masks. I was in the business of gingerly removing some of the veils that conceal people from themselves.' 'Gingerly removing the veils'—that's the phrase he used. He said, 'Of course, I was also in the business of leaving some of the masks right where they were, since some of them are tragically necessary for survival and shouldn't be touched because they have become part of the face.' Isn't that a remarkable way to look at it?"

"This does not sound like your ordinary real estate agent."

"He then said something that left no doubt in my mind that he would be very successful in this business. He said, 'A person's home is the biggest and most public mask of all.' And I have to tell you that I had never heard it put quite that way. He said, 'When I sell someone a house, I'm not selling them some true expression of themselves. I'm selling them a new mask to more effectively contain and conceal the dirty details of living.' "

"Wow," Harvey said.

"And, of course," Virginia added, "he wasn't simply referring to the objects people put in their houses. And I don't think he was just referring to all the dirty little secrets that families have, the nasty little things that people in families do to one another behind closed doors. I believe he was talking about the purpose of a beautiful home being, at the deepest level, a way to make up for the fact that we're all gradually falling apart. Physically crumbling. Losing our beauty and our youth and our dreams. That's what he meant by 'the dirty details of living.' That a lovely home, if you can afford it, takes the sting out of mortality. You're taking notes."

Harvey looked up from his notebook. "Just in case there's a midterm. Did he fit in all right?"

"Everyone adored him. He was one of my best horses. A terrific salesman. He had a particular knack with transferees. You know, every year three hundred thousand families are moved by corporations, and our market gets more than its share of them with so many businesses moving up here to the Tri-State Corridor. All these beleaguered pawns of the corporate chess game. But unlike most buyers, at least these men and their wives know what they want and they want it right away. To them, it's just another in a long line of temporary housing. It's virtually a science. They fly in for a couple days, you pack them into your car, and head for the subdivisions. Middle managers are looking for twenty-five hundred square feet minimum, upper management for three thousand. Master bedroom on the first floor, especially if the guy's older and has already hauled his ass around the country a few times. I tell you, Harvey, when the residential market goes soft, they're our meal ticket. There I go again."

"But I'm beginning to enjoy it."

"'Maybe I've been conducting too many real estate seminars," she said with a rich, snorting laugh.

Harvey leaned forward, elbows on the edge of her desk. "Virginia, when you say he liked the phrase 'Buyers are liars,' are you trying to tell me something?"

"Like what? All I meant was, Larry was very smart about selling."

"Are you saying he was good at manipulating people's emotions?"

"That would be the least charitable way of describing his abilities in this area. "As I mentioned, Harvey"—his name suddenly sounded impersonal, like a telemarketer's stilted technique—"an agent can't make someone buy a house they don't want. If that's what you're driving at."

"Is there something you know about Larry Peplow that you're afraid to tell me?"

"No."

"Virginia, surely you must've devoted some thought to how Peplow might've put himself in a position to be murdered."

"Oh, I have, Harvey."

"Well, then, did any of his clients have a reason to be upset with him?"

Schmauss swiveled in her chair to gaze out the window, past the ficus in the corner, into a bank parking lot.

"Hello," Harvey said, "are you there, Virginia?"

"There was one—oh, I don't know—impropriety," she said, her back to him.

"Yes?"

She rotated back to face him, saying with theatrical chagrin, "Look, I want you to know I absolutely don't approve of this sort of thing, and I let Larry know it in no uncertain terms. But the damage had already been done."

"Go ahead."

She shook her many bracelets down her wrist again. "This was about three months ago. Larry had been showing a house that we were the listing broker for to . . . let's call them couple A. They offered the asking price. The market's softened now, but this was just at the end of the boom and we were still getting asking-price offers. Now"—she flattened both palms against her desk blotter—"that very same day, another couple, couple B, who had been shown the house by an agent at another firm, also made an asking-price offer, on paper, with a thousand-dollar escrow check, which was conveyed to Larry by the other broker, which is customary. No problem, right? Larry simply conveys both offers to the seller. Except—and forgive me if you already know this—if you're an agent for the listing broker and you sell a house to one of your own prospects, you get a six percent commission—on the first hundred thousand, at least. If you sell to a buyer who's been brought to you by another agent, you split the commission with that broker and take three percent. This was a high-end house and the *difference* in the commission would be substantial. Of course, the agent splits *his* share with the agency, but we're still talking about a significant chunk of change for the agent himself. You follow?"

"Right behind you."

"So Larry did something unacceptable. They were both qualified buyers, but he didn't present both offers to the seller. He presented only his own client's offer, and they got the house. He told the other agent the seller was away for a couple of days. He closed his eyes, did the wrong thing, and doubled his payday. It's not the first time something like this has happened, I can assure you."

"And couple B discovered they'd been stiffed?"

"Ah." She held up a forefinger. "Couple A and couple B belong to the same country club. Need I say more? Mrs. A mentions to Mrs. B that they recently bought such-and-such a house and, this being the competitive North Shore, the purchase price is mentioned. So Mrs. B hits the roof, because she and her husband had made the exact same offer. No small thing. There's a saying around here, Harvey. 'In New York, it's what you do. In L.A., it's what you drive. In Chicago, it's where you live.' Suddenly I've got couple B in my office screaming at me. 'How come we didn't get the house? How come we didn't get the house?' I promised couple B I'd look into it. I went to Larry, who admitted what he'd done, and not without remorse. He'd pretended not to have received couple B's offer." She sighed. "I can't believe I'm telling you all this."

"Let me ask you something. Did couple B suspect Peplow of getting their offer first, then calling couple A, his own client, in order to elicit a bid from them—and a higher commission for himself?"

"No. And neither did I. I don't believe he would've been capable of that degree of treachery. In fact, I asked him that. He said he hadn't."

"So let me get this straight," Harvey said. "Larry's crime was limited to not conveying B's offer, so he could get the higher commission by selling the house to couple A?"

"Right."

"He didn't use B's offer as leverage to get a higher bid from A, therefore even more commission money for himself?"

"Right."

"A crime of omission, not commission?" Harvey suggested. "Did you tell the Garden Hills police about this?"

"No. No, I didn't."

"But why not?"

She cleared her throat. "Well, I didn't bring it up with the cops because—"

"Did you want to protect Larry? Even though he's dead?"

"No. Because I was protecting myself. If this thing had ever gotten out and gone before the North Shore Board of Ethics, or ended up on someone's desk down in Springfield at the Department of Education and Registration, Larry might've lost his sales license, and

Schmauss and Weevens could've ended up on the rack. So I called couple B back on the phone and told them I'd discussed their situation with Larry, and that the seller had considered both offers and made his choice, based on financing. There was nothing more I could do."

"You lied."

"I fell short of telling the whole truth."

"Couldn't couple B just call the seller to verify what you'd told them, and found out you were lying."

"No."

"Why not?"

"Because I personally called the seller, explained this unfortunate oversight, and the seller graciously agreed to corroborate my story. So whether couple B called the seller or not, and I don't know if they did, there was no one left to tell them the truth."

"You really went to bat for the guy."

"I valued him as an agent. I didn't want to lose him. I don't mind telling you that. Not that I'm proud for a moment that I lied to save his butt. But let me tell you, Cookie, this couldn't possibly have anything to do with his murder."

"Why's that?"

"Because, while buyers may die a thousand deaths over the purchase of a new house, they just don't kill agents. Because if this couple—"

"What's their name, by the way?"

"Upchurch. Look, Harvey, if the Upchurches had continued to suspect Larry of unethical conduct, surely they would've gone ahead and reported it, and it would've been investigated. Which they didn't and it wasn't. And that's why I neglected to inform the police. But since you asked." She let out a breath she seemed to have been holding inside for weeks. "You think it's possible that people would kill over something like this? Without first going through other channels?"

"You'd know a lot better than me."

"You'd be wasting our time to make anything out of it, but be my guest." She produced a phone book from her desk drawer and found their address and phone number with a loud turning of pages that involved much licking of her index finger. While Harvey wrote down the information, she said, "You'll keep me out of it, of course."

"Of course. Now, speaking of improprieties, Virginia, and I'll be very blunt, do you know if Larry was sleeping with anyone's wife?"

"Wife? No, that never occurred to me."

"Well, you know, single guy, all these women."

"Well, they don't call suburbs 'bedroom communities' for nothing, do they? Anyway, he dated. That much I know. The only girlfriend I know for a fact he had was someone named Lynn. A child. A lovely child, but a child. The word 'willowy,' it was invented to describe her. Have you spoken with her?"

"You're the first person I've talked to, outside of my brother. And he doesn't seem to know anything."

"There were a couple of women who came to pick him up here at work. No one I recognized. And I wasn't looking for wedding rings."

"He get along all right with the others in the office?"

"I never had any complaints."

"All right. I'm staying at something called the North Shore Suites Hotel, if any other ideas occur to you." Harvey looked at his notes. "This house the Upchurches wanted to buy. What development was it in?"

"That's the thing," Virginia Schmauss said. "An unfortunate coincidence."

"What? What's the thing?"

"It's in Rimwood Estates."

"Where Peplow was found murdered?"

"Yes."

"You were going to let me walk out of here today without volunteering that information?"

"Cookie, you don't think that *if* this sweet couple had it in them to kill Larry, that they'd be stupid enough to do it within a few hundred feet of the house they wanted so badly?"

"Virginia," he said, closing his notebook and getting to his feet, "I just want to be sure you're on my side of the street here."

"I'm with you, Cookie," she said, rising as well with a shifting of silk and a clatter of bracelets. "Because there's nothing worse for the real estate market than a high unsolved crime rate."

3

LARRY PEPLOW, IT turned out, had rented a house just six blocks away from Virginia Schmauss's office on Tander Avenue, the main thoroughfare, as it led out of the business district, and Harvey walked there under a blue June sky with high cirrus clouds like drops of cream in a glass of tinted water.

Once, in a moment of presumptuous self-reflection, he had told a *Boston Magazine* reporter doing a feature on local private detectives that he was in the "information business." But it was true. Information was his capital. As he walked east on Tander he felt better than he had an hour ago for the simple reason that Virginia Schmauss had volunteered under no particular pressure that Larry Peplow had stiffed some people named Upchurch. However, there were three kinds of information: good information, bad information, good information that was useless. The last was like Monopoly money. And this information—the aggrieved Upchurches—was that kind. Virginia Schmauss, of course, was no dummy. Even if the Upchurches just happened to be capable of murdering Peplow, or capable of hiring someone to do it for them, in the real world why on earth would they have him killed so close to the object of their frustration? The thing had a cheap feel to it. Yet the field next to Rimwood Estates could not have been a random choice. It was a place where Peplow had business; it was simply too much of a coincidence for him to be blown away by someone with no connection at all to real estate.

The house Peplow had rented sat just beyond town, where only a little of the sunlight sifted through the big maples and copper beeches overhead. It was an old white clapboard cottage from Coleridge's first generation of housing stock, past its prime, with a pitched roof, a porch that wrapped around one side, and some gingerbread. There was ample evidence of a rental's neglect. As he climbed the porch stairs, he almost lost his balance on a spongy, rotting step. The clapboard paint had flaked off in spots, disclosing an earlier powder blue. A beveled glass pane in the front door was badly cracked.

The police seal had been removed—a piece of the yellow tape was still stuck on a bush—and so had most of the contents of the house. He peered in from the porch and saw a dark living room, empty except for a slipcovered sofa and a dull green set of armchairs. In a community of opulent homes, some of which it was his job to sell, Larry Peplow had lived with someone else's furniture. Harvey would never know how Peplow had improved it, what touches he had added to make it, even for a while, his own.

"I don't like it one bit."

Harvey turned. The tiny voice behind him belonged to an elderly woman in a magenta jogging suit standing on the sidewalk with her arms folded defiantly in front of her. Perfect white bangs framed her cheery, crumpled face.

"I have to tell you, young man, I don't like it one little bit," she said.

Harvey came to the porch railing. "Excuse me, ma'am, but I'm working with the police. I'm an investigator."

"I wasn't talking about you, young man. I was talking about him." She jerked her chin up toward the house, as if indicating Peplow somewhere inside.

"You didn't like Mr. Peplow one bit? Is that what you mean?"

She danced up the walk toward him on her Reeboks. "I suppose he was all right," she said, stopping at the bottom of the steps. "But I don't like this murder business one bit. That's what I meant. We're not used to that sort of thing here. And to have that poor man—well, to have known him, and then have him be the one."

"You knew Mr. Peplow?"

"Young man, I've lived next door for fifty-three years"—she jerked her head toward the Victorian on Harvey's left—"and I've seen a lot of tenants come and go. I watched the Hibbard kids grow up here, before they all went off to school and the parents moved and started renting it out. When I moved to Coleridge, there *was* no expressway and it took an hour and a half to drive into the city along the lake."

"You certainly don't look old enough to've been here that long."

"Young man, even in this stupid jogging suit I look old enough to be your grandmother, and don't you think I don't know it, but thank you anyway for that nice compliment."

"It's nothing."

"Dot Chernoff."

"Harvey Blissberg."

"My husband and I jog every day and we used to see Larry from time to time. I made him a pie once. Now, *that's* something people don't do enough of for each other anymore."

"I couldn't agree more, Mrs. Chernoff. More pies would make this world a better place to live. Did you talk to him much?"

"Oh, we said hello often enough, but he wasn't a talkative fellow. Nice enough. Courteous man. Like you."

"Do you know why someone would want to kill him?"

"Heavens, no! Young man, I pride myself on being the kind of person who doesn't know people whom anyone would want to kill."

"You didn't know him to be in any kind of trouble?"

"Oh, he was in trouble, that's for sure."

"He was?"

"Any man who's got that many women coming and going is in

some kind of trouble. My husband, Abe, used to say it made him wish he was young again. And I told him, 'Abe, that boy Larry isn't young anymore, and you were *never* young enough for those sorts of goings-on, anyway.' "

"Goings-on?"

"Carrying on like that. That man should've been married and suffering like the rest of us." Her laugh sounded like birds twittering.

"What was he doing?"

"Sometimes they wouldn't come out till the next morning."

"Did you meet any of them?"

"No, I most certainly didn't."

"Well, that wasn't very nice of him, was it? Not to introduce you to his girlfriends. How many different girlfriends would you say he had in the—how long did he live here?"

"Almost four years, and there must've been three or four different ones."

"Three or four? For a minute, you made it sound like a revolving door."

"It's a lot of young women in my book."

"Do you know any of their names?"

"I may've been his neighbor, but I'm not nosy."

"Did you ever hear any loud noises or arguments coming from the house?"

"No, I didn't."

"Do you remember anything unusual happening in the weeks or months before he was killed?"

"No."

"Did he keep a regular schedule?"

"I'd be hard-pressed to say. You know these real estate people."

"I'm afraid I don't."

"Well, my Lord, they're out showing houses at all hours. Not like my husband, Abe. For forty-five years, he came home from work on the six-forty-one and walked home from the station and I'd have a martini and a big bowl of cashews waiting for him." She started jogging spryly in place. "Got to keep the calf muscles warm."

"I'll leave you to your running."

"Abe's home with a summer cold, so I'm jogging all by my lonesome today."

"Good luck," Harvey said. "I'm sure we'll be speaking again."

"Watch out, young man, or I might make you a pie," she said as she turned and flapped down the walk.

When Harvey was back in his car, he picked up the cellular phone and called the Upchurch residence in nearby Dancedale. A man with bigger fish to fry would be busy frying them, but he was a man with only one very small fish. He listened to the rings, envisioning a white wall phone jangling in a curtained kitchen, until Mrs. Upchurch herself answered.

He told her who he was and that he had information that Larry Peplow had sold to someone else a house that she felt should have been hers. She told him to come by around six, when her husband, Harry, would be home.

As he idled at a red light under a banner stretched overhead advertising the Coleridge Arts Fair, Harvey watched two attractive middle-aged women in long linen shorts pass in front of his car, shopping bags dangling from their tan hands. When one of them paused in the crosswalk and bent to scratch her thigh, a gold ladies' Rolex flashed sharply in the sun. In a camera store window to Harvey's left were two drastically enlarged color portraits of families. In one, a nuclear grouping of four in matching argyle sweaters posed against a Mercedes fender. In the other, a family of five with perfect teeth stood in front of blazing autumn trees with the family rottweiler, all in order of descending height. Next to the camera store was a sporting goods outfit. A headless mannequin in the window wore a black-and-orange athletic jacket with its back turned toward the street. The jacket said "Coleridge Collies."

The light turned green and he gave the Town Car a little gas.

Behind the wheel of a Jaguar passing in the opposite direction was a kid of about twenty, a gawky bird with a spiky purple plume of hair. Behind him was a teenage girl with ash blond hair driving a huge Olds Cutlass, talking into a cellular phone. College kids home for the summer, Harvey realized, enjoying the last days of sheltering wealth, a level of prosperity few would ever be able to duplicate themselves. He was surprised that people were still fighting over eight-hundred-thousand-dollar houses. America was bottoming out. How strange, he thought, to live in an America that suddenly had to prove itself to everyone; we're like a team that has blown a big lead at home. A town like Coleridge might be a theme park in a few years where, for the price of admission, angry Americans could experience the suburban wealth of a bygone era. The guided tour would wheel by a group of mechanical Mexican gardeners endlessly raking the yard of a Tudor house. *Please keep your hands inside the bus; those rakes are real!*

As he drove, the neighborhoods told the story of westward suburban expansion. Coleridge's business district gave way to leafy neighborhoods of bungalows and frame houses from the twenties and thirties, and after a mile to newer brick ranch houses and split-levels with scrollwork aluminum screen doors, and then the housing stock thinned out and Harvey saw, to his left and right, recent residential developments rising out of the farmland, looking naked with their inadequate foliage.

His car floated across the freight tracks connecting Chicago and Milwaukee, then passed a small strip mall with a brown mansard roof. Lodged between a Quik-Copy and a video store was an establishment with rice paper screens in the window called the Sunny Day Sushi Bar. An unlikely spot to find fresh sea urchin, but it was a world where farmers wore Gloria Vanderbilt jeans and gas stations sold Danish chewing gum. On the gravel shoulder, just before a road sign reading "Welcome to Garden Hills, Population 28,700," a woman in a straw sun hat was selling early corn and tomatoes out of the back of a pickup. She sat in a beach chair beside the brimming bushels, her ear pressed to a transistor radio.

Unlike Coleridge, the Garden Hills business district was lined with no-nonsense retail stores—a florist with graduation corsages piled high in the window in their clear plastic cubes, a luncheonette, and a dusty hardware store with a row of bright red lawn mowers, rototillers, and seeders parked in front.

He found the police station, a squat granite building on a balding patch of grass, and parked in one of the visitors' spaces. As he straightened his tie in the rearview mirror—if he had to impress anyone, it was Dombrowski, on whose good graces his own investigation would in some measure rely—he considered Larry Peplow, about whom so many seemed to know so little. He thought of what Virginia Schmauss said Peplow had told her: "I'm selling them a new mask to more effectively contain and conceal the dirty details of living." Well, talk about presumptuous self-reflection. He and Peplow had that in common, as well as an overdeveloped sense of privacy, and Harvey suddenly felt that he might have liked the guy.

4

"SIT DOWN, SON," said Lieutenant Walter Dombrowski, chief of detectives for the Garden Hills Police Department's Homicide Unit. He pointed to a wooden chair in his hot office and kept Harvey waiting while he pecked out another word at his hulking IBM Selectric. When he finally turned, his face was bubbled with perspiration; the old Fedder grumbling in the window seemed to be doing more harm than good.

Above his broad, creased, comforting face and strip of tan forehead, his silver blond hair rose stoutly in a brush cut. Behind gold-frame glasses his pale eyes appraised Harvey. He was somewhere in his fifties and looked more like a feed salesman than one of the suburbanites whom he served and protected.

"I've had as many as ten men on it and we're not netting out anything. First damn homicide in seven years, son, and it won't go down." He tapped the files on his desk labeled PEPLOW, LAWRENCE. "What do you need to know?"

"I'm not fussy, Lieutenant." He realized that Dombrowski was looking at him with an expression of intense scrutiny. "Is something the matter?" Harvey asked. "Do I have something on my face?"

"I'm just sitting here looking at you and wondering if you're really going to be any help or just get in our damn way here."

Something in Dombrowski's bearing, some little nut of panic, told him that the lieutenant knew that his unit was sorely in need of help. "I'm playing catch-up," Harvey said evenly, "so perhaps you could just tell me what you know."

"All right. He was found on his back in a grassy field, about a hundred yards west of the brick wall that goes around this Rimwood Estates out there. He'd been shot in the face from a distance of three or four feet with a hollow-point bullet from a Colt forty-five semiautomatic between, best guess, eleven and midnight. We found enough of a fragment in the grass to get a ballistic fingerprint. We didn't find the gun. There's just no more damn physical evidence to go on. No usable prints. No marks on him. No sign of a struggle. No sign of sexual activity. No hairs. No fibers. No footprints. Nothing left behind. We're satisfied he was done there. Someone looked the guy in the eye and blew him away. April seventeenth was a clear, cool night, and the grass was tall and dry. Trampled a bit where Peplow and his murderer walked out there, but that's all. A clean scene."

"I take it you don't think it was a thrill kill."

"No, I don't believe it was." The lieutenant took a sip of his iced coffee. "Peplow's car, an Audi," he went on, "it was back in Coleridge on the street in front of the home he rented, so my guess is he drove over to Rimwood Estates *with* his murderer. His car was clean. He was wearing pressed black chinos, a pink polo shirt, one of them alligator deals, and loafers with no socks. He was carrying his wallet, his keys, some Wrigley's Big Red gum, and a matchbook from The Nook, a coffee shop in Coleridge near his house. His wallet had seventy-seven bucks in it, Illinois license and registration, a United Airlines Mileage PLUS card, a Visa card issued by Fidelity, Coleridge Public Library Card, Cubs' schedule, and some other shit. You can have a look at it later. We got a copy of all his Visa charges for the last year, which you can also see, and a log of the toll calls from his house for the last year. That didn't amount to much."

"I imagine the fact the guy was the kind of guy wore alligator shirts, that's bound to make everyone around here jumpy."

Dombrowski smiled and patted the breast pocket of his western-style white shirt, which bulged with ballpoints and a pack of Chesterfields. "Well, yeah, the whole structure gets a little edgy. We've got Town Hall heat on this. But we also got budget cuts we're trying to work within. We're getting it at both ends. How was that Lake Superior whitefish last night?"

"Damn good," Harvey said. "A very superior piece of Lake Superior whitefish."

"Clarence never puts a bad piece of fish in front of you. You know, I've just about given up red meat. And that's saying something, since my idea of a green vegetable used to be club steak. You aware, son, that seventy percent of the protein Americans eat comes from meat? That's a crying shame."

"The bread pudding was also excellent."

"But good God almighty. I wish he'd cut back on the raisins some. I'm not a man who responds well to a lot of raisins."

"No witnesses to any part of it?"

"No one even heard the shot. See, this Rimwood Estates is a brand-spanking-new development. A couple of those big houses have been sold but no one lives there yet, except for this guy Vaultt. Jim Vaultt, the developer. He lives in one of the houses himself. He says he was at the movies that night over in Wahatan. If he wasn't, well, he would've had the opportunity to kill this fellow—and even if he was, he still could've slipped out—but he didn't have the inclination to kill the fellow, as far as I can tell."

"Nothing between them?"

"Peplow showed the houses to a few people. That's it."

"What about Peplow's background?"

"Ran an NCIC check on him. Negative. No priors and he wasn't currently wanted." Dombrowski tapped the folders again with one of those big square fingers that seems to predestine its owner to enter either law enforcement or professional wrestling. "Went through his address book, by the way, and came up empty. He grew up in upstate New York. Boonville, north of Utica. His father taught high school math, died a few years ago. Only child. Public school, went to Bowdoin College in Maine on a partial scholarship. High SAT scores, three-point-five grade average at Bowdoin."

"I understand he used to be a therapist."

"That's right. Got a Ph.D. and opened a clinical psychotherapy practice in Portland, Maine, in 1976. In 1988, he moved here."

"Never married?"

"Apparently not."

"Why'd he quit being a shrink and come here?"

"His mother said he told her Maine wasn't crazy enough. Too many therapists and not enough customers. He told her that when folks in Maine got agitated they'd go out and shoot a deer instead of seeking professional help. And maybe he wanted to make some money."

"Why here, though?"

Dombrowski took out his pack of Chesterfields, extracted a cigarette, and lit it. "We don't know. Aside from one of the guys he played basketball with, a guy he was at Bowdoin with, a Stuart somebody—his name's in the file—we haven't run across anyone from his former life here. And this guy Stuart hadn't been all that in touch with him over the years, but Peplow looked him up once he arrived. Maybe he just figured this was as good a place as any to make some money in real estate. The North Shore had one of the fastest-growing markets in the eighties."

"You checked with the Portland police?"

"Nothing. A speeding ticket." Dombrowski extended his lower lip and directed a strangely dainty stream of smoke toward the ceiling. "That's it."

"Did you talk to any of his friends in Maine?"

"Couldn't find any."

"How about former patients?"

"Peplow's files were not among his possessions here. His mother didn't have them either."

Harvey shifted his eyes to look at the county map on the wall behind Dombrowski. Coleridge, Wahatan, Dancedale lined up north to south along Lake Michigan. Garden Hills to the west. "What about his friends here?"

"There's your brother and his basketball buddies, but none of them really knew Peplow outside the gym. There's a girlfriend. A young woman named Lynn Nyland, some kind of freelance artist around here. Came in very distraught, and no acting job in my opinion. She told me they'd been out together five or six times. Struck me as a nice, lonely girl trying not to fall in love with a guy who had about fifteen years on her."

"What about his relatives?"

"A mother in upstate New York. With emphysema. We shipped the body to her after the ME was through with it."

"Anything I should know about it?"

"The body? You can go over the path reports yourself, but he had a trace of alcohol in his blood, something like point-oh-two—maybe a beer—and an Italian beef sandwich in his stomach. We found the place where he ate it—Zorro's, a sandwich shop in downtown Coleridge. The guy knew Peplow, an occasional customer. Said he came in alone that night around seven."

"Are you getting any help from the state?"

"We do our own laundry. Oh, there's a young buck up in Waukegan at the state's attorney's office who was sniffing around. He got it into his head this is a drug hit."

"Well?"

"Nothing in the big wide world to suggest he was involved with controlled substances. We combed his house."

"Then what's this guy in the AG's office going on?"

"He's just going on ego. He's a kid who grew up in the only poor neighborhood around here—they call it Fringetown, it's part of Coleridge—and my guess is that after he puts in his time up there he'd like to jump over to the right side of the tracks and practice some expensive law for the rich folks in Coleridge or Wahatan or Dancedale. Cracking this case would put him on the map. He's just headline hungry."

"What's wrong with Garden Hills? Don't you have any rich folks here?"

"When folks in Garden Hills get rich, they move closer to the lake. To Coleridge, Wahatan, and Dancedale." He held up a palm. "Now that's changing, of course. They've run out of real estate in those towns, but this country's not running out of rich people. There's still a lot of dough left over from the eighties. That's why you've got these high-end developments like Rimwood Estates. Eight-hundred-thousand-dollar homes where there used to be nothing but wheat, corn, and soybeans. Nice for the tax base, though. Oh, by the way, speaking of Fringetown, Peplow had been doing a little community work there in one of those youth action programs. Counseling some of the underprivileged kids one night a week. You know, to be poor around all this affluence here, it's enough right there to make you crazy. Guess he wanted to keep his hand in."

"Only the good die young," Harvey said.

Dombrowski grunted. "So what's our excuse?"

"I'm not that good. I imagine you've talked to the folks at this counseling center in . . . Fringetown, is it?"

"Its real name is Spruce Park. It's the working-class part of Coleridge. Families who've been here for seventy years watching the money pour in all around them. You know, they're the people who own the restaurants, the shoe repair shops, do the landscaping, teach gym at the high schools. We talked to the man who runs the program Peplow did his counseling for. He didn't know anything."

"There'd been no trouble between Peplow and any of the kids he was counseling?"

"Nope. Now, what else can I tell you?"

"You can tell me what your pet theory is, Lieutenant."

"I think his Oscar Mayer wiener killed him."

"You mean he had girl trouble?"

"I'm thinking he had wife trouble."

"He wasn't married."

"I'm thinking he had trouble with someone else's wife."

"But this Lynn Nyland you mentioned," Harvey said. "You said she was single, no?"

"I'm guessing he had other love interests."

"On what basis?"

"You talked to Virginia Schmauss?"

"This morning." The less said about the Upchurches the better at this point.

"She remembers two or three women showing up at the office for dates with him. This is over the course of the last year or so."

"Have you run these women down?"

"She couldn't give us their names or much of a description either."

"You didn't run across these women in his address book?"

"We found a couple who'd gone out with him or that he'd picked up. But they couldn't give us anything to hold on to."

"So you're just fishing."

"Son, around here a good-looking, red-blooded single man would be a fool to overlook the opportunities for some wiggly."

"It's that good around here, huh?"

"Son, who do you think's in these suburbs up here during the week between eight and six? About fifteen thousand housewives and mothers with boring sex lives and too much time and money on their hands. That's who. A guy like Peplow, he works up here in a job that normally entails a fair amount of contact with women who want to move up to a ten-room colonial in a better part of town, why you'd have to fucking lock yourself in your closet to miss that particular boat."

"I guess you would," Harvey said.

"The drawer in his bedroom nightstand was filled with two things. Cough drops and rubbers. Looked like he was running a fuckin' Trojan distributorship."

"So what d'you think he used the cough drops for?"

"Very funny."

"Lieutenant, everyone's got rubbers these days. At least he was practicing safe sex."

"Frankly, I think he dug his grave with his pecker. The man just plain liked wiggly."

"Lieutenant, if I may say so, your theory sounds more like an obsession than a suspicion."

"Last man murdered in Garden Hills was killed by his lover's husband. It happens."

Harvey looked at Dombrowski and decided to keep the Upchurches to himself. When you just had one very small fish of your own to fry, it didn't make sense to share it. "And you never heard Peplow's name before he was found in the field six weeks ago?"

"Nope," Dombrowski said.

"Who found him?"

"This guy Vaultt. The developer. He was walking around his development there the morning after, saw a flash of pink in the grass. His polo shirt." The lieutenant took something from one of the files and threw it across the desk at Harvey. "This is him. The real estate agency used it in one of their brochures. Looks a little bit like you."

Harvey put down the Parker Jotter and picked up the black-and-white photo. True, if you divided all men into eight or ten categories of physical appearance, he and Larry Peplow might be in the same group. They both had all their hair, although Peplow's was darker and he had heavy eyebrows like strokes of a black marker. The hair alone, well-defined and razor-cut, took five years off his age. His smile hung like a bright white hammock between his dimples. He was wearing a splashy tie, one of those wild geometric patterns like a bad dream. Harvey wondered briefly what the hell he was doing in a suburban police station twenty-five miles north of Chicago, trying to get the feel of a dead man's life. The details were already driving him crazy. "Can I hold on to this?"

"Be my guest."

"I'd also like to take the files and the path report to look at overnight. If I may."

"I ought to make you look at them here."

"If you insist."

"Aw, what the hell. Just have them back on my desk tomorrow morning at nine."

"Check."

"So," Dombrowski said, folding his arms behind his head. "You been a dick long?"

"A few years," Harvey said. "I used to play ball for a living."

"Yeah, I know who you are." Maybe it accounted for his relative congeniality. "I was anxious to see what kind of dick an old beat-up ballplayer would make."

"Do I look that bad to you, Lieutenant?"

"Let's just say your face is too old for a baseball card but not old enough for plastic surgery."

"That's kind of you."

"But you're in the right place, son. North Shore's got more plastic surgeons than cops. Half the women around here, you can't tell if they're thirty-five or sixty-five. Even my wife, now, she's saying she'd like to get her chin back up in the vicinity of her face."

"What're you going to do?" Harvey shrugged, amused by Dombrowski's preoccupation with diet and plastic surgery. It was as if he had absorbed the themes of upper-class suburban life by osmosis. Maybe the world really was becoming a better place if homicide cops were now watching their cholesterol.

"As you go about your business, son, I do have rules. You're playing in my league now."

"I'm well aware, Lieutenant."

"If a witness we've already talked to doesn't want to talk to you, I don't want to hear that you've been badgering them. If they don't want to talk, I want you to leave my people the fuck alone. What are you smiling at, son?"

"I'm sorry, Lieutenant. I was just admiring your fine knack for combining hospitality and hostility."

"The other rule is I want to know what you know——"

"——and you want to know it *when* I know it," Harvey finished for him.

"If not before."

"Count on me."

Dombrowski put out his Chesterfield. "And no talking to the press."

Harvey had never talked to them much when he played ball, and he saw no reason to start now.

5

AS HE HEADED east toward Rimwood Estates, Harvey picked up the car phone and dialed his brother's home number in Evanston. School was out, and Norman was spending his mornings in his study writing a scholarly paper on unreliable narrators in twentieth-century fiction.

"Hey, man, how's it going?" Norm asked.

"It's going all right."

"Accommodations okay?"

"Yeah. Just fine."

"Where are you?"

"In my rental, heading for Rimwood Estates. Listen, Norm."

"What?"

"You didn't tell me Peplow used to be a shrink in Maine."

"He was? A *shrink*?"

"Yeah, this woman Schmauss he worked for and Dombrowski, the detective, they both knew."

"I just assumed he had been . . . I don't know what I assumed, Harv, but, no, I didn't know he'd been a shrink. How interesting."

"Interesting?"

"Well, he *was* a good listener. I mean, you were so busy enjoying his curiosity about you that you only realized later that he hadn't told you anything about himself. I wonder why he quit."

"Dombrowski says he told his mother there wasn't enough business in Maine. Norm, the next time you want me to look into the death of a good friend of yours, could you arrange to know a little bit more about the fucking guy?"

"I had a feeling this might not work out."

"What're you talking about?"

"Look! You're already pissed off! You know, we can forget it if you want."

"The fact is, Norm, you didn't even know he was a shrink before."

"So what? Does that mean we couldn't have been friends?" Harvey could always count on Norm to get the tense right, even in anger. "I don't know a damn thing about your life anymore, Harv, but I still care about you! If someone blew you away, you think my attitude would be, 'Hey, I hadn't talked to my brother in six weeks, so who gives a flying frittata?' You think I'd take that attitude?"

Harvey was trying to concentrate on the conversation and still navigate. He was heading north now, through some undeveloped farmland, looking for Sky View Road. "Norm," he said, "you remember the time we were fishing with Dad somewhere in Connecticut and there was this big snapping turtle in the grass, only I didn't know it was a snapping turtle, and you told me to pick it up by the shell and bring it to you? And like a dutiful little brother I went over and picked it up and it just about bit my finger off?"

"No."

"You've got a convenient memory."

"Are you suggesting I'm withholding some information about Larry?"

"No. Of course not."

"So this is just your way of asking if this case is another snapping turtle?"

"Something like that."

"My God you're pissy. But I don't know. I don't know if it's a snapping turtle. Anyway, you like to put your finger in the fire a little bit, don't you?"

"I don't know about that."

"C'mon, Harv, don't you remember when we went to the circus at Boston Garden once and the lion tamer put his head in a lion's mouth and you said, 'Gee, that looks like fun'?"

"I don't remember that."

"Yeah, well, look who's got the convenient memory now. Hey, I don't think anyone ever thought you'd end up selling insurance. So when am I going to see you? You've already been here almost a day."

"You know, you don't have to stick me with a murder investigation to get me out here to see you. I'll come here just for the hell of it."

"Harv, you got some Valium there in the car with you? I think you need some Valium."

"That's very funny. Because you're the one who's agitated, Norm. You've been agitated ever since I retired from baseball. You can't cash in on your relationship to me like you used to."

"Ouch. That's a very ugly thing to say. But you're still invited to play basketball with us tomorrow at noon."

"You're dead meat on the court."

"Harv, you're not good enough to carry my knee brace."

"Norm, I'm going to make you wish you never learned how to walk." There it was, Sky View Road. Harvey turned right, heading east. "Did Peplow ever tell you anything about this guy Vaultt?"

"Who's that?"

"The guy who developed Rimwood Estates. The guy who found the body."

"No."

"Well, thanks again for all your help."

THE ENTRANCE TO Rimwood Estates, two brick pillars with concrete caps, was up a couple of miles on the left, across from

Behnke's Nursery. A brass plate that said "Rimwood Estates" was bolted to one of the pillars. Planted in the grass nearby were two For Sale signs and a painted plywood sign that repeated the name of the development, but with a legend underneath: "We Take the Worry Out of Living."

Harvey turned up the newly paved drive. Last night, on his way to Clarence's restaurant, he had stopped here for a minute but could make out nothing in the dark. Now he saw that the drive was bordered by freshly sodded berms planted with young maple saplings, beyond which tall grass and trillium stretched to the woods on either side. The development proper, enclosed by a new brick wall, loomed a good two hundred feet ahead. When he drove through the open wrought-iron gate, Harvey almost flinched at the sight. Arranged on two cul-de-sacs were a dozen large houses, some still in the late stages of construction, but each one an egregious mix of architectural influences. French provincial, Georgian, Tudor, Mediterranean, and colonial styles had been used in shameless combinations. The houses rose out of the shockingly green sod like big, bright toys.

Harvey followed a sign that said "Sales Office" to a house at the rear of the right-hand cul-de-sac, a huge, low, cedar-shingled contemporary with some incongruous stucco facing. He drove up between the fieldstone pillars and parked in the driveway next to a brown Mercedes 450 SEL whose vanity plate read VAULTT.

Harvey had no success getting a response with the doorbell, which played the first nine notes of "I'm Getting Married in the Morning," and was walking back to his car when a voice shouted, "I'm in the back! Just walk around."

He took the flagstone path around the garage and turned the corner to see a late-middle-aged man in the process of filling a small slate-lined pool in the backyard. He was sitting on a stone wall, loosely holding a green garden hose and watching the arc of water sparkle in the sunlight.

He got up, threw the end of the hose into the pool, and came toward Harvey, wearing a white terry cloth swim ensemble—trunks and short-sleeved top. He was all thickening torso and stumpy legs, with a meaty, handsome face and a head of dense, silvering hair.

"I'm Jim Vaultt. What can I do you for?"

"Harvey Blissberg," he said, taking his hand. "Sorry to bother you."

"Nonsense. But I can see you're not here to buy a house."

"Am I that transparent?"

"I'd say you're buying, but not real estate."

The world was full of men—not to mention baseball pitchers— who need to gain the edge on you right away, and Harvey knew he had just met another one. "I'm not buying," he said. "I'm looking."

"Let me guess. You're looking for information."

"You're very good at this."

"I'm a salesman, Harvey. It's my job to read people."

It was the second time that day someone had used his first name in such a way that Harvey didn't recognize it as his own. "So," he said, "what else can you tell me about myself?"

"What else can I tell you? Well, you dress better than a cop. Your suede loafers just wouldn't cut it back at headquarters. And that thirty-dollar haircut. You could be a journalist or a consultant or a sales rep, but you're not. So that leaves only one thing. You're a private investigator. Am I right?"

"Bingo," Harvey said with a tired smile.

Vaultt held up his hands in mock diffidence. "Please. A no-brainer. A man was found murdered just off my property here a few weeks ago. I've spoken with the local cops and I know they don't know shit. I was expecting reinforcements."

"His friends hired me."

"Friends?"

"He played hoops with a bunch of guys. My older brother's one of them."

"Ah. So he called on his kid brother?" Vaultt plucked at his big nose with a thumb and forefinger. He had probably not been a handsome youth, but success had given him confidence and confidence had made him attractive. "Sit down." They sat in wrought-iron chairs around a matching glass-topped table. Vaultt slapped his bare thighs with his hands. "So you're going to find Peplow's murderer?"

"That's right," Harvey said. "And you're going to help me." Vaultt's aggressiveness was contagious.

"Ah," Vaultt said, his eyebrows elevating. "Well, that's what I'm here for." Then he added with exquisite insincerity, "And I really mean that."

"It would be a shame to waste your uncanny ability to read people."

"If it were so useful, the cops already would have benefited from it. How long have you been on this case?"

Harvey glanced at his watch. "Eighteen hours."

"And you haven't solved it yet?" He laughed. "What do you know so far?"

"Nothing."

"Whom have you talked to?"

"A few people. I know that the company Peplow worked for was the listing broker for your houses here."

"But I retain the right to sell them directly myself," he said, eager for Harvey to know that no one called his tune.

"So be it. But he sold one of them."

"That's right. To Stanley and Beverly Howell. They'll be moving in soon."

"Now," Harvey said, "here's the interesting part. The same day the Howells bid the asking price, another couple also bid the asking price, but they'd come through another broker."

"I didn't know that."

Harvey relished Vaultt's denial for a moment before countering. "Yes, you did. Because Peplow neglected to present that other offer to you, the shit hit the fan, and Virginia Schmauss called you to ask your cooperation in covering up Larry's indiscretion by telling the aggrieved couple that you had been told of both offers."

"All right," Vaultt said with a smile, "I did know that. That's very good. Your brother would be proud of you."

"That makes you an accomplice to real estate malpractice."

"But I was never obligated to lie. By the way, your name sounds familiar to me. And there can't be very many Blissbergs floating around."

"I used to play baseball."

"The majors?"

"Boston Red Sox and Providence Jewels."

"That must be it, though I haven't followed baseball since I was a kid. But it's hard to avoid hearing the names. So what are you, then, some kind of investigative relief pitcher?"

"That's right. They call me in when the other arms get tired."

"Did you have a successful career?"

"Relative to my talents. I was even voted to the All-Star team my last year." Harvey shrank inwardly from his unnecessary boast. Obviously, he still missed the old, easy identity.

"Why was that your last year, then?"

But Harvey didn't feel like going into it, how his roommate that year was found murdered, how Harvey had figured out who did it, how baseball lost its charm and a new career had opened up for him. "I wanted my millions of fans to remember me at my peak," he said.

Vaultt laughed. "Yes, nothing's worse than a visible demise. It's bad enough to deteriorate in private."

"But back to the couple."

"Well, I don't think that a real estate agent's going to get murdered over an infraction. I mean, people aren't *that* crazy when it comes to houses. Can I get you something? A Pepsi?"

"No, thank you," Harvey said. "I assume you didn't hear the shot."

"I was at the movies that night, in Wahatan. But I did find the body the next day."

"What did you see?"

"I saw something in the grass—"

"I mean, what movie?"

"Oh. *Swing Time*," Vaultt said. "Fred and Ginger. That's a horrible sight, a murdered man. But I suppose you've seen your share."

"I try to keep it to a minimum. You must've felt terrible."

"*I* didn't murder him."

"I didn't suggest you had."

"Oh, but the cops were interested in me for a while. They even wanted to know whether Larry had a concealed interest in this development. See, they were thinking maybe I'd knocked off my partner in a business dispute. Cops are fools, Harvey. All they had to do was look at the loan documents. I don't have partners. I've got excellent relationships with my banks and don't need anyone else's cash. I've done very well in commercial real estate, and that's what's allowed me to indulge my little dream of a super residential development."

"It's good enough for you to live here."

"Oh, I'm just here until they're sold. Then I'll move on. I've got shallow roots."

"Did you know Peplow very well?"

"Only saw him here. In the short time Rimwood was on the market, he squired a few couples around."

"Who else did Peplow show your houses to? Besides the Up-churches and the Howells?"

"Can't recall."

"You don't keep track?"

"I'd have to check my book. In fact, let me go get it." Vaultt got to his feet. "I could use a Pepsi. You sure you don't want one?"

"Sure. As long as you're getting up."

"Be right back."

Harvey watched as Vaultt ambled off on his hairless legs, plastic clogs slapping on the flagstone path leading to the back door. He had known a big developer or two in his time. All that high-flying, risk-taking, water-walking bravado. None of them would be caught dead taking money from a bunch of guys who happened to play basketball with a future murder victim.

"Here you go," Vaultt said over Harvey's shoulder, depositing a tumbler of Pepsi and a dimestore ledger on the table. "I put the houses on the market March first."

"The cops see this?"

"Never asked for it."

Harvey opened the book and ran his finger down the first page. There were the Howells on the fourteenth of March, with Peplow's name next to theirs. The Upchurches were shown the houses on the sixteenth by a broker named Fine. He turned the page and found Peplow's name three more times: next to a couple from Dancedale named Scott and Marilyn Barger; Anthony and Evelyn Smaldone from Kenosha, Wisconsin; and Craig and Nancy Williams from Downers Grove.

"What do you remember about these other people?" Harvey asked. "What about the Bargers? Scott and Marilyn."

Vaultt cupped his hand over his mouth, pinched his nose, and breathed out. "I believe they were a, you know, mid-thirties couple. Very athletic looking. Great-looking lady. What houses does it say they saw?"

Harvey looked. "The Colorado and the Foxton."

"All right. They only saw two. Then I've got them right. Nice, athletic couple. She wore a tennis dress. They weren't all that interested. He showed them two—and that was that."

"What about the Smaldones? Kenosha, Wisconsin."

"Oh, yes. Window-shoppers. A dowdy couple. They couldn't afford it."

"The Williamses. Downers Grove," Harvey read. "They saw the Laurelwood, the Yale, and the Foxton."

"Close to retirement age," Vaultt said, eyes closed to picture them. "Pinched faces. Much too much house for them."

"None of these couples made an offer?"

"It would tell you there in the book if they did."

None had. Harvey opened his little spiral-bound notebook and recorded the addresses of the Bargers, Smaldones, and Williamses, aware of Vaultt's gaze.

"What's the price range here?"

Vaultt pressed his Pepsi glass against his forehead. "About seven hundred thousand to nine hundred thousand."

"Are you getting a lot of traffic?"

"Enough. But right now everyone's proceeding cautiously. I was hoping to beat the downturn in the market, but construction delays held me up a little. I'm not worried. When you get in this price range, buyer sensitivity isn't so great."

Harvey slugged down some of his Pepsi. "Back to Peplow for a minute. When you first met him, what did your phenomenal talent for reading people tell you?"

"Well—I was surprised he dressed as well as he did. You don't run into that many male brokers out here in the 'burbs. Most of them are divorcees or women whose kids have flown the nest. The men tend to be a badly dressed group of guys, a little sloppy around the edges. Guys with a high fudge factor in their conversation."

"And Peplow didn't have a high fudge factor?"

"No, he was kind of a straight shooter. Good sense of humor. Bright, bright guy. There was a twinkle."

"A twinkle?"

"Look, there's a moment when you're showing a house and the agent realizes his people aren't interested. It's almost like the oxygen suddenly gets sucked out of the room. Suddenly everyone's going through the motions. The prospect's trying to figure out how much longer to feign interest before telling the agent he's seen enough. The agent's desperately trying to prop up the prospect, furiously pointing out new features. But it's a lost cause. Peplow didn't do that. One of those times I was with him showing the houses. Peplow knew his people had no interest and, instead of pretending, he caught my eye, gave me a little kind of shrug to let me know *he* knew, and we were all out of there in three minutes. Saved a lot of wasted time. It's like he wanted me to know he was something better than an agent."

Harvey imagined the kick Peplow might have gotten out of being in other people's houses. It must have gratified his curiosity about people, but at a different level; no longer memories and dreams, but the secrets of physical reality. The untended rosebed, the bad artwork, the cheap slippers on the closet floor.

"What do you think motivated him?" Harvey asked.

"You're wondering about that extra commission he grabbed for himself?"

"You think he needed money in a bad way?"

"He didn't *look* like he was hurting. You think *you* wear expensive shoes."

"Did he ever mention any personal vices to you? Gambling, drugs?"

"No. Look, you have to understand, I don't think I ever had a conversation with him. But I'll tell you one thing—he wasn't a sweater. You know, someone who sweats stuff out." Vaultt stole a quick sip of Pepsi. "He didn't have an air of desperation, or even effort, really."

For a moment they sat in the big backyard, saying nothing, before Harvey closed his notebook. "Well, you're not much help," he said.

"Not for lack of trying," Vaultt replied. "And I really mean that. I'd rather not have Rimwood Estates go down in history as the place where a real estate agent was mysteriously murdered. I'm counting on you, buddy."

When Harvey climbed back into his car, Vaultt squatted down to window level and said, "Come back anytime."

"The field where Peplow was shot," Harvey said, "you own that land too?"

"No. That parcel still belongs to a farmer named Lundquist, who used to plant it." Vaultt slapped at a bug on his bare leg. "Lives in Wheeling. He sold me the Rimwood property."

Harvey started the engine. "Nice houses," he told Vaultt.

"Don't bullshit a bullshitter, Harvey. I didn't build them for people like you. I built them for people who think that wearing a large diamond to a dinner theater production of *Gypsy* is the height of elegance. Let me tell you something."

"What?"

"I'll even furnish these houses, if that's what people want. Down to the hand soap in the powder room."

"You're kidding."

"Harvey, there are some people who are baffled and defeated by the whole home-furnishing process. That kind of thing can ruin some marriages. If I showed you one of these houses, you wouldn't believe it. *Tchotchkes* already on the coffee table. I'll even stock the icebox for you. Fill the spice rack. I've got everything in there."

Harvey laughed. "Everything but people."

"People," Vaultt said, drowning out Harvey's laughter with his own. "A detail."

Harvey laughed. "Do me a favor, Jim."

"Anything."

"Point me in the direction of Dancedale."

On the way to Dancedale, with Vaultt's directions lying next to him on the seat, he lit a Lucky Strike from a crumpled pack that had already lasted him more than a week. Every day presented two or three moments that he liked to alleviate with a cigarette, and meeting Vaultt had been one of those moments. His thoughts turned to his impasse with Mickey; he wondered if he might end up alone, like

Vaultt. Maybe earlier generations had gotten it right after all: Marry
in the dark of passion and wake up later with the consequences. The
bloom was off the rose of his and Mickey's cohabitation. They had a
facsimile of marriage, but with all the loopholes of a liaison, so that
now, just when they might have needed the constraints of matrimony
to see them through this period, they were free to toy with escape. In
their worst moments lately, they dared each other to commit. It was
as if he and Mickey took turns standing on the high board while the
other shouted "Jump!" But plunging was not his forte, nor Mickey's.
With some sorrow, he finally crushed out his precious Lucky.

THE UPCHURCHES LIVED in a small Tudor on a curling,
shaded street. Harry Upchurch was a placid fiftyish fellow with a thin
voice. Under a drizzle of dark hair threaded with gray, his wife Liz's
face twitched with dissatisfaction. They served him a beer on their
screened porch and politely answered his first few questions while
taking well-timed sips of their vodka tonics. They had yet to find a
house that interested them as much as the Rimwood Estates house
that Peplow had screwed them out of.

Liz Upchurch's nervousness was almost beginning to make him
suspicious when Harry Upchurch pulled an envelope out of his pocket.

"I don't know if this'll ease your mind about us," he said, handing
Harvey a pair of used American Airlines tickets bearing their names
for a flight to Kingston, Jamaica, on April 12, with a return on the
nineteenth. Larry Peplow had been killed on the seventeenth.

Harvey looked over the tickets. Of course, if they'd hired a hit
man, they'd have arranged to be out of town, but—watching them
now take birdlike sips of their drinks—he dismissed the idea. This is
America, he reminded himself; people do not kill over houses. "I've
never been to Jamaica," he said. "How was it?"

"We recommend it highly," Liz Upchurch said. "It's a lovely place
to be when a murder's being committed two thousand miles away."

"So I've heard," Harvey said.

It had been the pro forma house call he had expected. On his way back to the North Shore Suites Hotel, Harvey pulled off the road at a little brick grocery store that advertised sandwiches and cold beer in neon. When the screen door banged behind him, a woman in a pilling cardigan looked up from the counter, where she had been reading a neatly folded tabloid. Behind her rose shelves of aging canned goods. In a dented freezer case near the door he saw some of the world's oldest ice cream novelties, growing molds of ice. How often, in this new land of malls and minimarts, did someone darken her door, in need of a can of Del Monte green beans?

"Can I help you?" she said from the gloom, haloed by racks of potato chips and packaged cakes.

"I'm just looking for a sandwich." Over her shoulder he saw some colorless meat bubbling softly in a pan on a hot plate. "What's that?"

"Italian beef," she said.

Harvey glanced again at the thin sorry leaves of meat. It was not a dish he was familiar with, but he was the son of a restaurateur who on family car trips had made a practice of ordering the regional specialties, especially any made from the more obscure parts of the pig. Harvey had inherited his father's culinary fearlessness. He felt sorry for food that most other people wouldn't touch.

"Sounds great," he said to the woman.

Maybe because she was so seldom called upon anymore to serve the public, the woman was determined to draw out the transaction. With a tremulous hand she took forever to laboriously arrange the meat on a roll and wrap it in paper and foil. When she finally handed him the sandwich, it was with the pride of someone who had just completed a commissioned portrait, and Harvey was so moved by her effort that he bought a tin of aspirin he thought he might need, and a pocket comb he didn't.

He sat on the concrete stoop in front of the store and ate with one hand while he used the other to disperse mosquitoes. Halfway through the sodden sandwich, he remembered with a shudder that an Italian beef sandwich had been Larry Peplow's last meal.

He wrapped up the remainder of it but continued to sit. He could feel the heat coming off the Town Car's hood a few feet away. Across the street, through the glowing rectangle of a split-level's kitchen window, he watched a family of four sit down to dinner. A platter was silently handed from one to another. The boy got up to get something from the refrigerator and sat down again. The mother poured a beverage from a plastic pitcher into four glasses. Harvey watched the tableau, framed in darkness, people growing older inside their houses.

6

THE NEXT MORNING, a humid, soupy Friday, Harvey sat in a tub chair in his hotel room, looking at his notes and listening to Scott and Marilyn Barger's phone ring in Dancedale. He was freshly showered and dressed in a pair of light olive green Italian wool pants and a pale yellow short-sleeved rayon shirt. While he waited, he caught sight of himself in the mirror over the chipped dresser: a tall man bracing himself for middle age, dark hair just long enough to suggest an idiosyncratic line of work. With some dismay, he realized that everything he was wearing, including the braided Italian shoes, had been purchased with Mickey's help from Marshall's in Watertown, Massachusetts. They had been together long enough to cede to each other their respective strengths. Mickey was his wardrobe consultant and ordered the wine in restaurants. He cooked for company and did the driving on long trips.

"Hello?" A woman's voice said in his ear.

"Is this Marilyn Barger?"

"Yes, it is. Hold on one sec." There was a sound like the ripping of cloth, and then she returned to the phone. "Sorry. I'm waxing my legs. Who's this?"

"Mrs. Barger, my name's Harvey Blissberg. I'm sorry to bother you, but I'm a private detective investigating the murder of Larry Peplow."

"Of who?"

"The real estate agent who was murdered in April."

"Oh, that thing."

"He showed you and your husband some houses there. As you may recall, his body was found near the development."

There was another ripping sound. "Of course. Now I know what you're talking about."

"I was wondering if I might speak to you about him."

"To me? Why?"

"Well, you knew him."

"I don't know if you call it knowing him. But all right." The way she said it reminded Harvey of a little girl's sullen agreement to complete a chore around the house.

"But this sounds like a bad time."

"Hey, I'm not Gerald Ford. I can wax my legs and talk at the same time."

"Have the police already questioned you?"

"No. By the way, have you seen those houses?" she punctuated the question with another ripping sound. "Ouch," she said. It could have been a reference to the asking prices.

"As a matter of fact, yes."

"Something, aren't they?"

"How interested are you in buying one?"

"Well, we don't exactly have that kind of money. But it's always nice to know what three-quarters of a million dollars'll buy."

"Have you found what you're looking for?"

"Oh, no. I want our next house to be perfect. We're taking our time."

"It's hard to find the perfect house," Harvey said.

"You can say that again. And it's got to be a happy house."

"A happy house?"

"You know, not a house that's been put on the market because of a divorce or someone died or something. I think houses have personalities that they get from the people who live in them."

"Well, here's hoping you find a very happy house. Did you spend much time with Larry Peplow?"

"No. The time he showed Scott and me the Rimwood Estates houses, and that's it. Then I think he followed up with a phone call to see if we were at all interested."

"Which you weren't?"

"Maybe if Scott has four or five great years in a row."

"What's your husband do, if I may ask?"

"He sells a line of women's accessories to the big chains. You know, scarves, belts, inexpensive earrings."

"What was your impression of him? Of Peplow?"

"I'd have to think about that for a minute." Another rip. "Listen, do you want to have lunch and talk about this?" she said. "You have a nice voice. Do you like Japanese food?"

He had promised Norm he'd play basketball at the Y in Winnetka.

"There's a new place in Garden Hills. Do you like sushi? I *love* sushi!"

"All right," Harvey said, "sushi."

"It's called Sunny Day Sushi Bar, on Route Forty just west of the freight tracks."

"I think I've passed it."

"I've got a tennis game at ten-thirty. Let's make it for twelve-thirty. Is that all right?"

"That's fine."

"Okey-dokey. See you then." There was another rip and she hung up.

Harvey turned and surveyed the case file documents spread out on the second bed and every available surface in the room. He had been up until two in the morning reading them. The room was papered with information of no particular use. He would need to talk to Lynn Nyland, Peplow's young girlfriend, whose statement to the police had been a series of halting, traumatized murmurs. In it, Nyland had mentioned a Coleridge man named Sy Pincus, a friend and tennis partner of Peplow's. Harvey made a note to call him. The remainder of the signed statements—from Virginia Schmauss; Eleanor Zerbst, one of his colleagues at Schmauss & Weevens; James Vaultt; Robert Marvis, Peplow's landlord; Norman (saying nothing at great and agonizing length, as only a professor of English could); and Preston Quinn and Stuart Silver, two of Peplow's other basketball buddies— added nothing to the negligible assortment of biographical data Harvey had collected.

Peplow's Visa statements for the past year had no suspicious pattern to them. He had used the card primarily at restaurants, all of them in the Chicago area; at clothing, discount pharmacies, and other retail stores on the North Shore; and for magazine subscriptions to *Sports Illustrated, Time, Car and Driver,* and *The New Republic.* He had charged no plane flights or train trips to the card. His long distance calls for the past twelve months were infrequent. His mother received the bulk of them, about one every two weeks, but they were short conversations suggesting little more than ritual contact with her.

At the time of his death, he had a personal liquid net worth of just over $100,000. Twenty-six grand and change in cash—a Coleridge bank savings account and a bank money market fund—and shares in three different Fidelity mutual funds—conservative investments—valued at almost $80,000. He also owned, he read in Peplow's accountant's statement, a cabin on Sebago Lake in Raymond, Maine, appraised at $50,000. He left only incidental debts, like credit cards and a local bookstore account. No life insurance policy, no known will; he had not expected to die.

Harvey collected the papers, refiled them, put the folders back in the brown accordian envelope Dombrowski had given him, and called his brother, Norm.

"I can't make basketball," he told him.

"That's too bad."

"I've got someone to interview."

"Okay. How's it going?"

"I forgot to tell you something else you didn't know about him. He was capable of playing fast and loose as a real estate agent. He cut some corners once to make a bigger commission."

"He did?" He could hear the disappointment in Norm's voice.

"It's not as though he was broke, either. He had some money, mostly tied up in mutual funds."

"But he still cheated?"

"Ignored one perfectly good offer sheet on a house because another offer would give him a bigger commission."

"You think this is what got him killed?"

"I have no idea, Norm."

"Listen," Norm said, brightening, "why don't you come over to the house tonight for dinner? Stu Silver'll be here. He knew Peplow at Bowdoin. Maybe you'll get something out of him. Also, Linda and Nicky are dying to see you. Nick's leaving for overnight camp tomorrow."

It was like a little jab in the ribs. "Nicky's old enough for sleep-away camp already?"

"Time flies, Harv baby. Where've you been?"

LIEUTENANT DOMBROWSKI WAS at his desk in the Garden Hills police station, smoking Chesterfields as he leafed through some reports, when Harvey dropped the case file in front of him.

"A real page-turner, huh?" Dombrowski said, motioning him to sit. "So, whatcha been doin' with yourself?"

"Following a lead I got from Virginia Schmauss yesterday." It had been a bust, so he felt free to talk. As Harvey told the Upchurch story, Dombrowski kept time with his bobbing head.

"You're making me look bad, Blissberg."

"What? I got a story out of Schmauss she wouldn't tell you? Anyway, it didn't pan out."

Dombrowski said, "They got an alibi for the night of April seventeenth?"

"They were in Jamaica. They showed me the plane tickets. But we know now that Peplow was capable of cutting corners."

"Who isn't?" Dombrowski lit another Chesterfield. "I hate this case."

"I'm not crazy about it, either."

"If people knew how hard it was to catch a killer, there'd be even more killing out there."

"So let's just keep it between us," Harvey said. "By the way, I talked to Vaultt."

"There's a piece of work."

"Looks to me basically like an eccentric rich guy with bad taste in houses."

Dombrowski nodded. "Yeah. Worked twenty years for a big commercial real estate development company in the city called Barson Mangum. Went off on his own a few years ago. Rimwood Estates is his first residential development. Divorced. One kid. No priors. No dirt."

"Anything else?"

"Whaddya want? His waist and inseam measurements?"

"Thirty-six, thirty," Harvey deadpanned.

Dombrowski scowled. "I wish I had something on him. He's exactly the kind of guy it'd be nice to have something on. We do have a little break, though."

"Yeah?"

"Lynn Nyland, his young girlfriend."

"I remember," Harvey said.

"We questioned her again, and like Virginia Schmauss, she'd forgotten to tell us something. She'd been telling us she was working at home alone on some sort of assignment on April seventeenth. Now she confesses that an ex-boyfriend of hers from Minneapolis, her hometown, was here visiting her that weekend. He arrived on Friday the fifteenth and flew back to Minneapolis on Monday morning the eighteenth—about nine hours after Peplow was murdered and before Vaultt discovered his body. The boyfriend's number showed up all over her toll calls, which we subpoenaed last week, and United Airlines provided us with the rest. One of my men's flying up to Minnesota to talk to him. Even as we speak."

"And what's Lynn Nyland got to say about this?"

"The usual. She didn't tell us because she was afraid we'd suspect him. You can't blame her, can you? She'd broken up with him eight months earlier when she moved here from Minneapolis, and he was trying to get her back."

"Was she taking him back?"

"Apparently not, but she also told us she wasn't really in love with Peplow."

"Yes, I read that in her statement."

"We think she's lying about that," Dombrowski said. "To protect her boyfriend. We think she's pretending it was nothing serious with Peplow."

"If the boyfriend killed him on impulse," Harvey reasoned, "he would have to have found a gun here on short notice."

"We don't know who his friends are. We're talking about a man with his own small business—graphic design consulting or some such. A guy like that might know his way around. Anyway, who's to say Nyland hadn't been tormenting him over the phone for weeks with stories about her love affair with Peplow? If you saw this woman, you might think she was worth fighting over."

"Gee, Lieutenant, you sound like this case has a chance to go down after all. Maybe I ought to drop my end of it and catch a Cubs game."

"As you wish," Dombrowski said.

"What's Nyland's alibi for herself and—what's his name?"

"Kevin Lahey's his name, and she said they ate at an Italian place in Fringetown that night. Which checks out. The place takes reservations and Lahey's name is right there in the maître d's book for the seventeenth. At eight. That takes them to, say, ten. Peplow was murdered between eleven and midnight."

"Very interesting."

Dombrowski fixed Harvey with his pale blues. "You wouldn't be thinking of heading for Minneapolis?"

"Really, Lieutenant. And horn in on your fun?"

7

AT THE LITTLE strip mall on Route 40, Harvey pulled his Town Car into a spot next to a white Chrysler LeBaron convertible. A Danielle Steel paperback novel was open facedown on the passenger seat amid a litter of change, hairbrushes, and gum wrappers. The floor was strewn with empty Hamm's beer and Diet Coke cans. A Kent cigarette, its filter kissed with lipstick and the rest of it a long gray tail of ash, lay in the open ashtray. Some teenager, Harvey thought as he passed, using her car as a purse.

The window of the Sunny Day Sushi Bar was filled with painted plastic facsimiles of its dishes, a Japanese tradition that was completely lost on Harvey, whose appetite was not generally whetted by plastic reproductions of the food he was about to eat. He opened the door, and the humidity was quickly replaced by the cool serenity of the decor. Through the black latticework that separated the entryway from the dim boxy dining room he saw a very attractive woman in a white polo shirt and tennis skirt put down her cup of tea at a table by the window and raise a hand in fluttery greeting.

"Yoo-hoo!" she called loudly.

When Harvey had threaded his way to her table, she thrust her French-manicured hand at him. As he took it, he felt a callus in the crook of her thumb, the price no doubt paid for a million ground strokes.

"Marilyn Barger, I'm glad to meet you," she said in one breath, shaking her shrub of brunette hair like someone in a shampoo commercial. "Please. Sit down."

From across the room he thought she might have been twenty-five. Proximity forced him to revise his estimate. Judging by the spray of tiny lines around her eyes, she had to be in her thirties, but she gave off an excited girlishness. With those large eyes, as dark as the black lacquered tabletop, and a full mouth, painted coral, she did not look at all like a woman who had been informed of her actual age. White plastic disks dangled from her ears, grazing her shoulders. She kept her chin down slightly when she talked, as though she'd read somewhere, maybe in *Cosmo,* that this gave you an air of irresistible mystery.

"Well," she said, "isn't this great? Sushi in the middle of no-where!"

"Next thing you know, raw tuna'll be on the public school lunch menus."

"Huh? Oh!" It took her a moment to recognize the remark as an attempted witticism. "That's funny."

"Thank you."

"Do you mind if I smoke?" She produced a pack of Kents from somewhere under the table.

"No. Go right ahead." He grabbed the matchbook out of the black ashtray and lit her cigarette. "So that's your convertible out front. I thought it was a teenager's car. You have a teenage daughter?"

"I don't have children." She said it sternly, as if denying a charge. "No, I'll take full credit for the mess. I know it looks like a dump—Excuse me, ma'am," she barked after a passing waitress, "but can we get some service, please?" She turned back to Harvey. "You should see Scott's. It always looks like he just drove it home from the dealer. He owns more Dustbusters than any man alive. But I *live* in my car."

The waitress was there, having shuffled up silently to the edge of the table in her white socks and sandals, where she stood with pen and pad poised.

"I'd like an eel hand roll, a *tekka maki,* a *hamachi maki,* and a California roll," she said without hesitation. "Inside out, but no flying fish eggs. And some sake."

Harvey quickly scanned the menu. "Sushi deluxe." When the waitress dipped and padded away, he said, "Boy, you order like a pro."

"Huh? Oh! Well, you get to know the names after a while."

"You eat here a lot?"

"I know every sushi bar from Waukegan to Evanston," she announced, turning her head to blow cigarette smoke away from the table. Harvey wondered if she was one of those suburban women for whom ordering sushi or knowing how to return purchases to Nieman Marcus without a receipt was the closest they came to a profession.

"What do you do?" he asked.

"I work on my backhand." She bent her right arm and flexed her elbow against her ribcage. "Elbow in, elbow in. Chip's going to kill me if I don't get it down one of these days."

"What do you do when you're not playing tennis?"

"I'm a party planner."

"What's that?"

"I plan people's parties for them. It's just a little business I run out of my house. You know, I think up themes, I plan the decorations, I plan the menus and the flower arrangements."

"Sounds like fun," Harvey said.

"Oh, that's me!" She said with a wink. "I'm a fun facilitator!" She bent over the little bowl of vinegared cucumber salad the waitress had quietly placed before her.

"Let's talk about Larry Peplow."

"Why? Am I boring you with all my chatter?"

"Not at all."

"Did you know that Dancedale North High School has its own suicidologist on staff? A young woman whose sole job is to counsel high school kids who might be thinking of killing themselves?"

"I didn't know that."

"A few years ago there was a rash of suicides on the North Shore. It was terrible. What was it? Too much divorce? Too much pressure to succeed? Too much money? Who knows? Did you know that the suicide rate for white teenage boys all over America has tripled in the last thirty years? How come so many young people have nothing to live for?"

Conversationally, she was all over the place. "Did you know someone who killed himself?" he asked.

"A woman at the club lost a son a few years ago, but I don't really know her."

"So what're you getting at, Mrs. Barger?"

"Getting at? Nothing. I just think it's pretty interesting. All these suicides and hardly any murder. Everyone here's too polite to kill each other. Have you noticed how all the teenagers around here say please and thank you? It's touching. But when they find a man murdered in a field, no one knows what to think."

"Do *you* know what to think?"

"No."

"What about Peplow?"

"What about him?"

"*You* asked *me* to lunch, Mrs. Barger."

"Please, please, please. Please call me Marilyn. 'Mrs. Barger' sounds like everything in the world I don't want to be. You know, kids, one-piece bathing suits, Retin-A."

"Did Peplow say anything out of the ordinary to you the day he showed you the houses at Rimwood Estates?"

"Yes."

"What?"

"He stood with Scott and me in the doorway to a nine-hundred-square-foot master bedroom and said, 'This is lovely, isn't it?' "

"That was out of the ordinary?"

"But it was hideous! It was an atrocious bedroom with fake flagstones on one wall!" She slurped her sake. "Of course, real estate agents lie all the time. That's their business, isn't it? They have this congenital flaw. If the house has a kitchen the size of a closet, they say, 'Notice how nice and compact the kitchen is. It gets away from the old barn-size kitchen.' If there's no dining room at all, they tell you that dining rooms are old-fashioned. 'And by the way, don't you think the current owners did a beautiful job of buckling this linoleum in the kitchen?' Why would you say the master bedroom is lovely when it's a piece of shit? But they do!"

Their raw fish was finally put in front of them and Marilyn just kept going. "Don't you love the colors? They're like decorator colors, all these whites and grays and pinks." She stabbed out her cigarette in the ashtray. "Who hired you?"

Harvey removed his chopsticks from their paper sheath. "Some friends of his brought me in from Boston to help investigate. Peplow played basketball with them."

"You came all the way from Boston?" Her enunciation was impeded by a mouthful of *hamachi maki.*

"My older brother's one of those friends. He's a professor at Northwestern."

"What a nice brother you are."

"Yeah, I guess he owes me one."

"So, the police don't have any, what do you call them—leads?"

The sake was giving Harvey a soft, gauzy feeling, and he said without thinking, "There's a school of thought that Peplow ran afoul of his girlfriend's boyfriend. The boyfriend was in Chicago that weekend from Minnesota. I'm thinking my services may no longer be needed."

"Did they find something of his at the scene?" A grain of rice clung to her upper lip.

"Oh, no, that would be too easy. The murder scene was clean."

"Not even some telltale hair, or a piece of thread or something? Something the murderer dropped?"

"Nothing."

"Oh, dear. If I ever murdered someone, I'd probably end up leaving my driver's license at the scene. That's how messy I am." She paused, pinching a piece of California roll between her chopsticks in midair. "You know, I just thought of another time I saw Peplow. A week or so after he showed us the houses, I ran into him at the Brookvale Mall. I remember he looked terrible."

"Terrible? How?"

"You know, tired and spacy. He was in a men's clothing store. I was shopping for some pants for Scott. I said something like, 'Hey, you look like the bottom just fell out of the real estate market.' "

"Yes? And what did he say?"

"I don't remember. You're not drinking your sake."

"Actually, I am," he said, and raising the ceramic cup, said, "here's to my short stay in the Chicagoland area."

"It would be a shame for you to come all this way and leave empty-handed."

"I haven't even seen the lake yet. All this talk about the North Shore and I feel I might as well be marooned in Kansas."

"Then allow me."

"Allow you what?"

"Let me show you Lake Michigan. Come on, one more sake and I'll take you for a ride. The clouds are lifting."

Outside the restaurant window the cloud cover had thinned, and a creamy sheet of sunlight was falling on the wheat field across the road. She insisted on paying for lunch and preceded Harvey out of the restaurant into the parking lot. He couldn't take his eyes off her tennis skirt, which fell in pleats over her small behind.

"Here comes the sun," she said. "Let's take my car." She slid into the driver's seat and began throwing beer cans, paper cups, and hairbrushes into the back. Harvey got in the passenger side of the convertible and sat back with his eyes closed. The sun had already begun to warm the vinyl upholstery. The sake had drawn a tight circle around his consciousness. Inside the circle, he was aware only of the sun and the sound of Marilyn's voice as she pulled out onto Route 40.

"You're not married, are you?" she said.

"Yes, I am," he replied, the breeze brushing his face.

"I don't believe it. I can smell marriage on a man and you don't smell married."

"I've been living with the same woman for a few years. It's as good as marriage."

"Nothing's as good as marriage. Or as bad."

"And at which pole do you and your husband spend most of your time?"

"We don't spend time at either pole," Marilyn said. "We kind of stay right in the middle. That's our secret."

"No pain *and* no gain."

"No. Live and let live."

"I bet having children would change that," he said.

"Not something we have to worry about. I don't want them."

"Ever?"

"Ever."

"No kids. That leaves a lot of free time."

"My backhand needs a lot of attention."

"Why don't you want to have kids?"

"I don't love him. That's one reason."

"Does he love you?"

"Probably not. But we don't love each other equally."

"A perfect marriage."

"It suits me fine. This way, I wake up every morning and know just where I stand."

In ten minutes, they were on Sheridan Road, traveling south along the lake in Coleridge. Marilyn turned off Sheridan onto a winding access road that snaked down through a ravine until they were met by the yellow metal arm of a security gate with a Restricted Entry sign bolted to it. Marilyn yanked the car into park and Harvey jumped out to open the gate. She drove through, Harvey swung the gate back in place, and they continued down through the trees, past a small water treatment facility, and came out onto an apron of blacktop abutting a filthy, rubbly strip of beach. Marilyn parked the convertible in a corner of the parking lot under some trees, facing the water. They were obscured from the treatment plant by more trees. Behind them, the thick green bluff rose sixty feet to the lakefront homes.

She killed the engine and shifted on the seat to face him with her newly waxed bare legs tucked to one side.

"Some beach," Harvey said, averting his eyes. They landed on the northern edge of the horizon, where Waukegan's smokestacks coughed lightly against the sky. "So this is the 'shore' in North Shore," he said.

"I read that with all the toxic waste some of the waterbirds that eat Great Lakes fish are giving birth to a lot of deformed young." She seemed to specialize in depressing tidbits.

When Harvey looked at Marilyn Barger again, she was smiling at him. "Tell me something," she said. "Are you as attracted to me as I am to you?"

Harvey felt the whole moment lodge in his throat. "I find you . . . yes, I find you attractive."

"Good, because I'd like to take a run at you, okay? What do you say?"

Before Harvey had any idea what she was talking about, she was on her knees on the front seat, struggling with his zipper.

"Excuse me," Harvey managed to say with a laugh.

"Let's give this fella a little fresh air and exercise," she murmured, curling her index finger through his fly and locating his stiffening member. Gently, she guided it through the opening and closed her warm mouth over the tip.

Harvey threw his head back against the car seat and sighed. In an instant they had passed through the plane that separates the world from its urges.

"Oh, my, yes," Marilyn said and began devouring its full length, going to work so softly and quietly that Harvey felt he wouldn't have been aware of her activity had he not been the object of it.

Now she ran the tip of her tongue up and down the shaft repeatedly, slowly, like she might be some kind of engineer checking for flaws. Now she was up to something else altogether: Her long pink mop of a tongue started flicking at him, licking him politely—it reminded him of a child tidying up a melting ice cream cone.

"You're very good at this," he whispered.

"It's not as hard as it looks," she whispered back and suddenly was plunging furiously in his lap.

He closed his eyes, feeling the sun on the lids. His temples throbbed, ached with desire. Yet, somehow, it lacked intimacy for him. All that contact down below, but he felt like a spectator, albeit with the best seat in the house. Looking down at the top of her head, Harvey had the fantasy of getting out of the car, leaving the relevant part of him behind for her continued use.

She had a gift for it. He wondered whether, like the child violin prodigy or the twelve-year-old with a preternatural curveball, she had sensed her destiny early in life. Since practice made perfect, Harvey imagined himself at the end of a long line of beneficiaries of her art. But this was unfair to her, he thought; he had no evidence she made a career of this. She was a woman of some substance, some intelligence, some irony. She was, after all, a tennis-playing, sushi-eating suburban wife. There was nothing cheap about what was going on, just sudden and whimsical. Two adults ducking out into the alleyway behind the theater of their lives for a hot taste of common humanity.

Yet, already, the guilt was bleeding through, spoiling the picture.

He tried to banish thoughts of Mickey. In their—what was it?—six or seven years together, he had kept his nose clean up to now. He conjured up Norm's disapproving face. He even seemed to hear his father, dead twenty years now, grumbling in the background.

Marilyn Barger finally pulled away and tilted her flushed face up at him. "Well, I can see you're going to hold out longer than I am." She smiled, breathless, and sat back on her haunches on the front seat. "Get in the back seat," she ordered him.

"What?"

"In the back," she said. "My turn."

Harvey obeyed, opening the car door on his side. Out on the blue chop of Lake Michigan, two candy-colored windsurfer sails skimmed by. He released the lever on the front seat and climbed into the convertible's cluttered back.

Somehow, in his brief absence from the car, Marilyn had removed her panties, but not her skirt, and assumed a new position. She was on all fours between the bucket seats, her hands on the floor under the dashboard, her legs swung over in the back. Harvey found himself between them, staring at an engorged pink and purple blossom just inches away. She smelled of Fracas and dried perspiration.

He pressed his mouth against her and began to return the favor. Her moans egged him on. As he sucked her, he reached under her polo shirt and slid her bra up and over her breasts. There was more there than he had suspected, big handfuls of flesh. His cock pulsed with new excitement. She arched her back as he found her nipples. Suddenly her tennis shoes crossed and locked behind his head and within a few minutes, just as Harvey's tongue and neck were starting to cramp, her muffled cries rose from the vicinity of the dashboard, and he fantasized that the perplexed occupants of the houses on the bluffs were standing on their patios, peering through the trees to locate the source of all the commotion.

Then she slithered into the back seat and eyed his cock, which now rested against his thigh in a diminished state. "Hey, don't get lazy on me," she said and proceeded to finish the job she had begun fifteen minutes before.

"My God," Harvey said, eyes closed.

"I have to remember to keep my elbow in," she said, and they broke up in nervous laughter.

She climbed back into the front seat and took a travel-sized box of tissues out of the glove compartment. On the lake, the two windsurfers had been joined by a third. A freighter now moved hazily northward on the horizon. Marilyn came back, cradled Harvey's cock in the palm of one hand, and gently cleaned him off with the other.

"It's interesting, isn't it, what you'll do when the situation's clearly presented to you." She plucked a wad of fresh tissues out of the box and wiped herself.

"You do have a beautiful body," he said.

"You never know with people, do you?" she was saying. "It's true. I have a lot of curb appeal, as they say in the real estate business. But you never know what people look like on the inside."

He barely heard her. His mind was already far away, preparing his defense for the court of his conscience, stockpiling extenuating circumstances. Harvey pressed the heels of his hands against his eyes for a second and then looked at the woman who, just two hours ago, had been only a name in Jim Vaultt's ledger.

"Now what?" he said.

"Well, you have to catch a murderer and I"—she straightened her polo shirt—"I have some grocery shopping to do."

When they were back on Sheridan Road with the wind drying their faces, she turned to him and said, "You look like you're in shock."

"Well, this wasn't exactly on my schedule today."

"Oh, c'mon. You can admit to a little thing like wanting to get to know me better. I mean, if nothing had happened between us, you would've gone off thinking, 'Boy, another missed opportunity.' "

"It's a long way from the thought to the deed."

"That depends whose map you're using."

They were leaving Coleridge now on Route 40, heading back to the sushi bar. Harvey felt as if the familiar scenery of his life had fallen away like flats to reveal the distant landscape of casual sex, a world he thought he'd left behind. In the major leagues, there had always been lobby-hanging, halter-topped baseball groupies, and a couple of them had worn down his resistance. Once, in Anaheim, there was a young woman whose ambition it was to sleep only with .300 hitters, but who in a pinch would relax her standards. He could remember her chattering as she stripped in his hotel room, her gold anklet, the tiny tattooed butterfly above her sparse pubic hair, his feeling that he had been conquered, not desired. He had affected the genial denseness of one of his more promiscuous teammates, pretended to be him in order to dissociate his best self from the events taking place in his bed. "I never fucked anyone older than twenty-five before," she said matter-of-factly when it was over. He was jolted as Marilyn's car crossed the freight tracks.

"Door-to-door service," Marilyn said, turning into the strip mall's lot. "That was fun." As though they had enjoyed a nice competitive game of singles. "If you stick around, we should have lunch again. Where are you staying?"

"North Shore Suites Hotel." He got out of the car and stood next to it. "Well," he said, "see you around the quad."

"You know," she said, "I could learn to like you. Well, be good!" She jerked her convertible into reverse and, pulling away, blew him a kiss without making eye contact. It was the only kiss they had exchanged all afternoon.

8

HARVEY IGNORED THE flashing red message light on his room phone, undressed, yanked on his bathing suit, and did twenty laps in the empty motel pool. Each time he tilted his face out of the water to breathe, he heard the semis hissing and spitting on Edens Expressway thirty yards away. He turned against the gritty turquoise wall of the pool and changed to the breaststroke. He ripped off four more laps of the crawl, a kind of penance, chugging away, grabbing fistfuls of water on his final furious spurt. He caught his breath while hanging on to the pool's lip, and after casting a longing look at the ladder, hoisted himself with a grunt to the cement deck. He toweled off, tied the motel's thin terry cloth robe around him, ascended in an empty elevator to his room, and called the switchboard.

Lieutenant Dombrowski had called and so had Mickey, from WGBH-TV in Boston. He pictured her in her Spartan office there, excellent legs up on her desk, pencil between her teeth, hand twisting her auburn hair as she mentally resolved a knotty transition in her documentary. He took a deep breath and dialed her office, fighting off one guilty thought after another. The effort Mickey had made on his last birthday, even tracking down a couple of former Providence Jewels teammates for the celebration. And, more to the point, what a hard-ass she was on matters of principle; two months ago, she had written a long letter of complaint to the parent corporation of their local supermarket, whose manager she had observed being cruel to a homeless person.

His guilt was badly sharpened by one thought in particular: her father. Bruce Slavin, mid-sixtyish public interest lawyer in New York City, was as admirable as his daughter—warm, intelligent, forthright, athletic, full of integrity and social conscience. From the start, Bruce had treated Harvey with great respect, on the assumption that his daughter would never choose to consort with inferior people. It didn't hurt that Bruce was also a baseball fan whose most prized possession was a ball autographed by Jackie Robinson in 1949. He had raised Michele to believe that for her anything was not only possible but probable. And so, by the age of twenty-five, she had become the best television sports reporter in New England.

But her father had one flaw, and it was devastating for a daughter who looked up to him in so many other ways: He couldn't quite keep his pecker in his pants. When Mickey was an undergraduate at Columbia, her mother discovered her husband's parallel universe of extramarital affairs and chose Mickey's shoulder to cry on. The marriage managed to survive, but not so Mickey's trust in men. Her view of marriage dimmed drastically the winter night that her mother taxied up to Columbia in tears to take Mickey out for Indian food and a revelatory mother–daughter chat. Mickey henceforth never wanted to find herself in her mother's vulnerable position.

"Mickey Slavin," she said.

As soon as he heard her voice, he could feel his guilt converting to anger. It was unfair; he knew it. But he couldn't stop it. It suddenly boiled up in him, a conviction that it was some shortcoming in her that was responsible for his behavior with Marilyn.

"Hi," he said.

"How are you?"

"All right."

"How's it going?"

"The cops may have their first real suspect. I'm thinking of bailing out."

"Then come home. I kind of miss you."

It was like a spike through his heart now. If only she'd reject him, he could justify his anger.

"I miss you too," he managed.

"There's some trouble with Duane."

"What?" he said with alarm. Duane, one of their two middle-aged, doted-upon Siamese cats, had been sneezing ominously when Harvey left Boston.

"Well, he still wasn't eating, so I took him to the vet, and it turns out he's got a nasty upper-respiratory infection. He's all clogged up and since he can't breathe through his nose, he can't smell, and since he can't smell, he won't eat. The poor thing. He's already dehydrated. He just gasps for air through his mouth. He's thin, Bliss."

"What'd the vet say?" Harvey suddenly felt as if Duane were dying for his sins.

"He rehydrated him with some fluids. I'm supposed to run a hot shower and throw him in the bathroom to see if that opens up his nasal passages. If that doesn't work, I've got to take him back and the vet says he'll show me how to feed him with a syringe."

"How long did the vet say it'd be before he starts eating?"

Mickey sniffled. "That's the thing. The virus could go away tomorrow or it could be weeks. He said Siamese are so sensitive to stress, that sometimes they just decide to stop eating altogether."

"You mean he could just starve himself to death? All because of a stuffed nose?"

She was crying now, a rare indulgence for her. "Maybe Duane's reacting to all the stress between us lately."

Harvey didn't know what to say. An animal who slept on your neck when he knew you had a cold was not above blackmailing you into working on your relationship.

"We're not falling apart, are we?" she said.

"No, babe."

"It'd be so tacky to have to break up after all this."

"Extremely tacky. Let's stay together."

"At least for Duane's and Bubba's sake."

"Otherwise, the custody fight would be brutal."

"You should've seen him at the vet's"—she backed away from the sore topic—"suddenly he was just this sick, listless animal, reduced to all his dumb, decaying . . . you know, *animalness*. All the things that make him Duane aren't there anymore. It's like his personality's disappearing, leaving just an anonymous animal behind."

"He'll get better. Poor guy. I'll try to get out of here tomorrow."

"You sound weird, Bliss."

"I do?"

"Yeah, you all right? You sound kind of remote."

"How's Bubba doing?'

"Oh, he's fine, but he keeps ignoring Duane."

"That's a brother for you. Give them both a kiss for me. Your work all right?"

"Fine."

"Good."

"All right. I love you, Bliss. Be careful."

"Love you too, Mick."

He slowly lowered the receiver into its cradle, breathed deeply, and dialed Lieutenant Dombrowski's number. The desk sergeant put him on hold, and Harvey caught himself reliving his tryst with Marilyn. He had forgotten how addictive it was, that fantastic, uncanny, first knowledge of a stranger's body. Were there really grown men who paid no price for their extracurricular activities? If there were, why wasn't he one of them? And if he were, would a woman of Mickey's caliber ever have had anything to do with him in the first place?

"Is that you, son?" the lieutenant said.

"It's me."

"Minneapolis didn't wash."

"Lahey?"

"Just wanted you to know. Wriska talked to him and could tell right away he wasn't the type. Too intellectual."

"Leopold and Loeb were no slouches."

The reference sailed by Dombrowski. "Lahey even showed him a recent letter from Lynn Nyland, where she talks about giving it another try," he said. "I don't know how many times you can go back to the drawing board, but that's where we're going."

"Too bad," Harvey said.

"Don't ever let anyone tell you there's no such thing as a perfect crime. A confession's the only way this baby's going down."

"Yeah."

"Oh, one other thing, Harvey."

"What's that?"

"Who's this woman Marilyn Barger you were talking to?"

The receiver froze in Harvey's hand. "What're you talking about?"

"C'mon, I'm talking about a woman named Marilyn Barger, that's what I'm talking about. You were with her earlier today."

Oh, Jesus, Harvey thought. "When'd you start tailing me, Lieutenant?"

Dombrowski laughed demonically. "We've just been keeping a periodic eye on you. What the hell."

"What's the matter? Can't you develop leads on your own?"

"Now, now, son. Don't take it personally. But this *is* my home court. So who is she and what were you talking to her about?"

"What'd you do? Run her plates?"

"At the Japanese restaurant. She isn't someone we've run across yet."

Harvey breathed a little easier; at least they hadn't followed them to the beach. "She's just someone Peplow showed some houses to once at Rimwood Estates. I picked up her name from Vaultt's ledgers.

Don't worry—she didn't deliver. I think she's just bored and wanted
to get out."

"Probably just wanted a little wiggly."

"I should be so lucky," Harvey said.

"You keep on checking in with me now."

"Fine, Lieutenant. But keep your fucking men out of my rearview mirror."

Dombrowski let out a large laugh and was gone.

Harvey opened his spiral notebook again and dialed the office
number of Sy Pincus, the older businessman who had been Peplow's
frequent tennis partner at The Tennis Club in Coleridge.

"Pincus Associates," the receptionist said. "May I help you?"

"Is Mr. Sy Pincus there, please? This is Harvey Blissberg. I'm a
private detective."

Within twenty seconds, a boisterous voice greeted him: "Private,
huh? I guess I better not put you on the speakerphone!"

"Mr. Pincus, my name's Harvey Blissberg. I'm in town to
investigate Laurence Peplow's murder."

"I confess! I confess! I only got four points off him the last set we
played and I couldn't take it anymore!" His voice fell an octave.
"Listen, I'm sorry. It's nothing to joke about." Yet it was clear
that Pincus was too old to waste precious time grieving over lost
acquaintances. The world threw so much at you, after a while some
things didn't do any damage.

"Listen," Pincus went on, "the problem is it's Friday afternoon
and we all get a little crazy here in the office. We're throwing a
birthday party for one of my salesmen and we have a very liberal
policy about champagne."

"Well, I won't take you away from your celebration—"

"Forget it! Everyone's passed out! I'm the last conscious person in
the office! Talk to me!"

"I'd like to ask you about him."

"There's nothing much to say. I've been through this with the police. They were very impressed with how little I could tell them about a guy I played tennis with for more than two years."

"Still. You never know. If I could talk to you, maybe something would click."

"Then stop in tomorrow afternoon at my house. We're having a little barbecue."

"I was hoping for some time alone."

"Don't worry. We'll have time alone. I've known my friends so long, who needs to talk to them anymore? It's like the old joke about prison inmates telling jokes by number they know them so well. They come over, they eat some potato salad, they go home! Six-ten Camden Court, just off of Sheridan Road. Come around three."

Next he called Lynn Nyland's apartment in Coleridge and left a message on her machine, leaving his hotel number and saying he'd try her again tomorrow. Then he took a long shower and dressed for dinner at the home of his brother, Professor Norman Blissberg.

"I FEEL LIKE one of those old ladies we used to see toe-clamming on the Cape during the summer when we were kids," he said at the dinner table when the conversation had turned to Larry Peplow. "I'm just poking around in the muck."

"Excellent simile," Norm said, helping himself to more of the vegetables Linda had grilled outside on the Weber.

"Except there is no muck."

"Okay," Norm said, "so it's not such a great simile. But 'clammed up'—" he added. "That's not a bad description of the man."

"Glad you approve, Norm," Harvey said, playing with the ceramic napkin ring. Since his last visit to Norm and Linda's big brick Victorian, they'd added several bourgeois touches, including an antique pine hutch and an expensive couch with rolled arms and down cushions.

"What's eating you?" his brother asked.

Out of the corner of his eye Harvey watched his sister-in-law shoot
Norm a scolding look. The other guest, Peplow's old college friend
Stuart Silver, a heavyset real estate agent with a full black beard to
which shreds of the evening's meal were clinging, seemed unaware of
the little drama.

"What's eating me?" Harvey said. "I'll tell you what's eating me.
Usually there's something to say about a dead man. A man leaves a
record. He had some unsavory associations, big debts, prior arrests.
Maybe he was seen arguing in a bar with a stranger. Or a friend comes
forward and tells the cops he'd warned the guy about drugs. *Something*.
Peplow doesn't leave a record. I've looked at the case file and it points
nowhere. All I know is he played basketball with you guys twice a
week and was capable of screwing clients out of a house when he saw
a bigger commission elsewhere."

There was sudden silence at the table, almost as if Harvey had just
this minute brought them the news of Peplow's death. Stuart Silver
raked his fingers through his beard. Norm pushed some grilled
asparagus across his plate, looking depressed. They were all at the age
when the disappearance of any friend packed a morbid punch. People
were starting to get crossed off the list of the living. At his mother's
seventieth birthday party the year before, Harvey had surveyed the
scene and thought it all looked like an old home movie of a party that
had happened long ago and the participants had all passed away.
When he mentioned it to Dr. Ellyn Walker, she said his fear of loss
was so great that it was easier for him to fantasize that everyone was
already dead than that they were living and he would someday lose
them. Maybe that was what held him back from marriage. If he
married Mickey, it meant he would someday die, and so would she.
But as long as they just lived together, maybe they would live forever.

"You know," Silver said, "the fact that he considered me a good
friend was really kind of alarming. My God, in four years of college
maybe I spent a couple nights drinking with him. Okay, now fast-
forward fifteen years. I'd had no contact with him. He was just a face

from college you might pass again on the street once or twice before you die. Suddenly, four years ago, I get a phone call from the guy. He's in Portland, Maine, and he tells me he wants to move to Chicago and get his real estate license. 'Hey, how are you, Stu, old buddy?' he's saying, like in the interim I haven't gotten married, divorced, and put on thirty pounds. Only the lonely do that sort of thing, right? So he moved here, I helped him find his job at Schmauss and Weevens, got him into our basketball game, and worried he was going to leech off of me socially or something. But he never did. He remained a complete mystery."

"Did you know he was a therapist in Maine?" Harvey asked.

"Well, sure. He told me he didn't want to spend any more of his life sitting in a chair listening to the same boring secrets and getting hemorrhoids."

Harvey wondered why Peplow told some he had been a therapist, but not others, like Norm. He wondered if Peplow didn't volunteer the information because it would make him seem less like a regular guy. "What was he like at Bowdoin?" he asked.

Silver picked a crumb of dinner roll off his beard. "Just a couple of snapshots in my head. He had a car, a vintage Mustang, and sometimes a girl in it. I remember him standing in the back of the college green at antiwar rallies. You know, the charming outsider. He was so good-looking and slick, my first thought was, he was a preppie from an eccentric old family or something. He sometimes wore a black cape lined with scarlet corduroy. I think he had monogrammed shirts. It was only later that I learned he came from some unhappy middle-class family in upstate New York. But we all outgrow our pretensions, don't we? He just seemed like one of those full-of-himself people who is still really interested in other people. You felt like he *got* you." Silver tapped the table with his fist.

"He once talked about you, Harvey," Norm said.

"What do you mean—how'd he know about me?"

Linda laughed. "C'mon, Norm brags about you all the time."

"When it came up in conversation that you were my brother," Norm went on, "he said he used to go down to Fenway to see the Red Sox when you were playing. He said you weren't afraid of outfield walls. I guess he'd seen you crash into a few."

Harvey swirled the Pinot Grigio in his glass. "Did Peplow ever bend any rules?"

The question caught Silver with a forkful of rice pilaf halfway to his mouth. "Now that you mention it"—he returned the fork to his plate—"yeah, there was one thing. The night before a midterm paper was due in, I think it was a lit. survey course we were both taking, he asked me to help him out and show him the one I had written. Apparently, he hadn't gotten around to writing one yet. Too busy ironing his shirts, probably. We had different section leaders so he thought he could get away with a little peek at my work."

"And you obliged?"

"I'm sorry to say that I did."

"Partners in crime, huh?" Harvey said with a smile.

"Well," Silver said, a little uncertainly. "Come to think of it, he probably felt we had some sort of bond. I certainly didn't feel it. But he never mentioned the midterm to me when he came here."

"He was a cheater," Harvey said.

"Let he who is without sin," Norm said.

"I know, I know," Harvey said to him. "You think I'm a prude."

"Not really. I just think you talk like one."

"C'mon, we all have secrets," Stu said.

"Not as big as Larry Peplow's, I'll bet," Linda said.

Norm said, "What's your secret, Stu?"

"This beard isn't real," Stu replied, pretending to begin to peel it off.

Norm laughed. "No, no. No fake beard looks as bad as yours."

"What's *your* secret, Norm?" Stu asked.

"Mine?" he said. "My secret is that I wish I could've been my brother."

"How sweet of you," Harvey said, mugging.

"I'm serious, Harv. What red-blooded American boy wouldn't want to play in the big leagues? You stopped appreciating that somewhere along the line."

"When you're in it for a while, it's just a high-paying job."

"Well, Harv, that's the difference between you and Pete Rose. He never lost his love for it."

"Not the only difference between Pete and me," Harvey said. "I only had to retire from the game. He had to be banned. Think of how many fewer hearts I broke when I hung up my spikes."

"Where have you gone, Harvey Blissber-erg?" Norm sang. "A brother turns his lonely eyes to you."

"Now, now, boys," Linda said.

"No joking, Harv," Norm said, "when you were playing, did you know that I used to begin the first class of the semester by introducing myself and then adding, 'And for the many of you who must be wondering, yes, I am the brother of baseball player Harvey Blissberg. And, incidentally, anyone of you who can stand up right now and tell me what his lifetime batting average is can waive the midterm."

"Well?"

"Well, of course, even the girls would take wild guesses in the hope of escaping the midterm, but no one ever did. It sure broke the ice, though."

"If you're telling the truth, I'm touched. If not, that's cruel."

Norm flexed his eyebrows. "It's cruel either way, considering what your batting average was."

"Don't let him talk to you like that," Silver said.

"Why not? It's one of his few pleasures in life, ragging me. But, it's true, I didn't come here to be maligned, especially by someone with the waistline of Cecil Fielder."

"You're just jealous. You could have a waistline like this, too"— Norm plumped his gut—"if you ate more food. Here." He pushed the chicken platter toward him.

Watching Norm—paler, heavier, a vaguely funhouse version of himself—Harvey pondered the difficult fate of brothers. It was to look in the mirror and see someone whose particulars were all too familiar, but whose sum was alien, inaccessible, opposed to yours. For it was one of Family's jobs to cast its members into cleverly distinct roles, to drive the bearers of all this genetically overlapping material into the safety of their own exaggerated identities. And so Norm had been the cautious, smart, political one, and to Harvey fell the part of the witty, rebellious one.

Harvey admitted to himself at last what his fantasy had been: to come to Chicago, identify Peplow's killer in a brilliant display of deduction, and fly out triumphantly while his only, beaming sibling stood proudly on the tarmac with his friends, saying, *"That,* boys, was my little brother."

But here he was at his first job-performance review, and his work was sadly lacking. On top of it, he remembered with a stab, he'd spent part of the afternoon in the backseat of Marilyn Barger's Chrysler.

9

WHEN HE PASSED from the hot, crickety night into the empty North Shore Hotel Suites lobby at eleven o'clock, Shari nodded to him from the desk.

"Mr. Blissberg."

"Hi, Shari."

"Have you seen Lake Michigan yet?"

"I have. Thank you. How's business?"

"Picking up. Tomorrow we've got eighty insurance people in for some conference."

"That should be exciting."

Shari inclined her head toward the far corner of the lobby. "Someone's been waiting for you."

Marilyn Barger got up from a tub chair and started toward him. She was wearing her official uniform—a tennis outfit. "Hi," she said, patting her shoulder bag. "I've brought the documents you asked for."

Harvey almost asked "What documents?" before it occurred to him that Marilyn was only trying to dispel Shari's suspicions that her visit was anything other than business.

"Yes," he said. "The documents. Good of you to come." Shari was bowed busily over her computer terminal. "Why don't we do this upstairs?"

As she preceded him to the elevator, she touched her own behind. Harvey was convinced that women did this only when they knew a man was looking at them, in the hope that it had somehow gotten smaller since they last checked.

In his room, Marilyn sat in a chair by the window, surveyed the room, and clapped her hands. "How's the investigation going?"

Harvey leaned against the dresser. "Well, it's not the boyfriend from Minnesota. The field's wide open again and I guess I'm back in business."

"Congratulations."

"Now, listen. This afternoon—" Harvey began.

"What about this afternoon?"

"I don't want you to get the wrong idea. That was just something that happened."

She made a pouty face. "You mean you won't cherish the memory forever?"

"Don't be silly. I filled three pages in my diary about you."

"You're sorry I came tonight."

"No, no," he protested.

"If you're worried about my husband, he's in Detroit, selling next spring's line of women's scarves."

"Your husband's far down on my list of worries."

"How can you say no to this body?"

"Only through the most strenuous suppression of my desire, I can assure you."

"Anyway, I'm here on business. I remembered what Peplow said to me at the mall that time."

Harvey sat on the edge of the bed, facing her. "What?" Anything sounded good to him now.

"It's funny I would've forgotten it until now."

"What'd he say?"

"Well, we got to talking about the houses at Rimwood Estates. I guess he could tell I wasn't all that interested in them by then, and he said, 'It's just as well, 'cause I came across some information about Rimwood, which I don't know what to do with, but maybe it's just as well you and your husband aren't really interested in that house there.' "

"Go on."

"All right. He said that he'd heard that there was toxic waste under Rimwood Estates."

"Toxic waste?"

"That years ago, when people were dumping stuff illegally, some plant in the area was paying the man who owned the land to let them bury stuff there. That's why he said it was just as well Scott and I weren't in a position to buy there."

"Who'd he hear it from?"

"He didn't say. He just said he stumbled on it by accident."

"He didn't tell you what kind of toxic waste it was or how long ago it happened?"

"C'mon, it was just something he threw out talking to me at a mall."

"What else did he tell you?"

"Just that he wasn't sure what he was going to do with the information."

"You're telling me the truth?"

"Yes."

"You realize what you're telling me, don't you?"

"I think so. If it was true and it got out, Rimwood Estates would be up a creek."

Harvey got up and began pacing back and forth at the end of the bed. Vaultt might've known and covered it up, but it wouldn't matter if Vaultt *knew* there was waste buried there or not. If it *was* buried there, he was cooked if Peplow made it public. The houses were already built. It might cost millions to clean it up. *If* it could be cleaned up at all. And even if it could be cleaned up, who'd buy an eight-hundred-thousand-dollar house on a piece of land that *used* to be a dump site? Harvey said, "Holy shit."

"But I was thinking," she said, "Peplow was killed right next to Rimwood Estates, right?"

"Right. In the field."

"Would the guy be stupid enough to do it there?"

Harvey brooded on this. In Rimwood's favor was that it was one place Vaultt could get rid of Peplow without being seen. No one lived in his houses yet. The field was hundreds of yards from the nearest people. Harvey's mind ran ahead into the maze of logic, looking for a route. Peplow goes to Vaultt, tells him about the rumor, and offers him his silence for a price. Harvey wouldn't put *that* past Peplow. So Vaultt discreetly has the land tested and the soil sample comes up positive. Peplow finds out and raises his price, infuriating Vaultt. Vaultt figures that Peplow hasn't mentioned the toxic waste to anybody else, so there wouldn't be a motive floating around to connect Vaultt to him if Peplow happened to die suddenly. Which he does. But who tipped Peplow off? Maybe some old-timer around here who knew all the dirty secrets before all the Midas Muffler shops and the malls started going up?

"Marilyn, try to remember exactly what he said to you at the mall."

"I've told you what I remember."

"Try. Did he say, 'Some guy told me,' or 'Some woman told me,' or what?"

"I'm pretty sure he just said he'd heard."

Vaultt had told him whom he bought the land from. A Scandinavian name. Lagervist? No, that was some novelist that Mickey liked and tried to get Harvey to read once. Arnquist?

"That's all I know." As she said it, she casually undid the top button of her tennis dress. "Well, that takes care of business."

"No, Marilyn. C'mon. Really."

"C'mon yourself. Don't you think healthy lust has its own rules. That we ought to observe?"

"No."

She got up and guided the curtains closed with the plastic wand. "Listen, I want you to know I'm a completely safe person to be mingling bodily fluids with. I don't make a habit of descending on helpless men like yourself."

"You could've fooled me."

She stepped out of her Footjoys and came over to sit cross-legged on the middle of the quilted pastel bedspread. "Look, I want to level with you, okay? Nothing much happens between Scott and me in the bedroom. It's not a big problem. It suits us fine. But it builds up. The moment you walked into the restaurant today, I thought, here's a man who can help me with my condition. And I looked at the way you looked at me and I thought, here's a man who wants to help."

"It's my famous poker face."

"Oh, stop it. Men wear their cocks on their sleeves. So, look, why don't we just start acting like a couple of healthy grown-ups who find themselves alone in a motel room?"

"Not that simple."

She suddenly reached out and took Harvey's hands in hers. "Harvey, don't you know that there're a few days set aside in every person's life when the usual rules don't apply? Just a few days out of a lifetime of good behavior when it's all right to screw up a little? You know, God once in a while turns his head and cuts us a little slack. You don't know that?"

He had to admire her grasp of the situation; she was so clinically proficient at every aspect of it, so discreetly indiscreet. Beyond establishing that he wasn't technically married, she had asked him nothing personal. It was as though she were throwing up a wall around him to obscure the rest of his life.

She had undone the rest of the buttons and slipped out of the top of her tennis dress. Her large breasts swelled out of a French-cut bra.

Before Harvey could register another protest, she cupped her breasts in her hands and said, "Let me tell you something funny about these."

"Put your dress back on, Marilyn."

"See, I've had these since I was fourteen. When I was a teenager, my mother was jealous of my breasts. My mother was small-breasted and I honestly don't think she could accept it. When I was a freshman in high school and couldn't get into B cups anymore, she kept buying me B cups. She didn't want them to get any bigger. She used to make fun of them. She used to say, 'You better not let any of the boys have a look at those, honey.' That's a great message to give a teenage girl, isn't it? Think about what kind of mother would do something like that. It can scare you. It really can."

"Thanks for sharing that with me."

"There's no need to make nervous jokes, Harvey." She reached down to undo the hook between the brilliantly white cups and her breasts sprang out. "Think of all the women around here who have expensive surgery to get what I got for free. And I didn't even know what I had for a long time" She licked the fingers of her left hand and began rotating a nipple, coaxing it erect.

"This is crazy, Marilyn. That's enough."

"Where's your sense of fun?" She took his hands again and drew him down to the bed. "Come here." She placed her right hand behind Harvey's head and brought him closer.

"This is crazy."

"The body of a twenty-year-old and the experience of a lifetime, huh?"

"There's a portrait of you somewhere aging in a closet."

"Come here, honey."

Harvey drew back at the endearment.

"Now what?"

"Tell me something."

"What?"

"Did you sleep with Peplow?"

She slapped him hard across the face, then quickly covered her breasts with her hands. "You're out of your fucking mind. What do you think I am?"

Harvey touched his tingling mouth. "I had to ask."

"You think I'm someone I'm not." She stuffed herself back into her bra and jammed her arms into the tennis dress. "I overestimated you. Let's just forget it."

"I'm sorry, Marilyn. I had to ask. Look, it's my job."

She glared at him, big dark eyes dancing with tears. "You're the one who's cheap, not me."

"All right. So you didn't sleep with Peplow."

"The point is, I don't sleep around."

"I understand that now. I'm sorry."

"All right." She sniffled. "I'm sorry I slapped you. It's not my style."

Harvey pressed two fingertips against his upper lip. "You do it very well."

"Beginner's luck."

Harvey leaned in to kiss the side of her neck. Her skin smelled like plums. His whole body ached.

"Don't try to make it up to me," she breathed.

"Hey," he breathed back in her perfect ear, "cut me a little slack."

10

WHEN HARVEY ROLLED through the second set of gates at
Rimwood Estates late Saturday morning, Jim Vaultt was standing in
the front yard of one of his exotic creations, directing workmen to
plant dogwoods. He wore a many-pocketed pale yellow guayabera
streaked with dirt. When Harvey came over and stood next to him in
the ferocious sun, Vaultt slowly removed his wraparound sunglasses
and said, "Good morning, Harvey."

"Morning, Jim. How are things?"

"Couldn't be having more fun if I tried." He signaled for a
workman to lug the sapling in his arms farther to the left. "I love
pushing nature around. It's my revenge for all the things nature has
done to me. To what do I owe this surprise visit?"

"Thought I'd stop by to see if you remembered anything else."

"You seem very cat-and-mouse today, Harvey. But the facts
haven't changed."

"Memories improve."

"Mine's not likely to."

"You were still at the movies in Wahatan on April seventeenth?"

"That's right."

Harvey took out his little spiral notebook and flipped it open.
"On April seventeenth the Wahatan Cinema was showing a Fred

Astaire–Ginger Rogers double bill. *Top Hat* started at eight-twenty and *Swingtime* at ten-thirty. *Swingtime* lasts a hundred and three minutes, so it would've let out at about ten or fifteen after midnight. Assuming it started on time."

"Now back over to the right a little!" Vaultt yelled at the workmen. "I want 'em to see that damn dogwood out the breakfast nook window!" He turned to Harvey. "That sounds about right."

"Did you see both that night?"

"Just *Swingtime*."

"During which time Peplow was murdered."

"That's what the medical examiner determined. Between eleven and midnight."

"Did anybody see you at the movies?"

"You're trying my patience, Harvey, but, yes, many people saw me there. Just nobody who knows me. So you're going to have to take my word I was there. But it's all academic unless you can think of a motive for me to kill this guy Peplow."

"Yeah, I'll have to work on that."

"Harvey," Vaultt said, watching the workmen, "do you have any idea what it's like being thought capable of murder? What it's like to have your character so thoroughly misunderstood?"

First Marilyn, now Vaultt—why was it he kept getting everybody wrong? "Haven't had the pleasure," he said.

"Well, let me tell you, it's very strange standing next to you and knowing that you are seriously considering the possibility that I was capable of shooting a man in the face, let alone had reason to do so."

"There's a first time for everything."

"Don't be a jerk, Harvey. You want me to save you some valuable time?"

"Sure."

"I didn't do it. I told you on Thursday I didn't do it, and that hasn't changed. In other words, I haven't in the interim remembered that I killed Larry Peplow."

"Oh, well." Harvey pressed on the sod with the toe of his shoe. "So let's change the subject. How about Fred Astaire?"

"You like him?"

"I have a high regard for someone who can do anything that well." Astaire, in fact, was fresh in his mind. A few months ago, in an effort no doubt to rejuvenate their relationship, Mickey had rented *Swingtime, The Gay Divorcee,* and *Top Hat* for the two of them to watch.

"Talk about grace under pressure," Vaultt said.

"Talk about making the hard stuff look easy. I love that number in *Swingtime*—'The Continental.' 'It's so en-chant-ing, the Cont-i-nen-tal.' " He sang in that voice that Mickey once described as "very beautiful except for its tunelessness." "The thing goes on forever, doesn't it? Does it still hold up?"

"Sure. Absolutely."

Harvey plucked at his shirt. The heat was intense. "Hey, Jim, what's a guy like you doing here, anyway? You don't have a family?"

"Divorced. My wife and daughter are in L.A. I'm a refugee from domestic life."

They watched a second workman puncture the sod with a shovel to make a hole for the dogwood. "Well," Harvey said, "I guess I better be going."

Vaultt squinted at the sky. "Kind of hot, isn't it, to be gumshoe-ing around?"

Harvey brushed some sweat off his hairline. "Well, you know, Jim, the pursuit of justice knows no weather."

"Very nicely put," Vaultt said. "Very nice."

"Thank you."

He left the developer motioning about the placement of a second dogwood and drove north toward the town of Wheeling. That morning he had called the public information officer for the Illinois EPA, a David Kimmel in Oak Park, and roused him from his Saturday-morning lethargy to answer a few questions about land pollution.

"You're telling me that no toxic substance has surfaced at the site?" Kimmel had said after Harvey told him about his third-hand report.

"That's right."

"You know the source of this rumor?"

"Not yet."

"Look, any toxin would have to have an exposure route that poses a threat. Like it would have to leach into the well water or the septic tank. Or, during construction, the earthmoving equipment might uncover it.

"But when a developer buys a piece of land to build on, doesn't he by law or something have to test the soil for possible pollution?"

"In Illinois, we've got something called the Property Transfer Act, but it applies only to business properties. Before a business property changes hands, a consultant comes in and does a paper-trail audit to determine if there're any problems. But not in the case of residential land."

"I see. Now, in your view, is it plausible that someone was paying off the previous owner to dump toxic waste or something on the land?"

"Oh, sure, it can happen. Every once in a great while, some excavation in the Chicagoland area turns up fifty-five-gallon drums of illegally dumped polychlorinated biphenyls."

"PCBs?"

"PCBs or PCEs—perchloroethylenes. It's scary how much illegal dumping went on before the 1984 land ban."

"And if it were discovered that a new housing development had been built on contaminated land, if it were made public, what would happen to the development?"

"First, your Field Operation Services guys would have to go out and take samples. There's a whole scoring process, and depending on the hazardous waste score, the problem would fall under one of several programs. If it was bad enough, it could end up under the federal EPA Superfund."

"Meanwhile, as far as the people living there—"

"You could kiss the development good-bye."

Harvey turned off the four-lane at a traffic light and came out from under a viaduct carrying the freight tracks between Chicago and Milwaukee to find himself in farm country only occasionally interrupted by an older middle-class housing development. He consulted the Post-it on his dash, where he had written the directions to Arnold Lundquist's house, and drove west.

Despite the cold and constant blast from the air conditioner's vents, his skin felt feverish and sticky. He shifted in his seat and pulled his matted pants from the back of his thighs. After Marilyn Barger had left his hotel room last night, he had barely had the energy to call Mickey in Cambridge to announce that he would be staying on for a while. Duane was no better, and Harvey got off the phone sickened with his betrayal, yet determined somehow to justify it. In any case, he could not feel with Marilyn's conviction that there were a few days set aside in everyone's life when the usual rules didn't apply. There was a trick to looking the other way, some psychological sleight-of-hand that could not be learned this late in life.

He had finally fallen asleep at two, sedated by two rationalizations. First, at Marilyn's insistence once again there had, technically, been no sexual intercourse. Second, that she had provided him with a lead that, if it panned out, would mitigate, if not excuse, his dalliance with her. Maybe Peplow had happened to run into someone who said, "Oh, the old Lundquist land. I remember when the old farmer was taking money to let PCBs be buried there back in the fifties." According to Kimmel of the Illinois EPA, Vaultt wouldn't have known of it when he bought the land and built on it. Only if Peplow had tried to blackmail Vaultt with it would Vaultt have found out, and then, quite possibly, killed him to protect his investment. But where was he going to find the information's source now, this needle in the North Shore haystack? Certainly Lundquist wasn't going to say, but the old farmer might give something away. Harvey would settle for a sense of where the lies were.

At the sound of the Lincoln Town Car coming up the gravel driveway of his pink ranch house, the white-haired Lundquist appeared on the front stoop in blue jeans and a western shirt. Harvey wondered how the man was able to stand at such an odd angle until he noticed the cane Lundquist was leaning on. As he shook the farmer's fibrous old hand, Harvey figured him for well into his seventies, although the brown face alone, as grooved and dry as an overbaked cookie, might have suggested something closer to a hundred-year-old Indian chieftain. A true relic, Harvey thought, sure to know a great deal more than he would ever say.

"You're asking me," Lundquist said when they were seated in the dark living room not far from the floor fan creaking in its cage, "if my old land was ever used as a dumping ground for chemicals?"

Harvey had tried to put it as delicately as possible, but he already felt the farmer's wrath. "You understand, I'm simply checking out a rumor. A man was killed on your property, the part you still own next to the housing development."

"I know that, son."

"I'm looking for a motive for that slaying." The house smelled wonderfully of fresh cake.

"You're asking me if there's some chemical I let somebody put in my ground that's eating away down there?"

"I'm not saying—"

"That I took money to let someone foul my land?" He tapped his cane unhappily on every noun.

"Mr. Lundquist, if it's true, I only want the information to help solve a killing and not to bring any unpleasantness into your life."

"You've already brought plenty and you've only been here five minutes."

"I'm sorry, sir. Can I ask you about this man Vaultt you sold your land to?"

"What about him?"

"Did you get to know him at all?"

"Only met him at the watchamacallit."

"The closing?"

"And I didn't much want to meet him even then. It was my daddy's farm and it beat me down a little to sell off any part of it. But my son's a computer programmer in Michigan and I was getting too old." He tapped his cane twice on the floor. "Is that about it now, son?"

Harvey stood. "That's about it, sir. I'm sorry to intrude."

Lundquist slowly raised his great frame from the Barcalounger and said, "Now, look here"—Harvey waited for a final denunciation—"as long as you're here, you might as well take some muffins home with you. The missus bakes up a storm every Saturday." He disappeared into the kitchen and came back with three muffins in a Ziploc sandwich bag, still warm through the plastic.

Lundquist had given nothing away. It was a half hour's drive from Wheeling back down to Sy Pincus's house in Coleridge. Harvey went through all three muffins.

Sy Pincus lived in a rambling, cantilevered contemporary house set into the side of a cool, wooded ravine near the lake. Vivaldi's *Four Seasons* floated out of the French doors onto a flagstone patio where a woman in a black service uniform circulated with canapés among several couples. Judging by the unforced laughter that rose into the trees above them, they were old friends. A leonine man in light pants and a frayed madras shirt came out of the crowd with a drink in his hand to meet Harvey at the edge of the patio.

"Sy Pincus!" he announced.

"I'm Harvey Blissberg. The detective who phoned you yesterday."

"Of course!" Pincus took Harvey by the back of the neck with rough bonhomie. "Glad to see you. Come over and I'll introduce you to my friends. At least they're people who *say* they're my friends, but what the hell!"

"Really, it's unnecessary."

Undaunted, Pincus introduced him to a man named Klinger, "the Cruller King of Chicago," and his wife, Ruth; to someone named Greco, "Your Man for Mattresses," and his wife, Donna, a cellist for the Chicago Symphony.

"I'm afraid it all means nothing to me," Harvey whispered to him during a lull in the introductions. "I'm from Boston."

"Boston! Home of the bean and the cod!" He grabbed a passing gray-haired woman and swung her around to face Harvey. "At least you can say hello to this wonderful specimen, my wife, Harriet. Harriet, this is Harvey Blissberg."

"Glad to meet you," she said tightly, casting a disapproving glance at her husband's drink.

"Harvey's in from Boston to investigate the murder of my former singles partner, Larry."

"I see," Harriet said blankly. She seemed unable or unwilling to integrate this information. "If you'll excuse me, I've got to run to the kitchen. You know—new caterer."

"Can I pour you a drink?" Pincus asked, but before Harvey could answer a man in his thirties with an expensive haircut stepped between them.

"Sy," the man said, "I wanted to thank you. Great party, but I've got to get back to Beth. Nice seeing you."

Pincus pumped the man's hand. "Georgie, I never got to ask you how things are in the commodities business."

"They're just great, Sy," the man said, anxious to leave. "Give me a call next week and I'll tell you all about it." He pulled out of Pincus's grasp and backed onto the gravel driveway, waving.

"You look more and more like your father every day!" Pincus called after him, then turned to Harvey. "That's Mr. Made-a-Million-This-Morning-in-the-Commodities-Market." He took a lusty gulp of his Scotch. "I remember when his father used to unload scrap steel right off the railroad cars by hand! Built an empire from scratch and still puts in a full day at seventy-four! But Georgie there buys and sells things that don't even exist yet and he's going to retire at the age of forty-five with all the money in the world. What kind of life is that? Plus he hits his overhead like a girl."

Pincus pointed to a man on the patio. "Now Ken Greco's got a son, he made a fortune inventing a foot-long egg for the food service industry that's got something like forty-eight center slices, and now he doesn't know what to do with himself. I'm telling you, Harvey, these young guys don't know what it means to build something. They should be working their butts off for the love of it! They don't have a knot in their stomach, that's what it is. Not one of them looks scared! Come on"—he took Harvey abruptly by the upper arm—"I'll show you where the booze is."

He walked ahead of Sy Pincus into the house, which held a gracious mix of antiques and contemporary pieces. The original art on the walls was impressive, except for one amateurish painting of a clown near the fireplace.

"An original Gacy," Pincus said.

"Not a name I know."

"John Wayne Gacy? Convicted in 1980 of killing thirty-three young men? Buried most in the crawl space of his house in Chicago?"

"You're kidding! That guy who worked children's parties?"

"Yes sir. That's how he spends his time. Sits in a windowless cell twenty-three hours a day painting landscapes, clowns, and Disney characters."

"That's ghoulish."

"A friend of a friend, a lawyer, got it for me. But Gacy's no longer allowed to sell paintings outside prison, so that Bozo there is virtually priceless. But I see you don't approve."

"I haven't formed an opinion yet."

Pincus turned to the bartender and handed him his glass. "Top me off there, please. Harvey, what're you drinking?"

"I'll have what you're having."

Pincus led Harvey into an adjoining room, most of it glass, looking out on a vast network of trees on the receding slope of the prehistoric ravine. They sat with their Scotches.

"So," Pincus said, running a hand through his silvery hair, "Larry Peplow."

"How long did you know him?"

"Oh, well, he must have joined the club two years ago. I'd say we played singles together pretty regularly. I liked playing with Larry because he never took advantage of my old legs by drop-shotting me to death. Guys my own age, Harvey, they dink you to death. But Larry, he hit out. Of course, he liked to blow eighty-mile-an-hour crosscourt forehands right by me. He had the killer instinct. Would've made a damn good salesman, if you ask me."

Harvey twirled the ice cubes in his Scotch. "But he *was* a salesman. He sold real estate."

"Selling houses? That's a woman's game. Larry had a knot in his stomach and fire in his belly. Not like the kids who grew up here."

"Did you socialize with him?"

"I think we had him over here for a party once. Other than that, I just saw him at the club. Between sets we'd sit and talk and watch the *alter kockers* hit tennis balls. The thing I like best about this kid, he laughed at my jokes. You ever hear the one about the man in his eighties goes to the doctor and says, 'Doc, when I was a young man and had an erection, I couldn't bend it. Now I can bend it easy. Doc, you think I'm getting stronger?' "

"Hadn't heard that one," Harvey said.

"You know, Harriet and I just celebrated our forty-fifth wedding anniversary. On our honeymoon, she sat on the edge of the bed and cried. This time, *I* sat on the edge of the bed and cried."

"Did you—" Harvey began.

"So Moses says to God on Mount Sinai, 'Now let me get this straight—the Arabs get the oil and we get to cut off the tips of our *what?*' " Pincus paused to suck down some Scotch.

"Mr. Pincus, can you remember what you talked about? Did he ever reveal much about himself?"

"I remember one time, we talked about our mothers."

"Your mothers?"

"I told Larry, when I was a young man, mine used to throw herself across the door to keep me from leaving home. When I told Larry that, he said, 'I wish I'd had one like yours.' I said, 'But that's not love, Larry, that's *meshuga,*' and he said, 'I never loved my mother, and I don't believe she ever loved me.' He said, 'My mom's a cold fish.' "

"Did he ever mention anyone he was in trouble with? Anyone who might've wished him harm?"

"I take it his mother's not a suspect."

Harvey acknowledged the quip with a courtesy laugh. "Anybody?"

"Not that I recall," Pincus said.

"Did he discuss his work with you?"

"No. I never got the feeling he took it all that seriously. Real estate wasn't exactly a calling for him. He seemed to be in a kind of holding pattern. You know, I kept offering him a job selling for me, but he wasn't interested. I think he was afraid that if he worked for me, he couldn't beat me in tennis anymore with impunity."

"Did he ever talk about the years he was a shrink in Maine?"

"He never mentioned it was Maine, but, yes, he did say something about being a shrink." He took a thoughtful sip of his drink. "I think he was unhappy with a job where the progress was so slow and difficult to measure. I don't think he had the patience for it. With a house, of course, you either sell it or you don't. I would guess, also, he preferred the gamble of working on commission."

Yes, Harvey thought, Peplow would have liked the big hit better than the steady drip of patients' fees into his bank account. "Did he gamble?"

"I doubt it. I couldn't even get him to bet on our tennis games."

"Did you get the feeling he needed money?"

"Nope."

"Let me ask you something else—a shot in the dark."

"Shoot."

"Did he ever mention that he'd gotten hold of some damaging information about a real estate development?"

"I don't follow."

"Did he ever mention he had something on somebody. A developer."

Pincus's eyebrows flicked almost imperceptibly. "You're talking about information he could, let's say, convert into cash?"

"Yes."

"You're talking about blackmail. That's serious stuff."

"Hey, the guy was murdered. He was into *something*."

"What kind of information are you talking about?"

"Peplow might've found out that a housing development had been built on an illegal toxic waste site."

"And used it against the developer?"

"That's right."

"But why? He wasn't poor."

"I know," Harvey said. "I wonder if he could've been in it for the game."

"That's a hell of a game, Harvey."

"What was his manner like?"

"His manner? Well, he had a mouth. He yelled a lot on the court."

"At you?"

"At me, at himself when he made a bad shot, at the ball, at the racquet. You name it." Pincus finished his drink and shrugged. "I wish I could help you more."

Harvey nodded. He had gotten a better interview than the Garden Hills cops, but it was all stuff around the edges. He was going over old ground here.

"Help yourself to some food," Pincus said, rising.

"Thank you."

Pincus stood over him, his big capped teeth flashing. "You know the one about Moses comes down from Mount Sinai?"

"Afraid not."

"Moses comes down from Mount Sinai and tells everyone, 'The good news is we got Him down to ten. The bad news is adultery's still in there.' "

As Harvey was helping himself to poached salmon and cucumber sauce at the buffet table, he watched a tall young woman in a yellow silk blouse approach. She looked like a stalk of wheat. Her beauty was only a bit less beautiful for being somewhat common. She was the blond you passed in a convertible on a sunny day, or the one in the background of a beer commercial, running her hand through some guy's hair.

"Sy tells me you're the private detective."

"That's right."

"My name's Lynn. Lynn Nyland."

"The girlfriend," Harvey said. Her wispy loveliness sent a flutter through him. Dombrowski had thought her worth fighting over.

"I got your message on my machine. Do you wanna talk on the patio? I left my drink there."

They walked outside and sat down. Between her espadrilles and the hem of her skirt there seemed to be three feet of legs.

"So you're a friend of the Pincuses?" Harvey asked.

"Well, not really. I met them through Larry. Larry took me to the club once and introduced me to Sy and then we saw them once at a lecture at the Coleridge library. I think they're just taking pity on me, having me here. It's nice of them, though. Everybody around here is so nice."

She had a hurt, lost quality, and already Harvey felt protective toward her. He tried to recall the transcript of her interview in the case file. Her father a pilot for Delta, her mother deceased. She had moved from Wayzata, Minnesota, to Coleridge five months before to pursue a career in commercial art. And her boyfriend in Minnesota, Kevin Lahey, had been, for a minute and a half, a suspect.

"How'd you meet Larry?"

"I'm ashamed to say. I let him pick me up. While I was having breakfast, of all things." She bit her left thumbnail, and when she took it away, he saw that she had been gnawing it pretty good, only that nail.

"Where?"

"At a place called The Nook in Coleridge. We were sitting a couple of stools apart at the counter and he asked me to pass the cream. He said, 'You don't look like you're from here, either.' I don't know how he knew that, but it was one thing we had in common. We were both outsiders. And single. You know, you can always blend into a city, but a suburb belongs to families. Anyway, I was lonely. And he was funny. I remember he said, 'Can you believe seventy cents for a cup of coffee? Why, I remember when a cup of coffee cost only sixty-five cents.' "

"Tell me why you moved here."

"The real reason?"

"Yes."

"I thought I should get away from my dad."

"The Delta pilot."

She looked at him with mute surprise. "Yeah. My mom died my last year in college and I came home to look after him. And it got to be sort of a habit, looking after him. All of a sudden I was twenty-eight and still living at home. So I decided to move to Chicago and take classes at the Art Institute and, you know, freelance." Most of her sentences went up at the end, as if she wasn't sure her listener would approve. "Only I was scared to live in the city, so I just took the train up to the North Shore. I got off at the town that looked the nicest and rented an apartment. But I think I'm going back. As soon as I finish the assignment I'm on."

"Well, you've been through a lot."

"I wouldn't recommend it."

"Can you tell me about your relationship with him?"

"We went out maybe a dozen times over a two-month period."

"You told Lieutenant Dombrowski five or six times."

She blushed. "Oh. Well, I guess I tried to minimize it."

"Why minimize it?"

"I don't know. Because I was scared?"

"Of what?"

"Just scared," Nyland said. "Here was this guy I liked and suddenly he was murdered." She sniffed back tears.

"It's all right," he said.

"The cops just sent someone up to Minnesota to question my old boyfriend there who was visiting me the weekend he was killed. I'm really blistered that they thought he would have anything to do with it."

"They were suspicious because you told the police only this week that Kevin was here the weekend Larry was murdered."

"I know. I should've told them before."

"But you were scared."

"Yeah. You know, he didn't have anything to do with it."

"I believe you. And, by the way, so do the cops."

She sighed with relief and pulled the cocktail napkin from under her drink to dab her eyes. "Good."

"Did Larry know about Kevin?"

"Yeah, he knew. I told Larry a lot of stuff. He was real easy to talk to."

"Was he jealous?"

"Hardly. Listen, I don't think he loved me. He took an interest in things, in my life, but like an older brother or something. A father figure."

"Did you love him?"

She contemplated her ravaged thumbnail. "It was bigger than a

crush, but too small to be love. You can't call it love when you know
it's not real or that it's not going to last."

She was not a complete innocent, then. Harvey looked down,
troubled by the illicit thrill it gave him to ask a beautiful stranger
such personal questions. Sometimes his job made him feel like a
voyeur, except what he peeped at was other people's feelings.

"But I felt safe," she added, bringing the thumbnail to her
mouth. "He just made me feel so special."

"How'd he feel about you?"

"I don't know. Maybe it was, I was easy to be with. I looked up
to him, and I suppose he enjoyed that. He was much older."

"Did you—forgive me for getting so personal, you don't have to
answer this—but you did have a sexual relationship with him,
didn't you?"

"Yes."

"Was there anything unusual about it?"

"I don't know what to say. He seemed normal to me. I mean,
there was nothing kinky. He never spent the night, though. And the
couple of times we were at his place, he'd drive me home, you know,
like at two or three in the morning."

"Did that bother you?"

She thought for a moment with her lower lip tucked under her
front teeth. "I guess it would've been nice to wake up next to him.
But he was a pretty private person. Look, I mean, I suppose I had no
business with a much older guy. I knew it couldn't lead anywhere.
But—" She stopped and clutched herself and looked across the ravine.

"Yes?"

"I guess I was grateful for the experience. I'd spent a lot of time
caring for my dad and not enough time growing up."

"Did he tell you much about his life?"

"No, not really. I know he grew up in New York somewhere. And
that before he'd come here, he taught literature at Boston University."

"He told you he taught literature?"

"He liked to quote this poem, 'To His Coy Mistress.' Something about Time's winged chariot drawing near."

"Excuse me, but did Larry say how long he taught there? Why he quit?"

"He said his ex-wife had left him for another man back east. A few years ago."

"What else did he tell you?"

"Not much, really. He just really made an effort to make me feel special. That's what I remember most now. He took me to a lot of nice restaurants."

"What did the two of you talk about at all these dinners?"

"Oh, he asked me a lot about my family, my childhood. He was very sympathetic about my mother's death—you know, since he'd lost his at a young age."

"His mother's dead?"

"Yeah, and it was a pretty terrible death. Cancer. She held on forever. He said it marked him for life."

"How so?"

"He said it made him afraid of commitment."

"He was letting you know, right? Not to get too serious about him?"

"I guess."

"Anyway, so he liked knowing about your past."

"He was interested in how I felt about things, you know, my reactions to stuff. Everything from how my day had gone to what it was like being a high school cheerleader. He was really a great listener."

"Did he ask you much about your boyfriend in Minnesota?"

"Yeah, I talked about Kevin. And Larry was real supportive. He'd give me advice about Kevin and how just because we were apart now didn't mean we wouldn't be together later."

"Comforting stuff, huh?"

"Yeah, like a father. Or a psychiatrist; he really didn't want me to get too attached. Anyway, that's why it made me so mad that the cops would suspect Kevin."

"When was the last time you were together with Larry?"

"The Tuesday or Wednesday night before he was—you know. I think Tuesday."

"Did he say anything significant to you? Did he seem to be in trouble of any kind?"

"No. He was the same as always. We ate Chinese, played minigolf, and then we went back to my place."

As Harvey wandered through the airy rooms looking for Sy Pincus, to say good-bye, a hand on his shoulder stopped him near the baby grand. It was Ruth Klinger, the wife of the Cruller King. She was a woman in her fifties with a deep tan, a simian jaw, and a surgically improved nose that looked like a pinch of clay. With the absurd casualness of the drunk, she leaned against the piano to keep her balance and said, "Sho you're trying to figure out who killed Larry Peplow."

"Yes," Harvey said over the Pachelbel, "and if you know who did it, I'd appreciate it if you told me."

"I don't know who did it, but I will shay this, and I'm only telling you becush you're a detective, unnerstan'?" One of her eyelids was drooping. "He came to my housh in Feberry to appraish it and damn if he didn't jump me in my own bed. He marched right into my housh and he took me to bed"—she leaned closer, virtually laying her heavily perfumed head on Harvey's shoulder—"and gave me the besht fuck I've had in ten yearsh. And I'm shorry he'sh dead."

Poor Lynn Nyland, he thought, turning away from Ruth Klinger's sickly sweet breath. But Harvey was less interested in Peplow's lies than in the lies of the still living. Like Virginia Schmauss's failure to tell the police about Peplow's unethical conduct. Like, possibly, Marilyn Barger's saying she hadn't slept with Peplow. Like, possibly, Jim Vault not actually having been at the movies that night.

Harvey moved away from the woman, saying "Excuse me, ma'am, but my ride's here."

"Besht in *twenny* yearsh," Ruth Klinger said.

Because if Vaultt had gone to the movies to see *Swingtime* on April 17, surely he would've known that "The Continental" wasn't in *Swingtime* at all. It was in *The Gay Divorcee*.

11

AFTER TWO TRIES, he reached Larry Peplow's mother in Boonville, New York.

"No sir, my boy didn't ever gamble or run with a bad crowd." She stopped to draw an emphysemic breath. "He got values from me. We didn't have a lot of money"—she drew another loud breath—"but we were rich in values."

Your boy was in his forties, he wanted to tell her; and he had a name: Larry.

"Oh, he fell in with a bunch of bad actors in junior high, but I just put my foot down. I don't mind telling you. I kept my boy in the house with me after school for, well, it had to be two or three months. His father was strict too." Another laborious breath, like a snore. "Milton was a teacher, you know. Kept him out of a class trip to Albany once when he talked back to us at dinner."

"Mrs. Peplow, Larry spoke with you regularly?"

"Oh, yes sir, we kept in close touch."

"Did he indicate to you in any of your phone conversations that he was in danger of any kind?"

"He most certainly did not, and if there had been a problem in his life, I like to think"—he waited for her to complete a raspy intake of precious air—"I would have been the first to know about it." It was like chatting with Darth Vader.

"And your son never married, is that right?" He felt short of breath just listening to her.

"No sir, he didn't."

"Did that surprise you?"

"I guess my boy never found a girl who made the grade. You know, the Lord made a lot of seconds."

"When he changed careers, Mrs. Peplow, did Larry consult you?"

"I remember what he said to me. He said to me, 'Mother, selling someone a house they love will make them happier than anything I can do for them by listening to their troubles.' And that was good enough for me."

"All right," Harvey said. "I can't think of anything else. Thanks for taking the time to talk to me."

"You're most certainly welcome, sir."

"CONTENTS OF HIS pockets on the night he was murdered."

In the evidence room of the Garden Hills police station Dombrowski held out a plastic bag to Harvey. In it was a nondescript wallet, three sticks of Wrigley's Big Red chewing gum, a matchbook from The Nook in Coleridge, and a bunch of keys hanging from a soft blue rubber disk that said "Wahatan Audi—Sales and Service."

Dombrowski laid the bag on the table in the middle of the room lined with blue lockers. "His shirt," the lieutenant said, pinching another, larger plastic bag, dangling it in front of Harvey's face.

Harvey sat at the table and turned the bag over in his hands. The back of the pink Lacoste shirt was dark—virtually black—with dried blood. What had until now seemed to be as much an intellectual exercise as anything—In this picture can you find the man who killed this man?—suddenly, at the sight of Peplow's ruined, once inhabited shirt, lost every abstract quality. Harvey pictured Peplow's last instant of life, staring at the gun. You were there. Then you were not there. Life was a troubled moment between eternities.

Lieutenant Dombrowski leaned his large frame against a row of lockers and said, "You still seeing the Barger woman?"

How he wanted a drink of water. The Scotch at Pincus's had dehydrated him; Peplow's shirt and Dombrowski's surveillance were not improving his salivation. "What do you mean, am I still seeing the Barger woman?"

"Son, I'm just wondering if you've been using my case to get yourself a little wiggly."

"Right. Sure." Harvey glanced at the smiling photo of Laurence Peplow lying on the table, the one from the Schmauss & Weevens brochure. Peplow smiling with that big crescent of white teeth. Salesman's teeth.

"We saw her car at your motel last night."

Harvey turned the photo over and looked up. "Lieutenant, how come you're so much better at tailing me than you are at solving murders?"

"Relax, son. I had a man in the area. I sent him over to see how you were doing. When he got there, the Barger woman was just getting out of her car."

"Why don't you quit wasting your precious manpower on me?"

"It's a tribute to you, son. We figure anyone you're interested in, we're interested in."

"She came over to tell me a story she'd remembered about Peplow."

"What kind of story?" The unlit Chesterfield in the corner of his mouth jumped up and down as he talked, like a conductor's baton.

"She'd remembered that she'd run into Peplow once at a store and he mentioned that he had some information about the land Vaultt built Rimwood Estates on. That there'd been some illegal dumping there years ago. Toxic stuff."

"That the decedent could use to blackmail Vaultt?"

"That would be the idea. You ever hear something about that?"

Dombrowski shook his head. "Why is it that people tell you things they don't tell us?"

"You got me. Charisma?"

"Yeah, yeah. Take the needle out of your arm, son. So, you believe her?"

"I don't know. But in the absence of any real beliefs, disbelief's a luxury I can't afford."

"Let me get a piece of paper so I can write that one down."

"Don't bother," Harvey said, bluffing in the direction of his wallet. "I've got it printed up on cards."

Dombrowski had turned to yank the first of two large cardboard boxes out of the locker. "So that's why you want to look at his shit—in case he jotted down some notes about this alleged dumping?"

"I figure a guy who cheats on a college midterm and real estate commissions just might possibly be capable of extortion."

"You never told me about the midterm."

"His old college classmate told me. Stu Silver."

"Shame on you, son. We had a deal."

"Lieutenant, I can't tell you every last detail. Give me some damn room to operate. When my information reaches critical mass, you're at the top of my list of people to call."

Dombrowski placed the cardboard box in front of Harvey. "Here're some of the goodies we took from his house. Plus his Rolodex from work."

The two boxes were filled with papers and books. For almost an hour Harvey sorted through them while Dombrowski sat across from him smoking Chesterfields. In one pile Harvey laid everything that had no value—junk mail; blank Schmauss & Weevens Multiple Listing/Exclusive Right to Sell Agreements, Purchase and Sale Agreements, Marketing Performance Reviews, and open-house sign-in sheets; scraps of paper with grocery lists on them and errand reminders; magazines and paperback books.

After half an hour Dombrowski laughed. "What'd you expect, a neatly printed note that said, 'Here's the name and number of the fart who told me about the illegal dumping'?"

"Something like that."

"Maybe the state EPA would know."

"They're already checking for me," Harvey said.

"Son, maybe you and I should go over there with a backhoe and just start digging for fifty-five-gallon drums."

The second pile, when Harvey was through separating the contents of the boxes, contained an address book, a large Weekly-Minder appointment book, a Rolodex from work, and an assortment of business cards that the police had found scattered about his desk at work and his study at home. The cards all represented businesses from the area: printers, florists, interior decorators, investment counselors, a hair salon. The only one that Peplow had written on was the last, a card for The Hair Shack in Coleridge. The name Trish was written in pen across one corner in script that Harvey by now recognized as Peplow's spiky hand. Harvey carefully set it aside.

The Rolodex bulged with the names of prospects and business contacts. Vaultt's name and number were in it and so was Stu Silver's, but not Marilyn Barger's or Norm's. Harvey looked up at Dombrowski and asked, "Did you find any leads in here?"

"No," the lieutenant said. "We spent our time working over the address book."

Harvey picked up the red dime-store address book and quickly thumbed through it. Names, addresses, and numbers had been entered in several colors of ink and pencil. Stu Silver and Sy Pincus were in there, but neither Vaultt, Barger, nor Norm Blissberg were. Under *P*, Peplow's mother was listed as "Florence Peplow."

"What'd you find in here?"

"Not much," Dombrowski said. "I put two men on it and they called everyone they could track down. No one could think of a good reason why someone would waste Peplow."

Harvey held up the little book. "Can I take this with me for a day or two?"

"I don't like to fool with the chain of custody. Something could happen to it. But I'll tell you what." Dombrowski picked up the phone to summon his aide. "I'm going to give you a printout of all the people in that book we reached or tried to reach."

"Thank you, Lieutenant," Harvey said. "Now let's see about this." He handled the vinyl spiral-bound appointment book.

"Don't get your hopes up, son. Peplow didn't have an appointment to get blown away on April seventeenth."

Harvey happened to open the appointment book to the second week in May. It was blank. He had been dead a month. He leafed back to the week of April 17. That afternoon he had had an appointment with someone named Marcus at three. A phone number was conveniently written down next to the name.

"You talked to this person Marcus?"

Dombrowski nodded. "Peplow showed them a house in Wahatan. Nothing doing. Middle-aged couple with three kids."

Harvey glanced ahead to the following week. Peplow had written down an open house on Sunday. On the next day, Monday, he had had an appointment with "Trish." The Hair Shack. On the Wednesday after his murder, he had been planning to attend a Realtors National Marketing Institute seminar. Harvey leafed back through the two or three weeks leading up to his death. There were names all over, four or five or six a day.

"Those names," Dombrowski said from across the table, "they're just people looking for a house."

A uniformed female police officer came in and Dombrowski said, "Susie, would you please pull the Peplow case file and make a copy for this gentleman of all the three-oh-twos relating to the people in the decedent's address book? There's also a sheet of negative results."

"Yes, sir."

"Thank you, Susie."

When she'd left the room, Dombrowski said, gesturing at the evidence-laden table, "Look at all this jetsam." He clucked. "You know a good psychic?"

"Yeah," Harvey said, "the more you know, the less you know."

Dombrowski sighed. "My kingdom for a stray hair. Something, anything, the lab could DNA fingerprint and we could get on with our lives."

"How many men you have on this case now?"

"Four."

"Do I hear a back burner being lit?"

"I needed to pull manpower away for a rape case in Dancedale. Somebody's hit three women in the last month, and the heat's moved there. But let's be blunt, son. If Peplow was a local with a lot of relatives making a lot of noise, I'd still be throwing everything I've got at the case. But the man had the bad luck to be from out of town."

With some help from a gas station attendant in Dancedale's leafy Tudor business district, Harvey found the Barger house in a neighborhood of modest but well-kept houses. The street was blazing with hydrangeas. The arching drizzle from a couple of oscillating sprinklers looked like tinsel in the sun. Two girls raced down the street on Rollerblades, twittering.

Marilyn's Chrysler LeBaron was in the driveway of her clapboard cape. Harvey pressed the doorbell and then waited on the front stoop. This was what Larry Peplow had been doing for a living, he thought, ringing doorbells, giving housewives free appraisals, occasionally something more, while their husbands were grinding out a living in the city. Why couldn't this case be a simple matter of a violently jealous husband rubbing out his wife's lover, just as Dombrowski had thought? Because Peplow was killed at Rimwood Estates, that's why. What husband would have bothered to drive him there, of all places, late at night? He had driven there with someone, someone with whom he didn't expect any trouble. There had been no struggle.

Harvey rang again, and after another thirty seconds the door opened to reveal Marilyn Barger in a lime bikini whose top, two tiny iridescent flags of Lycra, was pathetically inadequate to its designed task. She was wearing a stripe of zinc oxide down the bridge of her nose.

"Well, hi!" she said through the screen door. "I didn't hear the doorbell at first. I was catching some late sun in the back."

"I happened to be in the neighborhood."

She cocked her head. "Gee, we can't seem to leave each other alone, can we?"

"You don't seem to believe me."

With both hands she yanked upward on the strings of her bikini top. "That you just happened to be in my neighborhood? I'm not stupid, Harvey."

Why *was* he here? "I'm here on business," he said.

"Oh, goody."

"Can I come in?"

"Wait there. Let me put something on. Since this is business." She left him on the stoop and returned quickly in a royal blue, yellow, and green kimono full of birds and pagodas. She opened the screen door and came out, saying, "C'mon, we'll walk around to the back."

The emerald yard was primly enclosed by a picket fence and a border of daylilies. In one far corner was a matching garage-size outbuilding connected to the house by a brick walk that fanned out near the living room sliders to become a patio with two cheap chaise lounges. He was familiar with the model from his wanderings at Caldor. Barger took off her kimono and slowly reclined in one of the chairs. She squirted some sunscreen into her palm.

Harvey sat on the edge of the other lounge chair. "Is your—"

"He's playing golf," she said, reaching for her sunglasses on the little table next to her.

"Ah."

"Don't worry, he's harmless," she said, rubbing the sunscreen between her hands. "So what's your business?"

"I'd like to ask you a few more questions."

She smiled patronizingly. "Yes, Harvey, go ahead." She began applying the sunscreen to one long leg, stroking up from her ankle with both hands, kneading her calf.

"Did Larry really tell you about some information he had about illegal dumping at Rimwood Estates?"

"Don't you have any new questions?" Now she squirted a white line of sunscreen along the top of her thigh and started to massage it in, working it around to the back of her leg, then slowly drawing the cream up to her crotch.

"It's not checking out yet."

"I'm not surprised. Anyone could've told him about it."

"The farmer who sold Vaultt the land was having none of it."

"What would you expect him to say?"

"You're sure Larry didn't say any more about it? Mention a name?"

"Old question again. No."

"Why would he tell you anything in the first place?"

Her hands stopped. "You tell me." Then she went to work on her other leg, stroking and pressing.

"I don't know why he would confide in you." Harvey glanced up at the shuttered white house behind her. It was well maintained, but hardly a house at all compared to the minimansions at Rimwood Estates. "You'd only met him once before, right? When he showed you Rimwood?"

"Now, Harvey"—she said it as though speaking to someone with a mental impairment—"haven't you ever told a stranger things you wouldn't tell your best friend? It's a flaw of human nature. I guess I was confidant-for-a-day."

Of course, she was right; and, conversely, a guy like Peplow could also play basketball with guys for years and never tell them anything. But he said, "Somehow I don't believe it, Marilyn."

"Why would I lie to you?"

"You saw him more than you're saying."

"*Bzzzzz*"—she imitated a game show buzzer—"Wrong."

"Did you know him at some time in the past?"

"*Bzzzzz*. Try again."

"Did you go to school with him?"

"I never met him before he showed Scott and me Rimwood."

"Where'd you go to college?"

"Champagne–Urbana. University of Illinois. Class of seventy-eight."

That made her thirty-five or thirty-six. "Marilyn, there's something you're not telling me."

She stopped rubbing her legs, removed her sunglasses, and observed him coldly. "I've told you everything. I realize it's not much to go on, but it's what I've got. This guy Peplow showed us a few houses and then I ran into him at the mall. If you're going to solve this murder, you're going to need more than me to do it. Okay?" She sighed, picked up the bottle of sunscreen, squeezed a small pool of it into her hand, and began rubbing it on her breasts.

Harvey watched her in amazement. She stroked her own breasts with the idle delight of someone caressing a cat. It was as if her body didn't quite belong to her. He cast a glance around the yard for some distraction while Marilyn continued to blend lotion into her cleavage with flattened fingers.

"What's that?" He nodded in the direction of the garage in the corner of the yard.

"That's my warehouse."

"Your warehouse?"

"I told you. I'm a party planner."

"That's right. I believe you referred to yourself as 'a fun facilitator.' "

"Let's put it this way. When you've had a party planned by Marilyn Barger, you *know* you've had a party." She laughed self-mockingly.

"What a strange occupation."

"The suburbs are a strange place."

"What do you keep in there?"

"Well, for starters I've got a nice collection of *papier-mâché* parrots on trapezes. Just in case you're thinking of a tropical-theme party."

"Can I see them?"

The musty, baking little building was lined with metal shelves filled with frosted wreaths, plastic pelicans, multicolored kites in the shape of fish, bowls and platters, beads and ornaments and silk flowers and tree branches coated in silver glitter. There were boxes of cheap salad bowls and champagne flutes. In one corner there was a hand truck, in another a helium tank.

"These are just bits and pieces," she said as they stood in the hot dead air. "When I do a party, I go out to Pier One or one of these discount places and I scavenge." She picked up a large wreath. "I picked these up for two bucks apiece. The trick is to shop the day after the holiday you're shopping for. I got these the day after Christmas—for next year."

"And these?" Harvey pointed to a box of red light bulbs.

"Oh, I did a party for a couple in Wilmette. The theme was 'A Cold Day in Hell.' I had huge blocks of ice illuminated by red bulbs. And all the food was red. I found red canvas at three cents a yard at a mill outlet. Oh, yeah, and the invitations were singed at the edges. Neat, huh?"

"Very creative."

"I like to create realities," she said.

"Not me," Harvey said. "I like to figure out what other people's realities are."

She opened her kimono and fanned it. "It's a hot day in hell in here, huh?"

"Let's not get any ideas, Marilyn."

"I don't have any ideas."

"Good."

"What is it—you think everything I do is for your benefit?"

"Then for whose benefit is it?" he asked.

"It doesn't have to be for anyone's benefit."

She turned and dragged a forefinger along the dusty edge of a shelf piled high with miniature beach balls. "You know, don't take this the wrong way but I have no great stake in our little affair going on. I'd be perfectly satisfied if we never touched each other again."

He was surprised that her words hurt. Everything confused him now. In little more than a day, their relationship had already passed through too many phases.

"But I do like you," she said.

He didn't know what to say. The reassurance was belittling.

"Okay?" she said with a conciliatory smile.

"So, what *is* your maiden name?"

"Oh, now you're playing the detective again."

"That's right."

"Advantage Blissberg."

"I'm just curious."

"No, you're not curious. You're suspicious. You're thinking of checking up on me to see if I am who I say I am. Maybe to see if I really did go to the University of Illinois. Well, be my guest. My maiden name is Samuels. *S, A, M, U, E, L, S.* Now let's get out of here." ·

She led him out of the garage, where the air was much cooler than he remembered it. All that was left of the sun in the backyard was a rhomboid of light in the patio. As they walked down the path, a heavyset six-footer in a striped polo shirt and pressed chinos came through the slider dangling a brown bottle of Hamm's beer from his left hand. He walked with the rolling gait of a former jock.

"Hi, hon!" he shouted.

"Hey, Scott!" Marilyn said with tinny good cheer and walked to her husband's side, standing on tiptoes to peck his cheek. "How'd it go?" Her whole tone of voice had changed; the vixen had been suddenly invaded by the spirit of a suburban housewife.

"Hon, you're looking at a man who broke eighty today."

"That's my boy."

He looked at Harvey and stuck out a hand. "Hi. Scott Barger." His short, neatly parted hair was graying upward from the temples. His broad face was freshly roasted from a long afternoon of sun.

"Harvey Blissberg," Harvey said as Scott slammed his hand into his.

"Scott, Mr. Blissberg's a private detective."

"A private detective. Now *that* sounds interesting."

Marilyn patted her husband's forearm. "You remember that fellow who got murdered a couple of months ago in Garden Hills."

"Oh, yes."

"The agent who showed us all those big ugly houses?"

"Sure."

"Mr. Blissberg's been snooping around the North Shore trying to find some answers."

"Is that so?"

"He came by to see if we could tell him anything, you know, based on our one encounter with him."

Harvey had to hand it to her. For a moment, he almost believed himself that he and Marilyn had just met. Didn't her husband wonder what they were doing coming out of the garage in back? Apparently not, judging from his bland, untroubled demeanor. He seemed like a man missing a dimension, a man mystified by nuances. Someone who thought poetry was for girls.

"How 'bout a beer?" He raised his Hamm's, forefinger plugging the bottleneck.

"No, thanks. This was just a shot in the dark and I guess I missed."

"I insist," Scott said.

"No, really."

"Scottie, he's probably got a lot of other people to see."

"Naw, c'mon, have a Hamm's." He threw his arm around Harvey

and drew him toward the house. "It's not every day you get a chance to talk to a real private detective. Now, me, I'm just a salesman, women's accessories. . . ."

Marilyn excused herself and went upstairs to change out of her bathing suit, leaving the two men alone in the kitchen. Harvey tensely waited for sufficient time to pass before he could leave without offending his host. He learned far more than he had ever hoped to about the recession-proofness of women's headwear and the perennial popularity of tube tops. He felt so disconnected from the aimless conversation that it might as well have been piped into the room from another source.

"Excuse me," Harvey said. "Where's the bathroom?"

Harvey took aim at the pale blue toilet bowl in the powder room off the kitchen. He felt nauseated now. His own weakness with Marilyn had carried him away from the case, from his job, from himself, and into this nasty territory. A year ago he was in a suburban Boston nightclub with Mickey, and he had spotted a married man he knew dancing with another woman, burying his face in her neck right there on the dance floor. He had turned away quickly, with a shiver of disgust, to avoid embarrassing both of them. But how did you turn away when it was you that you wanted to turn away from?

He washed his hands with the scented oval soap, dried them slowly on the Bargers' elaborately monogrammed towels, and listened to Marilyn's footsteps overhead coming down the stairs.

12

AFTER A FEW desultory laps in the hotel pool that night Harvey sat naked on the bed in his room, nursing a second can of Hires root beer from the machine down the hall. Over the air-conditioning's tremolo he listened to a golden oldie rock-block on FM radio mixed with the sound of eighteen-wheelers passing outside on Edens. Spread out before him, unread, were the photocopied documents Dombrowski had given him: the reports of the phone calls his people had made to seventy-six of the people in Peplow's address book.

Shari at the front desk had moved him to a new room on the third floor, an unsettling mirror image of the first. The remnants of a room-service meal of Lake Superior whitefish—vastly inferior to Clarence's—sat near the door on one of those chrome carts that reminded Harvey unpleasantly of a hospital gurney, adding to his sense of being somewhere he did not want to be.

He picked up the 302s, but his concentration was immediately broken by thoughts of his visit to Marilyn Barger. He couldn't quite put his finger on what bothered him most. Surely, not the short shelf life of his dalliance with her. If anything, he could already feel the burden of guilt lifting, his mind downscaling the infidelity to the status of a mere bad episode, a flaw in the human condition. Now that it had been exposed to her domestic reality, his ardor was curdling.

Was having to shoot the breeze with Scott in the kitchen, that bizarre piece of business, what bothered him? Harvey was sure that Marilyn had never told her husband about her second encounter with Peplow at the mall and his mention of the illegal dumping. Either she was lying about it—it had never happened—or, like so many couples, they simply didn't talk to each other. Harvey couldn't get it out of his head that she *had* slept with Peplow, and that was the reason she had never mentioned the second encounter to Scott.

Maybe what ate at Harvey was knowing that he and Mickey too had reached a stage of mutual benign neglect. He winced at the thought of Mickey lying next to him in bed a few weeks ago reading an article in *Vogue* titled "Ten Foolproof Ways to Refresh Your Marriage." Passion didn't need any advice from magazines. But what was that peck on Scott's cheek about? Probably nothing more than one of those small public displays of affection that survive the worst marital devastation. On the other hand, he did seem sort of devoted to her, painstakingly making her Bloody Mary in the kitchen, proudly explaining to Harvey that she liked it with a splash of Rose's lime juice.

Harvey yawned and began working his way through the seventy-six reports. Each one noted the person called, the phone number, the address, the time called, the subject's relationship to Peplow, the last time the subject had seen or talked to Peplow, whether the subject had noticed anything unusual about him, and the interviewing officer's name. The yield was disappointing. One woman who lived in Chicago told the police she was flattered her name was in his book—they'd met briefly in a bar—but that he had never called. Two other women listed had dated him once or twice, but none in the last year. The police had talked to his insurance agent, his accountant (who was later interviewed in person to determine that Peplow had not had any unusual financial dealings), and an old college classmate, now living in Oak Park, whose number Peplow had apparently been given by someone else; the classmate had not heard from Peplow since graduation day more than twenty years before. All but two people had been unaware of his murder at the time the police called, although both the *Tribune* and the *Sun-Times* had carried items within two days of the crime.

Harvey picked up the single sheet of paper at the bottom of the stack that listed all the negative results. There were twenty-two names and numbers. According to the printout, ten of the phone numbers were no longer in service, seven belonged to people who had inherited the number and did not know a Laurence Peplow, and three of the phone numbers didn't answer after repeated attempts to call. When the police tried the remaining two numbers, they had gotten a recorded message saying the call could not be completed as dialed. One of the numbers was listed in Peplow's address book as belonging to "S. L. Gen'l Store" and the other to an "F. Walls."

Your call cannot be completed as dialed, your call cannot be completed as dialed. . . . Harvey drifted toward sleep. He had wanted to call Mickey to find out how Duane was doing, but with all his reading tonight he had conveniently forgotten. Why hadn't she called him? Was she working too hard herself on her documentary about gender and competition? Or did she intuit at long distance, as only she could, who could tell you at a glance which couples at a party were in marital distress, that he had run afoul of his dick? Gender, he thought, almost asleep . . . To be a man was to live oppressed under a dictatorship of the dick, to do constant battle with that little flap of flesh. . . .

He awoke with a start in the pitch black room and sat up in bed. The clock radio said 1:47. For all their diligence, the police had overlooked the obvious. The reason their two calls could not be completed as dialed had to be that the telephone exchanges didn't exist in the Chicagoland area. Harvey was certain that they were Portland numbers, written down without the area code. "S. L. Gen' Store" had to be the general store in Sebago Lake, Maine, where

Peplow had a cabin. It was a number he would need from time to time. What about F. Walls?

Harvey switched on the nightstand light, and his room jumped rudely to life. Squinting, he found the area code for Maine in the front of the North Suburban Chicago telephone book and dialed 207-555-1212. He took the sheet of negative results and laid it next to the phone.

"Directory assistance. What city?"

"Portland, please. Do you have a number for an F. Walls listed in Portland?"

"One moment, please. I have an office number for a Dr. Frederick Walls in Portland. That's the only F. Walls. Would you like it?"

"Please."

Somewhere in Maine, the operator hit a terminal key and a computer's voice said flatly, "The number is . . . 5 . . . 5 . . . 5 . . . 3 . . . 8 . . . 9 . . . 7." The voice repeated it, graciously advising Harvey to please make a note of it.

He did, right next to the number for Dr. Walls on the negatives sheet. The two numbers matched.

Harvey turned off the light and fell back on his pillow. Well, it was something. Of course, given his luck, Dr. Walls would turn out to be the podiatrist who had removed Larry Peplow's plantar warts.

When he awoke again, the clock said 4:14, and Harvey, with the aimless determination of a sleepwalker, got up and went to the window. He pulled back the heavy draperies and stared at the expressway. There was a lot of traffic for the middle of the night. The swimming pool, its lights extinguished, looked like a piece of black velvet thrown across the cement. He fought to recall what had awakened him.

After Marilyn Barger had come back down the stairs to rejoin her husband and Harvey, there had been more small talk, then Marilyn had left the kitchen again, and Scott was rhapsodizing about what a great country it was where you could travel around selling knockoffs of Chanel scarves to Wal-Mart, pull down good money, and still have time for your golf—all as if the framers of the Constitution had had just that sort of freedom in mind. Golf, Scott said, that was hobby numero uno, but he liked to dabble in home improvements. And he pointed out the door of the kitchen to a large room with a vaulted ceiling and said that he and a contractor friend had done that work together. What work? Harvey asked. Well, Scott said, that used to be the attached garage. Now it was a combination den/playroom with a pool table and a large-screen Hitachi and a couple of cream-colored leather armchairs. It's not quite finished, Scott said, we still need to put the molding up, but what do you think? Harvey said it looked like a real professional job.

And, of course, Harvey had been distracted from making the vital connection—distracted by his trespassing on their marriage, by his need to escape their house with its flowerbeds and its falsehoods. But now he knew what had bothered him so much about that visit.

The Bargers had recently turned their garage into a den, a job that it would have to have taken the two men—Scott and his friend—several months to finish. Yet just eight weeks ago Scott and Marilyn Barger were looking for a new house at Rimwood Estates, at a time when the conversion of their garage had to have already begun.

If you were seriously planning to sell your current house, you might paint the interior or the exterior or put on a new roof in order to make your property more salable, but you wouldn't undertake to turn your garage into a den to house your pool table. Was that why Marilyn had walked Harvey around the *outside* of the house to the backyard, why she had tried to convince her husband later that Harvey was too busy to come inside for a beer? Because the last thing she wanted Harvey to see was any evidence that they hadn't been interested in buying a new house at all?

If Marilyn and Scott Barger didn't go to Rimwood Estates with Larry Peplow because they were really interested in buying a new house, then why did they go?

Harvey went to the door of his room and double-locked it, then took his little five-shot Smith & Wesson Model 60 from the desk drawer, removed the clip holster, laid the stainless steel revolver under his pillow, and went back to sleep.

The phone rang, and before he knew what he was doing, he had Mickey in his ear.

"I woke you," she said.

"No, you didn't. I'm still sleeping."

"Want me to call back?"

"No, it's all right. I think I'm up now. What time is it?"

"Ten. Sunday morning."

"That's nine here."

"Excellent deduction," she said. "No wonder you're a detective. How are you?"

"Okay. You?"

"Okay. Duane's not so hot, but I've been keeping him alive. I've been feeding him with this big syringe for the last two days. It's like stuffing a Strasbourg goose or something, except he's not getting any fatter."

"What's the vet say?"

"He's not making any predictions. If I can keep him alive until the virus goes away and he begins eating on his own again, we'll be all right. But the vet says that at his age Duane might just give up. Those sensitive Siamese. He's down to seven pounds, Bliss. I think he's just depressed."

Mickey was deftly steering the conversation toward their relationship, and he wanted no part of it, not at this hour. "Isn't there something the vet can give him to stimulate his appetite?"

"He tried some antihistamine that's supposed to have that effect, but it didn't do the trick."

Harvey heard a pathetic bleat in the background. "That's him?"

"You want to talk to him?" Mickey considered it one of his very best traits that he was not embarrassed to talk to animals on the phone.

"Hell, yeah. Put him on." He waited a second until he heard faint congested breathing on the other end of the line. "Hey, Duane," he said, "you okay, babe?"

The cat responded with a weak sound of recognition.

"Now listen to me. I've spent a good part of my life not breathing through my nose and it's not the end of the world. You've just got to tough it out, Duane. Don't wimp out on me."

"He seems to know it's you." It was Mickey again. "So how's the case?"

"Oh, I've got a few dots. If I can connect them, maybe I'll have part of a picture. Basically, I'm collecting lies. I'm in the lie-collection business. I've got my eye on someone with a shaky alibi, but no motive yet, just rumors. I've got a woman this guy Peplow once showed a house to who says Peplow was in a position to blackmail this guy, but it's still pretty soft." Harvey thought that bringing up Marilyn Barger might help detoxify the situation, but his stomach was turning over on him.

"How much more time you figure you need there?"

"Depends on how many dots I can connect in the next couple of days."

"Okay," she said with no emotion.

"What's the problem?"

"It's just part of the pattern, Bliss. Whenever I try to discuss what's going on between us, you don't want to hear about it or you leave town on a case. I can't get a real hearing." She paused for a sigh of exasperation. "Look, it's not that our problems are so terrible. It's that you don't want to face them and your refusal to face them is creating all these ancillary tensions."

Leave it to her to use a word like "ancillary" at nine on Sunday morning. He tried to concentrate on what she was saying, but the flow of his attention, the flow of his feeling, was blocked. Why had he let this thing with Marilyn ever happen? Was his fear of loss so

great that he'd throw away his relationship with Mickey now just so
it couldn't be lost later?

"You think it's enough to say, 'But I know we'll always be
together.' But it's not. You've got to learn to listen to me."

He had been saying to himself for months now that Mickey and
he would come out of this nosedive sooner or later. He boasted to
friends that they were joined at the deepest levels. He liked to tell
Mickey that he could see them together in forty years, heading for the
shuffleboard court. And she would say, It's not forty years from now
that I worry about. It's getting through the next two days with you.

"I want to feel like we're ready to spend the rest of our lives
together," she said. "I want to feel like you're not trying to escape.
That you're not about to run off with some floozy."

"Floozy? First ancillary, now floozy."

"Yeah. There's a certain basic commitment that's missing."

"You haven't exactly been trying to drag me to the altar."

"If I have to drag you, I don't want to go in the first place."

"Mick, you seem to forget that you have this monumental fear
of marriage."

"It's not marriage I fear. It's a bad marriage. I won't be trapped."

"It's beginning to feel like a self-fulfilling prophecy," he said. The
call was a depressing reprise of so many recent conversations. "Mick,"
he said, "you know I love you. And I'll do better. How's the
documentary going?"

She sighed deeply, her way of informing him he wasn't getting
away with anything by changing the subject. "Just fine. You know,
when you look at this footage of how differently boys and girls play in
the sandbox, it's amazing men and women can stand to be in the
same room."

In the shower later Harvey pressed his fingertips into his scalp,
working up a shampoo lather. The cranium—what a fragile shell it
was for all that trouble within. He shuddered at the image of a bullet
passing through Peplow's brain, plowing through all those folds.

Afterward, Harvey shaved, dressed in a pair of jeans and a light blue rayon shirt, and thought about calling Norm to see about taking in a Cubs game. The team had a young outfielder he wanted to see in action, but he saw the negatives sheets on the dresser and instead dialed the office of Dr. Frederick Walls in Portland. After four rings the recorded message said, "This is Dr. Walls. Please leave a message at the sound of the beep and I'll get back to you as soon as I can."

"Dr. Walls," Harvey said, pacing with the phone in his hand, "my name is Harvey Blissberg. I'm a private detective investigating the murder of a Laurence Peplow in Chicago. I would appreciate it very much if you could try to reach me, either at my hotel here or possibly on my car phone. I'm calling on Sunday." He left both numbers and thanked the machine.

Harvey hung up and sat on the bed. He was waiting, waiting, waiting for a pitch he could hit.

13

ON MONDAY MORNING, he telephoned the registrar's office at the University of Illinois to confirm that a student named Marilyn Samuels had indeed graduated in 1978 with a bachelor of arts degree. Then he spent what was left of the morning down in the hotel's modest exercise room, sampling the Nautilus machines and logging twenty minutes on the Stair Master. The physical vanities of a former professional athlete do not die easily, and he stole glimpses of his labor in the full-length mirror. In any case, the last thing he needed was to disgrace himself on the basketball court at noon in front of his own brother.

Back in his room, the message light on the phone was twitching. The desk clerk informed him that Marilyn had called. It was an event he wasn't quite prepared to act on. He dressed, got in his Town Car, and headed for the Winnetka YMCA.

While consuming a banana and two Bartlett pears, he tuned in an all-sports radio station and listened to callers' passionate opinions about recent White Sox lineup changes. This was followed by yesterday's baseball scores. Men he had never heard of had hit home runs, hurled six-hitters, and otherwise lived up to, or not lived up to, their early-season promise. He felt a twinge of obsolescence, lit a Lucky Strike, and finally called Marilyn back on the cellular.

"What's up?" he said.

"Well, I called you to say I'm sorry about yesterday," she said. "I was a little rough on you."

"I think you said everything that needed to be said, Marilyn."

"You're sulking."

"It's my natural demeanor."

"For your information, I was having a bad day. Scott and I had to go see my father last night. That always puts me in a foul mood."

"What's that?"

"He's got Alzheimer's."

"That's no fun."

"Daddy was never any fun to begin with."

"I'm sorry to hear that."

"Yeah . . well, you know."

"You have a very cute house." Harvey paused while he passed a Mercedes tentatively navigated by an elderly woman; somehow she reminded him of a child carrying a large tray of food. "I'm surprised you're looking for a new house, especially with that brand-new den of yours." During the short silence that followed, he cracked the window and flicked his ash into the warm wind.

"Wait a second," she said. "You think I've been lying to you about looking for a new house? Because Scottie was in the midst of renovating ours?"

Harvey said nothing.

"You never heard of wives dragging their husbands to see bigger and better houses they dream of moving into, and the husbands going along even though all they want to do is stay in the old house with the smaller mortgage and maybe renovate the garage and put in a couple of big leather chairs and sit in one of them drinking Hamm's?"

"There's just two of you, Marilyn. Why do you need a bigger house?"

"What do you want me to say?"

"Don't let me put words in your mouth."

"I know how it must look to you now, but sooner or later we're moving to a nicer place."

"You mean a 'happy house.' "

"Exactly. Ask Scott. He'll tell you about all the arguments we have about this."

"Uh-huh."

"It's amazing, but you really think I do know something. Excuse me, but perhaps you'd like to tell me what reason I could possibly have to be hiding anything?"

Harvey ground out his Lucky in the ashtray. The fact was he couldn't tell her.

"You seem to forget how this whole thing started, Harvey. You found my name on a list of people this guy showed houses to. So you called me."

"And you asked me to lunch," he said.

"What can I say? I'm a bored suburban housewife! I found the idea of a murder investigation titillating. Look, it beats pedicures and bake sales. And if you hadn't turned out to be so damn alluring, we never would've spoken again after that lunch. So it's my fault."

"You probably say that to all the guys."

"Fuck you, Harvey. If I were you, I'd try to find out a little more about that piece of land and who might've buried what there who-knows-when." She took a breath and said, "Let me tell you something. I'll tell you why you keep thinking I'm guilty of something. You're projecting. It's because *you're* guilty of something and you can't take it and you keep trying to pin it on me. We fooled around and you don't like yourself for it and now you keep trying to make me pay for it. And I'm sick and tired of it."

"Uh-huh."

"Anyway, I also called to say that cop Dombrowski's called me in for questioning this afternoon. I know I shouldn't be surprised."

"I have a deal with him," Harvey said. "I pass along interesting stuff I know." But she had already hung up on him.

. . .

AFTER HIS TEAM lost the first game at the Y to a dubious collection of overaged gym rats that included his brother Norm, Harvey
went to the water fountain to cough up some ancient phlegm and
then slumped on the courtside bench. One of Harvey's teammates sat
down next to him with an exaggerated sigh. He was a lawyer in his
thirties named Preston Quinn, whose ardor for the game vastly
exceeded his skill at it. He had read Quinn's statement to the cops.
There had been nothing in it.

"Hey, we almost came back and won it," Preston said.

Harvey watched his brother miss a jumper to start the second
game. "Yeah, but Stu Silver kept pumping in those rainbows."
Peplow's old classmate from Bowdoin had turned out to be a superb
long-range shooter.

"Nice block on your brother, though." Norm had made the
mistake of trying to drive past Harvey on a fast break. "You really
stuffed him good."

Harvey toweled off his forearms and made a face. "Well, I've got
an inch and a half on him."

"Hey, c'mon," the lawyer said, "it was a nice play! And you
must've loved doing that to your own brother."

"Okay"—he broke into a smile—"it pleased me more than I
can say."

"That's the spirit."

"Hey!" one of the players on the floor screamed to another. "Pass
it while we're still young!"

The teams were moving up and down the scarred floor, middle-
aged men determined to wring the last juice of youth from their
creaking bodies. A waddling software consultant attempted an absurd
move at the top of the key.

"Way to shake and bake, Tony!" someone at the other end of the
bench called out.

"Funny how the mind keeps saying 'Michael Jordan,' " Harvey said to Preston, "even when the body's saying 'coronary.' "

"Whenever someone tried something fancy like that, Larry used to say, 'In your fuckin' dreams!' That was Pep's phrase."

Harvey turned to him. "Hey, Preston, did he ever say anything to you about a developer he might've had the goods on? Anything about a piece of property filled with toxic waste? Anything like that?"

"No."

"No hint of trouble?"

"No."

"What about the fact that he used to be a psychotherapist? He ever talk about it?"

"Not to me. Stu happened to mention it one day. That's the only reason I know."

Harvey watched the court as he spoke. "It doesn't seem like any of you guys got to know him that well." Norm banked in an unlikely runner, and Harvey called out, "Norm, you're breakin' my heart with those shots."

"Eat my Reeboks," Norm replied as he backpedaled downcourt on rejuvenated legs.

"You know what it's like," Preston was saying. "Eighteen guys show up to put on their gym shoes and pretend to be best friends for a couple of hours. Then we leave the Y in eighteen different cars." The lawyer pointed to the balding ectomorph who had just stolen a rebound from Norm and laid the basketball back in for an easy two. "Eric there. I played with Eric there for three years before I found out he owns some of the hottest little advertising shops in Chicagoland."

By the time they were all toweling off in the locker room, he had still learned nothing new about Peplow. He couldn't be sure how much his brother or any of these men really cared about him. It was frightening how easily and quietly people passed beyond your affections. It was just a regular pickup game. And yet the joking and taunting all around him in the Y's gray aisles of dented metal lockers was a kind of intimacy.

A restaurant-chain purchasing agent named Tom was saying, "No, the definition is, if you wife finds out, it's infidelity."

"No, no, no," Norm said, rubbing some antifungal paste between his toes. "It's only infidelity if she leaves you."

"What if you don't put your prick inside her?" asked Eric. "What if it's just some other part of your body? Is *that* infidelity?"

"Some other part?" said a black anaesthesiologist named Emile. "Man, if you're not putting one of three parts of your body in a woman, that's not infidelity—that's *stupidity*."

"Hey, I know what *your* M. O. is, Emile," Eric shouted. "You put the woman into a deep sleep before you spring into action."

"That's right. If she's not conscious it's not infidelity."

"Okay, okay, okay," Preston the lawyer said, "let's get technical for a minute."

"Preston, go play with yourself," Emile said.

"Hey, if I could find it I would. Okay, say that the tip of your prick is right *there,* but it's not inside. Is that infidelity?"

"Is it erect?" asked the purchasing agent.

"I don't know about yours," Preston said, "but mine sure is."

Norm looked up. "Wait a second. You're saying your prick is *touching,* but it's not inside?"

"Yeah."

"That's not sex, Preston."

"If you've gone that far, man, why not go the extra foot?" Emile said.

"Foot?" said Eric. "C'mon, Emile, some of us aren't that fortunate."

"You know, it's different for Jews," Norm said. "For a Jew, just looking at lingerie ads is considered infidelity."

No stereotype was inadmissible. It was the kind of camaraderie that used to be his steady diet. "Hey, Preston," he said, "so what was Peplow's definition of infidelity?"

Preston looked up, but Eric replied. "He didn't need one, did he? Poor guy wasn't married."

"Doesn't mean he didn't have an opinion."

"Anybody remember what Larry's position was on the subject?" Preston called out. Some of the faster dressers were already leaving, saying good-bye over their shoulders.

"Position?" Tom said. Harvey could see the bad joke coming. "His position was anything that didn't hurt his back." There were several groans.

"Pep didn't like to schmooze it up as much as a lot of us," Norm said. "He had some dignity about it. Kind of a little above it. Like you, Harv."

Harvey laughed. "Oh, yeah, right. Normie, you seem to've forgot how much time I logged in major league locker rooms. It's just that I've used up all my good lines."

Norm tied his shoes and said, "C'mon, baby bro', I'll take you to lunch. I'm losing too many brain cells listening to this crap."

IN HIS CAR, following his brother's Volvo to a favorite haunt of his in Evanston, Harvey pulled a business card out of his pocket and punched in the number for The Hair Shack in Coleridge on his cellular. He asked for Trish.

"I'm afraid she's busy with a customer right now," the man said. "Can I help you?"

Trish had a slot open at five that afternoon, and Harvey reserved it.

As he tailed his brother down Sheridan Road through the leafy, dormant Northwestern University campus, his phone rang by his right knee, startling him. He couldn't imagine who it was, since his brother, Norm, fifty yards in front of him, didn't have a car phone. Had he given the number to Dombrowski?

"Hello," Harvey said.

"Is this Harvey Blissberg?" a man said evenly.

"Speaking," Harvey said although he thought it would seem more appropriate to respond: "Driving."

"This is Dr. Walls in Portland."

"Ah, yes." Harvey tried to collect himself. Basketball had released too many endorphins. He felt soft around the edges. "Thanks for getting back to me."

"Your message said that Mr. Peplow was murdered?" Dr. Walls said in a measured voice.

"Yes."

There was a three-second pause on Walls's end. "What were the circumstances?"

"He was found shot through the head in a field here north of Chicago about seven or eight weeks ago."

"Chicago," he said.

"He had been living here for the last few years."

"I see."

"He was practicing as a real estate agent in the area."

"I see. Are there any suspects?"

"No suspects. That's why I'm here."

"You said you were a private detective."

"That's right. I'm trying to plug a few holes in the official police investigation."

"Who hired you? If I may ask."

"Some of Peplow's friends here."

"I see."

"Forgive me, Dr. Walls, but I'm afraid I don't know who you are. I found your name among Peplow's things. What exactly was your relationship to him?" Please don't be the podiatrist.

"I once treated Mr. Peplow."

"For what?" Harvey followed his brother down a side street.

"I'm a psychiatrist, Mr. Blissberg."

Harvey braked for an oblivious yellow dog. "I see. Were you *his* psychiatrist?"

"For a time. In the mid-eighties."

"Had you spoken to him since then?"

"No, I don't believe so."

"Your name was in his current address book."

"That may be, but I haven't spoken to him in years. I didn't know about his death."

Norm pulled into a small parking lot near the business district, and Harvey maneuvered his car into an empty space three down from Norm's.

"Is there anything you can tell me about him that might help me? To be honest, we're not making a great deal of headway with the case."

"No, I don't think so."

"You can't, or won't?"

"I'm afraid my position doesn't allow me to make that distinction."

Harvey put his car in park and left the engine running. "So even if you did know something that would help me, you wouldn't tell me?"

"Well, of course, that would depend."

"On what?"

"I imagine if a patient told me that the Mafia was after him for a debt, was threatening his life, I might tell the authorities that I had been told this."

"You would tell them when?"

"I wouldn't tell them just to be telling them, if that's what you mean," Walls said.

"You mean, you would tell the authorities only if your patient was found dead, say, at the bottom of Casco Bay?"

"That's an indelicate way of putting it."

"Well, you know private eyes, Doctor." Harvey tacked. "Were you treating Peplow as part of his training?"

"No."

Norm came to Harvey's window and gave him a questioning look. Harvey shook his head and waved Norm away. "So he came to you because of problems he was having."

"That's why people consult psychiatrists."

Norm pantomimed that he would meet Harvey at the restaurant next door and left. "May I ask you what—you know, generally speaking—what you were treating him for?"

"That's confidential."

"You know, Doctor, the man is dead. He's been murdered. What does that do to your confidentiality?"

"Nothing. I have a patient waiting for me, so I'm afraid I can't talk any longer, Mr. Blissberg."

"I'm trying to find the murderer of a man who used to be your patient. If there's anything you know that would help, it would be appreciated."

"I want you to know that I understand your situation and I wish I could help you."

"But you have no information, or you have some but can't reveal it?"

"We've already covered this," Walls said with just the slightest trace of impatience. "I obviously know some things about Mr. Peplow's life, but whether it would be helpful to you, I just can't say."

"Why did Peplow stop being a therapist?"

Walls sighed lightly. "I don't know. He may have been disenchanted. Being a therapist is not for everyone."

"Is that a general observation or are you talking about Peplow now?"

"That's a general observation. Now, look, I'm sorry but I have to go."

"Dr. Walls, am I barking up the wrong tree?"

"I'm not in a position to know that."

"But, Dr. Walls, you *are* in a position to tell me if there may be something in his past I need to investigate."

"A person's past is a very large and complex matter, Mr. Blissberg, and I can claim only to know some aspects of Mr. Peplow's. And I can't say whether any of those aspects would be of use to you. But we're going in circles now. I've told you, I can't discuss former or current patients."

"Unless the Mafia has been after them?"

"The Mafia was not interested in Mr. Peplow. I knew of no direct threat to his physical well-being."

"You're in a position to save me a lot of legwork and trouble."

"But I'm unable to do that. On principle. And now I must really go."

14

"WE TAKE THE Worry Out of Living." The motto on the painted
plywood sign stuck in the grass near the Rimwood Estates entrance
had taken on, in the light of Peplow's murder, an unpleasant irony,
and as Harvey drove between the brick pillars on Tuesday morning,
he wondered whether to mention to Vaultt that it might be bad for
business. A chain of North Shore weekly newspapers was keeping the
homicide alive in the public's mind through an occasional police
blotter squib about the investigation's difficulties. Harvey's participa-
tion had been noted in the latest accounts, although he declined an
interview with a young female reporter who had tracked him down at
the hotel.

As he passed through the second, wrought-iron gate that marked
the entrance to Rimwood Estates proper, a state trooper in dark glasses
stopped his car with a raised hand and crouched by Harvey's window.

"May I help you?" he said.

Through the windshield Harvey saw what looked like an incursion
of benign alien gardeners. Several men in bulky yellow disposable
paper suits, rubber gloves, booties, hard hats, masks and protective
goggles were working in the yards of some of Vaultt's houses. An
unmarked white panel truck was parked in the road.

"My name's Blissberg." He gave the trooper a look at his Massachusetts private investigator's license. "I'm cooperating with the Garden Hills police on the Peplow investigation. What's going on?"

"State EPA. They're taking some samples."

Harvey saw that one of the aliens was not holding a gardening tool after all, but a hand auger he was drilling into the ground. "Is Lieutenant Dombrowski here?" he asked.

"He's over there." The trooper pointed away from the EPA technicians to two men in the driveway of a neighboring house. "Back up and leave the car outside the gate. And be careful. There may be gases."

When Harvey approached the two men on foot, Vaultt was holding a battery-operated fan in front of his face and Dombrowski was saying to him, "We'll replace the sod. You won't know they've been here."

"Like hell I won't. Now get these goons off my lawns." Vaultt's face was doubly red, from the sun and his outrage. He was wearing a guayabera again, this one of the palest green. "Well, if it isn't what's-his-name," he said, spotting Harvey.

"Greetings, Jim. Lieutenant. I just came by to chat, Jim, so imagine my surprise—"

"Get these goons off my grass!" Vaultt shouted at Dombrowski again, waving his fan at him. "Just because some broad says Peplow said this land is polluted doesn't mean you can come storming in here. You have no right. This is my baby."

Dombrowski dragged a handkerchief across his face. "If the land's polluted, the public has a right to be protected."

"You have no evidence that it is."

"Just bear with us."

Vaultt turned to Harvey. "Suppose you tell me exactly what this woman told you."

"She said she ran into Peplow and he told her that he had heard you built on some toxic waste."

"That's bullshit. Who did he say told him that?"

"She said he didn't say."

"Then it's just a lot of fucking she-said-he-said. And even if you did find something, what the hell would that prove?"

Dombrowski and Harvey looked at each other, wondering whose job it was to make the obvious connection for Vaultt.

The lieutenant gave in and said in a bored voice, "The theory is that Peplow might have tried to blackmail you with the knowledge."

"Go ahead," Vaultt said with his hands on his hips, "I'm dying to hear the rest of this."

"That if it was true," the lieutenant continued offhandedly, "and it was made public, your baby here would be down the toity."

"So I killed him?"

"It's only a theory, Vaultt."

"Oh, and a very excellent one!" Vaultt said contemptuously. "After all, who wants to spend several hundred thousand dollars on a house just in order to get leukemia? Except, why the fuck would I kill him here? I may be a developer but I'm not a fucking idiot!"

"If you killed him here," Harvey said, "no one would have seen you with him. This place is empty except for you."

"How'd he get here? Huh? How'd he get here? He didn't have his car. And you know as well as I he was killed here. And *if* I just happened to kill him somewhere else, I'd have to be doubly dumb to bring him back here and draw attention to myself."

Dombrowski adjusted his sunglasses on the bridge of his nose. "He could've driven here. You could've had an argument and shot him. Then you drove his car back to his house and parked it. And you came back here and put the keys back in his pocket."

"What'd I do, call a cab? Or did I walk the five miles?"

"It's just a theory," Dombrowski said.

"I could drive a fucking fleet of trucks through the holes in it."

Harvey felt that something wasn't right. There was an off note here; the antagonism between Vaultt and Dombrowski was too casual. Of course, it might have been the heat, draining the conversation of its natural energies, but suddenly Harvey wondered if Vaultt and Dombrowski weren't just going through the motions for his benefit, if the EPA had been called in merely for the record. Dombrowski was scrubbing the side of his neck with his hankie. Vaultt's beefy face wore a placid expression as it received the battery-operated fan's breeze. Two guys in their fifties, maybe with a secret between them. Did Vaultt have a problem that only Dombrowski could safely get rid of? No. More likely, Vaultt had taken care of it himself and had hired Dombrowski to make sure no one ever figured it out. It would explain why the murder scene was so clean. It would explain the surveillance. It would also explain Dombrowski's openness with Harvey; Harvey's arrival on the scene did not threaten Dombrowski's self-esteem as a cop because the lieutenant had not in fact failed to find Peplow's murderer. He had succeeded in protecting him. So far.

For a moment the temperature could have been in the fifties, not the nineties. What if it wasn't Vaultt who was the odd man out here, but Harvey? How could he begin to expose the connection between these two men? And to whom would he expose it? Before he could think of bothering the Lake County prosecutors with it, or the feds, he'd have to have more to offer than these stomach-churning, paranoid conjectures.

Or was it just out of frustration that Harvey was breeding this cover-up hypothesis? Be rational, he advised himself: The only motive Dombrowski could have to cover for Vaultt was money. And it would have to be a lot of money because Garden Hills did not need an unsolved murder on its books, and Dombrowski had better things to do than have his homicide unit be thought incompetent. Harvey fought back the conspiracy-theory urge.

But it was suspicious that Dombrowski would overlook the obvious, and now Harvey interjected it quietly. "Jim," he said, "the theory isn't that you killed him here and drove his car back to his house. The theory is you picked him up. You picked him up and drove him back here, telling him you wanted to discuss his price."

"And then I popped him? This is such bullshit I can't believe it."

Dombrowski spread his hands, palms down, the mediator. "Look, Jim, the rumor about the dump is out, so at this point we need the EPA tests to dispel it."

Vaultt looked away, toward the woods at the back of his development. "Anyway, I was at the movies."

"I'm not so sure about that," Harvey said.

Dombrowski turned to look at him.

Vaultt's head snapped around. "What do you mean, you're not so sure? What the hell is this?" He looked very close to busting either Harvey or Dombrowski.

"Nobody saw you there," Harvey said. "Besides, you're a little hazy about what movie you went to."

"What're you talking about?"

"You told me you went to see one movie, *Swingtime,* which began at ten-thirty on the night of Peplow's murder. When I came by here on Saturday, I asked you how the musical number 'The Continental' stood the test of time when you saw it, and you said it stood up fine."

"So?"

"So 'The Continental' isn't in *Swingtime.* It's in *The Gay Divorcee.*"

"You mean I'm supposed to fucking remember which movie some dance number is in?"

"I think so," Harvey said, "when it takes up half the movie."

"This is all just purely theoretical, of course," Dombrowski said, lighting a Chesterfield. He seemed eager to dissipate the tension. "That's a new haircut, isn't it, son?" he added, turning to Harvey.

Harvey ran his hand over it. "She didn't leave it long enough in back." The only privileged information that Trish at The Hair Shack had been able to provide yesterday was that Peplow's hair had been unusually dry.

"You guys are really jerking me around," Vaultt said, hands shoved into two of his guayabera's many pockets. "And I really mean that."

HARVEY HAD A lunch of gyoza and salmon teriyaki at the Sunny
Day Sushi Bar and drank two very cold Kirin beers to improve his
reality. The conspiracy theory was clinging like a bad dream. If only
he could establish a relationship between Dombrowski and Vaultt.
Find somebody who had seen them together. Go back and talk to
Pincus, Lynn Nyland, Virginia Schmauss. Visit the morgue of the
local papers and see what kind of trouble Dombrowski may have had
in the past. The thought tired him out. After a bowl of green tea ice
cream he showed Peplow's grinning photo to the waitresses. Maybe
one of them would say she had seen the gentleman here with
Dombrowski. But no one recognized him.

Behind the wheel of his Town Car again, Harvey sought some
relief from his new speculations about Dombrowski. He pondered
how to pry open Dr. Frederick Walls's end of the case. Walls was not
going to put out, and who could blame him? Harvey did not want to
think that the good Dr. Ellyn Walker of Lexington, Massachusetts,
would ever divulge a harmless anecdote of his, let alone a confidence
of any value, even if he were dead and beyond the reach of worldly
disclosure. The dead were defenseless. Yet what Walls knew, however
unrelated to the murder, might have its uses, and the thought of all
that information being held in escrow annoyed the hell out of him.
He would have to find another point of entry into Peplow's past.

Harvey drove by a stable, a stand selling early raspberries and flats
of annuals, a housing development called Crystal River Glen. Then
his car phone buzzed by his right knee.

"Hello?" he said.

"Mr. Blissberg."

"Yes?"

"This is Dr. Walls in Portland."

Harvey sat up straight behind the wheel. "Yes. How are you?"

"How's the investigation going?"

"Not very well, thank you." He drove by a junior high school, the second of the day named after JFK. A small fleet of yellow buses sat serenely in the parking lot.

"I wanted to ask you a question."

"Certainly," Harvey said.

"I was simply wondering whether, in the course of your investigation, you had come across a certain name."

"Such as?"

"Terry Charette." He said it too matter-of-factly, as if he were just shooting the breeze.

"No, I haven't."

"No, no, of course you wouldn't've. I was simply wondering."

"Who's Terry Charette?"

"He's the only individual I can think of who might've wished Peplow harm."

"Why?"

"I can't say."

"Who is he?"

"I can't say."

"Was, or is, Charette a patient of yours?"

"I can't say."

"What's his relationship to Peplow?"

"I can't tell you that either."

"Where do I find this person?" Harvey said.

"In Portland. It may help."

"Help me more."

"I'm going to give you his phone number."

Harvey fumbled for his Parker Jotter in his shirt pocket and scrawled the name and number in the margin of the *Chicago Tribune* lying next to him on the velour upholstery.

"You're not going to tell me why I'm calling this person?" Harvey asked.

But the line was dead.

15

IT WAS AS if the camera, after having being trained on the same scene for much of the movie, had finally started to pan right. But what now came into view was a long shot, filmed from such a distance that the action, if indeed there was any, was impossible to make out.

When he returned to the North Shore Suites Hotel, he immediately phoned the membership office of the American Psychological Association in Washington, where a woman told him that a Laurence Peplow, formerly practicing on Noonan Street in Portland, Maine, had voluntarily resigned his membership in 1988 and left no forwarding address.

Then Harvey began calling the number Walls had given him, only to keep getting Terry Charette's answering machine. He had no message to leave, in fact no way to know why he was even calling, so he hung up carefully each time during the gruff recording. Between calls Harvey lay on one of the double beds in his room watching *The Third Man* on PBS, followed by a cooking show in which a clergyman-chef, one of those mesmerizingly gentle fellows who sees the face of God in the lowly lentil, sautéed and assembled a variety of vegetarian dishes. He was entranced. As a teenager he had helped out in the hot, clanging kitchen of his father's suburban Boston restaurant. There were times when he dreamed of extending his culinary dabbling into a career. He dreamed not of a cooking show—he would never be able to manage the pious patter—but a rustic restaurant somewhere in New England where each day would bring its small and predictable satisfactions. It was odd how hard it was to end up doing what one merely loved.

The cooking show chef signed off with a tribute to "the friendly little fava bean," and Harvey rolled into a sitting position on the bed and tried Terry Charette's number again. It was six in Portland.

"Yeah?" said a tired voice after the third ring.

"Is this Terry Charette?"

"Yeah, who's this?"

"My name's Harvey Blissberg. I'm a private detective."

"Yeah? What's this about?"

"I'm helping to investigate the death of a man named Laurence Peplow."

During the short silence that followed, Harvey killed the television set with the remote control and picked up a pen on the nightstand.

"Did you know him?" Harvey asked.

"I don't know if I did or not. Who's asking?"

"Like I said, I'm a private detective. I don't know what more I can tell you. Some friends of his hired me."

"So, like, how did he die?"

"He was murdered."

"Murdered?"

"Outside of Chicago."

"Chicago," he repeated, just as Walls had.

"He was shot in the head in a town called Garden Hills."

"Jesus." He said it with genuine surprise.

"Did you know him?"

"How'd you get my name?"

"From a shrink named Walls. Are you a patient of his?"

"Walls? Never heard of him. Where're you calling me from?"

"Chicago. You didn't know about his murder?"

"No."

"Will you talk to me?"

"Why?"

"Because you knew him."

"I didn't."

"He was a therapist in Portland until a few years ago," Harvey said. "Were you a patient of his?"

"I told you I didn't know him."

"A colleague?"

"No."

"Now, look, why won't you talk to me?"

Charette just breathed into the phone.

"Maybe if I give you some time to think about it," Harvey said. "What if I called you back tomorrow? Would that be all right?"

"I don't know."

"Can I ask you what you do for a living, Terry?"

"I'm a carpenter."

"Let me give you my phone number here in Chicago, just in case you feel like talking." He gave him the hotel's number and the car phone number, too.

"Listen. Are there, you know, any suspects?"

"No. That's why I'm interested in anything you'd have to say, Terry."

"Okay" is all he managed.

"I'll give you a call tomorrow. Is there a work number you can give me?"

"No."

"All right then. I'll be in touch. Good-bye."

"Good-bye."

Charette had been vaguely hostile, but ambivalent. Not defensive enough to have killed Peplow—the murder seemed to be news to him—but still hiding something of significance. Dr. Frederick Walls had not sent Harvey on a wild-goose chase, even if Charette really didn't seem to know who Walls was. Why would Charette have wished Peplow harm?

Harvey called home. He was about to hang up when Mickey answered the phone on the sixth ring.

"How's Duane?"

"The same," she said. "He won't eat on his own. I was just cleaning up the bathroom. The walls were covered with bits of Friskies Turkey and Giblets."

"Why?"

" 'Cause sometimes when I stick the damn syringe in his jowl and fire away he jerks his head and I end up spraying the walls with it."

"I'm sorry I'm not there to help out."

"Yeah." She managed to compress anger, resignation, and spite into a single syllable.

"How's Bubba doing?"

"He's fine. Except for an occasional sniff of Duane's head, he just goes about his business. Kind of reminds me of you."

"Please. I hardly ever smell your head."

"When are you coming home?"

"It's only been five days, Mick. Anyway, I'm coming east."

"Is 'east' some sort of euphemism for home?"

"I'm going to Portland, Maine. I think I've got a break in this case."

"When?"

"Tomorrow. You want to come up and meet me? I could use a little wiggly."

"Wiggly? What the hell's wiggly?"

"You know, a little horizontal amusement."

"Bliss, you sound like a jerk."

"C'mon, Mick. Put away the knives."

"No, I'm serious. You're talking like a jock. Anyway, even if I wanted to come to Portland, I can't. I have to stay here and look after Duane."

"Oh, right."

"Unless you think your sexual needs are more important than Duane's survival."

"I just want to see you. Maybe I'll drive down after I've checked out this lead."

"I'll be here."

"You sound so excited."

"This is not an exciting time in our relationship."

"Are you keeping busy?"

"Well, I'm having dinner with Paul tonight."

"Who's Paul?"

"You know, Paul Sarnes, my executive producer on the project."

Harvey had met him once, an angular ex-academic with one of those beards that looks more like grooming negligence than a deliberate attempt to grow facial hair. "You going to go?"

"Why not? He's divorced and I'm effectively single."

"Don't taunt me, Slavin."

"I'm sure he just wants to talk shop."

"Have a good time."

"Of course, if it turns out he's interested in a little horizontal amusement," she said, "I'll just have to play it by ear."

He lay on the bed feeling a woolly depression begin to cover him. He recoiled at the thought of going out to eat alone in one of the cheery mall restaurants nearby with their bacon bits and individual loaves of bread, but a room service dinner smacked of incarceration, so he slipped into his loafers and wandered into the warm buzzing dusk.

When he returned to his room, Harvey booked a noon flight Wednesday to Portland. Then he opened his address book and looked up Dr. Ellyn Walker's home phone number. "In case of emergency," she had said when she gave it to him. It made Harvey feel worse off than he thought he was. What was he going to do, call her up in the middle of the night with an especially thorny dream? Was he closer to putting a gun to his own head than he believed? But here he was, dialing it at nine o'clock from his bed.

"Hello?" she said.

"Dr. Walker?"

"Yes?"

"This is Harvey Blissberg."

"Oh, hello."

"I thought I'd get an answering machine."

"Sorry to disappoint you," she said. "What's up?"

"I needed a little help."

"Can it wait till our regular hour?"

"I'd sort of rather it didn't."

"Okay."

"Is this a bad time to talk?"

"Go ahead."

"I just wanted to run something by you. But first of all, I'm going to have to cancel tomorrow's session. I'm still in Chicago on a case. I don't remember what I told you about it."

"You said it was something your brother asked you to do."

"A friend of his—really an acquaintance—was murdered here in Chicago several weeks ago. A real estate agent who used to be a psychotherapist in Portland, Maine. He was a clinical psychologist Ph.D. But here's the thing: I stumbled on this guy's former shrink in Maine, a Dr. Frederick Walls. Do you know him, by any chance?"

"No, I haven't heard of him."

"Anyway, I called the guy and all he would say was, yes, he had seen Peplow—that's the murder victim's name, Laurence Peplow—that he had seen him as a patient for a while in the mid-eighties. But he wouldn't give me any more than that."

"Therapist–patient confidentiality. It's not taken lightly, even when the patient is dead. You remember the recent flap caused by Anne Sexton's psychiatrist?"

"Not offhand." All Harvey recalled was that she was a poet who killed herself.

"Her psychiatrist had tape-recorded her sessions and made the tapes available to Sexton's biographer. It caused quite a stir. Anyway."

"But, Dr. Walker, here's the thing. Walls called me back this morning. And he gave me the name of someone else to call in Portland. He said it was the only person he could think of who might've wished Peplow harm."

"So he had second thoughts about not getting involved?"

"Yeah, I guess. So when I called this guy, Charette, he was pretty evasive. He wouldn't say if he knew Peplow or not. The only thing he told me was that he was a carpenter. Oh—and that he was not a patient of Dr. Walls's, nor had he been one of Peplow's."

"We don't know why Peplow stopped practicing?"

"No. I called the American Psychological Association and they list Peplow as having voluntarily retired in 1988. Earlier, when I asked Dr. Walls why Peplow had quit being a shrink, he said something abstract about his possibly being disenchanted. He said, 'It's not for everyone.' But he wasn't saying this was necessarily true of Peplow." Harvey caught his breath. "Is there any way you can find out any information for me about Frederick Walls?"

"I can look him up for you in the directory. What is he, a clinical psychologist, a psychiatrist, an analyst?"

"He said he was a psychiatrist."

"Just a moment."

She returned to the phone in a minute, saying, "All right, let's see. Walls, Walls. Here he is. Frederick Walls. This is the *Directory of the American Psychiatric.* Well, he seems perfectly kosher. Born 1931 . . . MD at Michigan, interned at a VA hospital in Rochester. . . . Let's see, residency in Connecticut, associate clinical professorship . . . a couple of prestigious fellowships . . . prison programs . . . chief of psychiatry at Beller Hospital in Portland . . . headed ethics committee of Maine Psychiatric . . . private practice. I'd say he's something of a heavyweight."

"How can I find out more about Peplow's therapy with him?"

"You can't. I know of a case where even the FBI couldn't gain access to the psychiatric files of a suspected felon."

"I didn't think the answer would be yes."

"If third-party payments were involved, it's conceivable you could find out what Walls's diagnosis was by getting hold of the insurance forms that have to be submitted. I don't know how easy that would be. But, in any case, any diagnosis would be vague and possibly misleading. Many therapists will simply put down 'anxiety neurosis' because it covers so much ground."

Harvey wondered for an instant what she had put on his insurance claim forms. "Sad Former Ballplayer Syndrome"?

"Mr. Blissberg, was this man Peplow a successful real estate agent?"

"Apparently. It also appears that he shaved corners."

"In what way?"

"Failing to convey a competing offer for a house once because that way—by conveying only the other offer—he would earn a higher commission."

"Interesting."

"What's interesting?"

"Well, the real estate profession, even if you're not shaving corners, is a profession of dual allegiances."

"Because you represent both the seller and the buyer?"

"Let's just say it's a field where you find a certain number of people who are good at rationalizing improprieties. It presents opportunities to manipulate others for your own financial benefit."

"But many professions do that."

"That may be true. Tell me something. As far as you know, what were Peplow's relationships like?"

"Well, he seems to have been very personable, but private. He seems to have asked a lot of questions and answered few."

"Sounds like a therapist," she said with a little laugh.

"And he wasn't married."

"How old was he?"

"Forty-four."

"Never married?"

"Is that significant?"

"I don't know. Was he gay?"

"No. He seemed to have a certain number of casual relationships with women. I spoke to a young woman he had been seeing for a few months when he was killed. She was about fifteen or sixteen years younger than he. She fell kind of hard for him, even though she figured it wasn't for real. What she didn't know was that he lied to her."

"What was the lie?"

"That he had formerly taught college English. He never told her he had been a therapist." He had also lied about his mother, Harvey recalled—that she was dead.

"But he had mentioned his former career to others?"

"Yes, to some friends, to his employer. His employer said he had given her a whole rap about real estate and psychotherapy both having to do with masks."

"But he hid it from the young woman."

"But why hide it from her?"

"I don't know. Perhaps he was only hiding it from himself in her presence. Well—" she said, indicating the end of the conversation with a slight shift of tone. "So I'll see you a week from tomorrow, then."

"Yes, a week from tomorrow," he said. "I appreciate the, uh, consultation."

"You're welcome. Good luck with your case."

When he put the phone down, he felt strangely abandoned. This privileged contact with her outside the confines of her office had been titillating. He was quite sure that none of her other patients were in a position to consult her on murder investigations. He wondered what she thought of him. He was suddenly and uncomfortably aware of wanting to impress her. It was unsettling how quickly she had insinuated herself into his thoughts, how quietly she—about whom he knew next to nothing—had moved into his heart.

He became aware of a light tapping at his hotel room door and from his bed called out, "Who is it?"

"Marilyn," said a voice in the hall.

16

"BOY, IT'S A lonely life, isn't it?" she said, standing in the doorway in her pleated tennis dress and Footjoys, surveying the clutter.

Harvey hastily gathered up a few articles of dirty clothing and plunged them into an open nylon carry-on on the floor. "Don't just stand there. You might as well come in."

"Afraid someone might see me?" she asked, but closed the door behind her and sauntered over to sit in the tub chair by the window. She dropped her shoulder bag at her feet.

"As a matter of fact, the last time you were here the Garden Hills police were watching."

"Me?"

"Me, but you showed up." He now collected some of the notes scattered on the bed and slipped them into his briefcase on the floor. "What is this, some sort of courtesy call?"

"I didn't want to leave it with you sulking."

"You like your affairs to end with a bang instead of a whimper?"

"I wouldn't go that far."

Harvey leaned against the wall by the window and looked down at her. "Where's Scott this time?"

"Why're you so interested in my husband?"

"Someone's got to be."

"He's away on business again, selling the Christmas line. Boxed goods."

To his immense chagrin, Harvey was already fighting arousal, the familiar pressure in his pants. There had been only one point he could have said no to her and meant it, and that was at the beginning four days ago, though it seemed like four weeks now. Once you had broken the plane of physical knowledge, you could not simply resurface at will. Whatever anger or suspicion passed between them, the truth was that he felt powerless before her sheer availability. And being kissed off by her the other day had only clarified and freed this desire for her.

"He says you used to play baseball," she said.

"Yeah. It's how I frittered away my youth." It surprised him that she hadn't known such a central fact about him. It was amazing how much of a relationship can be spun from so little thread.

"Scott was impressed. But, you know, he's such a jock. Were you good?"

"I was blessed with some ability."

"I like baseball," she said. "I think those thin socks they wear are sexy. Scott's taken me to a few Cubs games, but I never pay any attention to the players' names."

"I was in the other league. The American."

"So how'd you get from baseball to detective-ing?"

It was one of the few questions about his life she had bothered to ask; why was she starting in now with the commonplace inquiries? Anyway, it was too late and too beside the point to share even that part of his past. "Now that's a long story," he said. "Too long."

"It must be weird to peak so early in life."

"Not if you find another mountain to climb."

"Did you just make that up?"

"I believe so."

"I'll have to remember it. That ought to be in that book."

"Bartlett's Quotations?"

"Yeah, that's the one." She took a pack of Kents out of the bag at her feet and lit one with a lacquered lighter. "You don't mind, do you?" she said after the fact.

"Go ahead."

"You remember on Saturday when I told you I liked you?"

Harvey just watched her, wanting her. His bond with Mickey had sprung a leak, and now his feelings were spilling all over the place.

"Well, I meant it," she said, simultaneously exhaling smoke and picking at the corner of her mouth with a fingernail. "I get a charge out of you. I wished we could have met some other way."

"It would've ended the same."

"So it's ending, is it?"

"Yes."

"Well, I'm sorry to hear that."

"I'm leaving tomorrow," he said.

"You're quitting?"

"The action's moved elsewhere."

"Oh." She put out her cigarette after two hurried puffs and didn't even ask where. "I suppose you'll just put me out of your mind when you go back to"—she hesitated—"your other life. You know, when Scott told me you'd been a baseball player, I figured, well, maybe you're not as much of a straight arrow as I thought. You've probably had your share of baseball Annies."

Harvey laughed. "Since when do you know that term?"

"Like I said, I like baseball. In a previous life, I probably hung around outside of locker rooms. What did you do in a previous lifetime?"

"Beats me."

"Maybe this is your one and only one." She threw him a little laugh and tossed her short hair. "Hey, why don't you sit down already? You're making me nervous standing there."

He sat opposite her on the corner of the bed and shrugged.

"You're shrugging."

"I don't know what to say. I'm kind of beat." A yawn rose out of his throat and he looked away, covering it.

"Maybe a little recreation would perk you right up," she said.

"What?" He looked up.

She leaned down and pulled a ribbed plastic vibrator from her handbag.

"For chrissakes, Marilyn."

"What's the matter?"

"Oh, c'mon. Put that thing away."

"Meet Johnny."

"What, no last name?"

"We're intimates."

"I've only seen those in movies."

"Welcome to the movie of real life." She turned it on and held it, buzzing, in her lap.

"Real for you, maybe."

There seemed to be nothing in the room now but the ivory-colored, almost beautiful object in her fist.

She said, "If you want, you can just watch. I don't mind."

She uncrossed her bare legs and slowly brought the tip of her humming toy between them and up against the panties under her tennis dress. She released a long, low sigh.

"I guess I'll go down the hall for a Coke. How long do you think you'll be?"

"Don't make me laugh, Harvey." She slumped lower in her seat and hung her legs over the arms of the tub chair. She made another low animal sound through parted lips. "Did anyone ever tell you that you don't have a very sexy name?"

"We can't all be named Johnny."

"It's kind of old-fashioned. But I like everything else about you"—she squeezed out a moan—"I really do." She closed her eyes, excluding him from her pleasure, but opened them after a brief moment and stared at him with wild stillness. "Come here," she breathed, "there're a few things Johnny doesn't know."

She reached out her free hand and took his wrist and pulled him to her in a room now layered with the humming and buzzing of her toy, her moans, the air-conditioning, and the muffled traffic outside on Edens Expressway.

They ended up sitting side by side on the stiff carpet at the foot of the bed, panting as they stared at the ceiling.

"You probably never knew how much fun you could have without actually screwing," she said.

Harvey grunted.

"It's so much easier when you just do what you want."

"Civilized society can only tolerate a few of you at a time."

She laughed. "God gave some of us more than the average amount of desire."

"Now, I wouldn't go blaming him or her for your behavior."

"Oh, no, I take full responsibility."

Later, when she was reapplying her coral lipstick in front of the mirror over the dresser, she said to his reflection, "I hope they find something."

"You hope who finds what?"

"I hope they find some toxic junk at Rimwood Estates."

"The EPA was digging there this morning."

"Gee, that was fast."

"Speaking of which, how'd your talk with Dombrowski go?"

"He's unhappy with me for not remembering more. Or I should say with Peplow for not telling me more." She plumped her hair with her fingertips. "I never liked that guy Vaultt in the first place. I thought he was creepy."

"He definitely needs a new wardrobe consultant."

She picked up her handbag and faced Harvey. "Well, I better dash. I hate teary good-byes."

"You know perfectly well no one's going to start crying."

But her eyes were already moist. "Do you think there's a romantic inside me trying to get out?" she said, wiping the tears away with disdain. "Anyway, it's been real." She kissed him abruptly on the cheek. "You know where to find me the next time you're in Chicago tracking down a mystery killer. But I won't count on hearing from you."

"You never know."

"If I run into one of Dombrowski's men on the way out," she said at the door, "I'll tell him we were just talking baseball."

Portland, Maine

17

AFTER DUMPING HIS bags in his room at the Edwards Hotel, Harvey threw down a couple of cold beers at a yuppie bar on Commercial Street in the Old Port and walked to his car along the piers streaked with light, past Di Millo's Floating Restaurant and Marina and the clusters of chic, converted waterfront condos, most of them built in the eighties and many of them already on the auction block. Portland was much smaller than Providence, but it reminded him pleasantly of the city where he had spent his last, eventful year in baseball, all clutter and bricks and streets not much bigger than alleyways. The air was scented with the remains of last night's lobster dinners piled high in rubber barrels outside the restaurants. The bulky red brick E. Swasey & Co. Glass Ware building loomed ahead of him in the twilight. It was good to be back in New England, in a city that was already old when Garden Hills was still wilderness.

He was filled with the buoyancy of being in a new place, the sense that his consciousness had been wiped clean, that for the moment nothing was contaminated by the past. It was only a grace period, he knew, and one made more graceful by the two drinks—four, if you counted the two glasses of burgundy on the plane from O'Hare that afternoon—but Harvey would take any buoyancy he could get as he climbed into in his new rental and headed north on Commercial past the Customs House. Already he missed the Lincoln Town Car; the cramped, sensible Toyota Tercel made him feel that he had traded in a measure of dignity. At the end of Commercial he jogged onto Fore Street, doglegged partway up Munjoy Hill, and parked in front of an old two-story gabled brick house that looked down over a grassy lot to the Bath Iron Works with its massive blue dry dock, over the U.S. Navy frigates, and, to the left, over Portland Harbor sparkling in the warm reflected sunset.

He climbed the flight of wooden stairs and knocked on the door. Heavy footsteps approached on the other side, and the door was opened by a man in his thirties, shorter and heavier than Harvey, with broad French-Canadian good looks and wide-set eyes. He was holding an open can of plum tomatoes. He looked like an overinflated Robert Goulet, except that the black mustache, allowed to grow long, flopped over his mouth.

"Yes?"

"You Terry?"

"That's me." He wiped his hand on his jeans.

"I'm Harvey Blissberg."

When the name registered after a second, the features of Charette's face made a fist. He quickly ran his eyes over Harvey—the unpolished loafers, the unconstructed navy linen sportcoat, the soft leather briefcase he'd bought at T.J. Maxx for a mere fraction of its retail value. "You don't waste any time, do you?"

"Is this a bad time to talk?"

Charette held his position in the doorway. Over his shoulder Harvey could see a renovated apartment with plenty of bookshelves and a tasteful grouping of inexpensive furniture from Workbench. The random-width pine flank floors had been sanded and tung-oiled.

"I'm cooking dinner," he said.

"Let me take you out for a lobster."

"My girlfriend's here. And I've got nothing to say to you, anyway."

"I was really hoping we could talk."

A stringy-haired young woman in cutoffs and a T-shirt appeared behind Charette and said, "Ter, the garlic's burning. I need the tomatoes."

"Here." Charette held out the can of tomatoes behind him without taking his eyes off Harvey. "And put the water on to boil." The woman came forward to take the can, smiling apologetically at Harvey.

"Sorry to intrude," Harvey said to her, but she was already returning to the kitchen on bare feet.

"Please leave me alone," Charette said.

"You knew Laurence Peplow. I need to talk about him."

"I didn't know him."

"Then you knew *of* him."

Charette glared at him. He was not someone who suffered from a need to fill silences. Harvey looked down at Charette's nicked, callused hands, disproportionately large for his body, and the work jeans smudged with grease and sawdust.

"Look, my man," Harvey said, taking a tone worthy of Charette's respect, "there's nothing up my sleeve. This shrink Walls obviously felt you would help me solve this man's murder."

"I don't know anything about his murder."

"Let's say I believe you. Still, you know *something* about Peplow."

Charette drew down one end of his mustache into his mouth and sucked on it. "I'm really not interested, buddy, okay? I'm making spaghetti sauce." He turned his head. "I'll be right there, Nance," he called out. "Too bad you had to come all this way for nothing."

"Nice bookshelves."

"What?" Charette turned to look at them.

"You do that yourself?"

"I'm a cabinetmaker."

Harvey could make out the book titles on the shelves closest to the door. "You do a lot of reading?"

"What's it to you?"

Harvey opened his palms at shoulder level. "Hey, I'm just making conversation 'cause I don't want you to close the door on me. I don't want to put any pressure on you, you know, but I think you're my last shot at cracking this thing."

"I think you're wrong."

"You mean I'm wrong because you don't have any information, or I'm wrong because you're not my last shot?" Harvey was so damn tired of asking questions. "Look, if there're other people I can talk to, tell me. Just tell me who they are and I'll stop bothering you."

He folded his arms across his chest and said, "I have a feeling you're going to stop bothering me anyway."

"Terry, Terry," Harvey muttered. Fatigue had given him a certain equanimity. "That kind of brave talk doesn't work any better on me than it does on you. Let me just explain something to you. If a cop shows up here someday who knows a little more than I do right now and he asks you to come down to the station for a few questions, you're probably going to look back and wish you'd dealt with me."

"I guess I'll just have to take my chances."

A bolt of weariness hit Harvey's brain. It felt like a mental brownout. The beers and the travel were catching up with him. The smell of frying garlic in Charette's kitchen made him aware of how long he'd gone without eating.

"All those psychology books yours?" Harvey said, flicking his eyes at a shelf of paperbacks.

"I'm a college graduate."

"Just curious. Anyway"—Harvey held out his hand—"sorry to interrupt your cooking."

Charette—surprised to see the offered hand—looked at it for a second before pumping it once and softly closing the door in Harvey's face.

Harvey drove back down to the waterfront and ordered two one-and-a-quarter-pound steamed lobsters at Di Millo's, a converted ferryboat. He sat and thought, crumbling pieces of a dinner roll. He went to the public phone by the kitchen and opened the yellow pages to "Carpenters." There, under "Charette Carpentry and Cabinetry" was his home phone number and the address on Munjoy Hill. The lobsters came, and he performed the thorough surgery on them that was, after thirty-odd years of lobster eating, second-nature to him. When he was through with the claws and tails, he opened the body and picked out the knuckle meat and scraped the morsels out of the legs and tail fans with his teeth. He spread the tomalley on pieces of cracker and ate them.

When his big-boned waitress had cleared the debris and brought him a decaf, Harvey touched her arm.

"What's your name?"

"Dena."

"Dena, can you do me a big favor?"

She reached for the saucer filled with those little plastic thimbles of nondairy creamer. "Don't tell me—real cream for your coffee, right?"

"No, I want you to make a phone call for me."

"A phone call?"

"It's worth twenty bucks to me, and I'll even write down what to say. You ever done any acting?"

She cocked a hand on her hip. "What do you think this job is? Your think I'm naturally nice to strangers? What kind of phone call?"

"I'm an out-of-town detective here on business and I need some information from someone who won't suspect it's me who's asking."

"My boss wouldn't like it, me making phone calls on a busy night."

"If he sees, you'll just say it's an emergency. Your mother, your cat."

"I don't have a cat."

"How about a mother?"

"Yeah. All right."

While Dena left to deliver a check to another of her tables, Harvey took out a small spiral notebook and wrote: "Ask for Terry Charette and say: 'Hi, my name's Dena and I got your number from a friend at work. I'm thinking of getting some cabinets made and you came highly recommended. But first I wondered if you could maybe give me the names of two or three references—you know, like people you've done work for. Would that be all right?' "

Dena looked it over when she returned. "What if he doesn't have references or he won't give them to me?"

"Not likely to happen, but if it does, just say thanks, and you'll be in touch. You want me to stand with you at the phone?"

"No, it'll just make me nervous."

Harvey put a folded twenty in her pocket.

She came to his table a few minutes later with a scrap of paper and three names and numbers on it. A Cathy Susi in Cape Elizabeth and a Robert Steltz and a Eunice Claherty in Falmouth Foreside.

"You did great," Harvey said.

"Thanks. Now how 'bout some pie?"

BACK AT THE Edwards, Harvey called Lieutenant Dombrowski at his home in Garden Hills, Illinois. "It's Harvey Blissberg."

"And what would this be in reference to, son?"

"This is just a courtesy call, Lieutenant, to let you know I'm in Portland, Maine."

"I'm hurt you didn't let me know you'd left town."

"I hate good-byes."

"Our deal was, you let me know what you know."

"And I told you I would when what I know reaches critical mass."

"What's this 'critical mass' shit? You got something on Peplow out there?"

"I'm just checking out his background."

"You found a jealous husband, son?"

"No sir. Not yet. Have you heard back from the EPA?"

"Not yet."

"All right. I'll check in later to find out the results."

"Where you staying?"

"It's called the Edwards Hotel."

"You doing any good eating there, son?"

"I had a couple of one-and-a-quarter-pound Maine lobsters to-night." Harvey smacked his lips loudly into the receiver. "Sweet as could be. Right out of the water. Drawn butter and Delmonico potatoes."

"Stop smacking your damn lips, son. Don't do this to me. You know, by the time they get to the Midwest, those lobsters are so damn tense from the flight not even Clarence can make 'em taste the way they ought to."

At eleven he called Mickey in Cambridge a hundred and ten miles to the south. Duane was holding steady but still not eating on his own.

"What's happening in Portland?" she asked.

A sudden memory ruffled him. Several years before, it must have been their first fall together, he and Mickey had driven through Portland after his last season in baseball and eaten lobsters somewhere along Commercial Street. Afterward they had raced through a heavy downpour to the car, parked on a dark side street, and made love behind windows fogged with condensation. He imagined the arc of their relationship being described in a PBS documentary. "But it was only a few short years," the narrator would intone, "from their passionate lovemaking on the streets of Portland, Maine, to Mickey Slavin reading articles in women's magazines on how to improve her marriage." The future had too abruptly become the present, turning the benchmarks of courtship into grating anecdote. He knew that Mickey was remembering Portland too and that she, not wishing to disturb their impasse, would fail to mention it.

"Maybe I'll come down in a day or two and see you," he said.

"That would be nice."

"How was your date with Paul?"

"It was fine. He's pretty broken up over his divorce."

"Hunh," Harvey said. Curiosity was not a sin he wanted to commit at the moment. "And the documentary? How's it going?"

"Oh, it's so slow. This endless rearranging of bits and pieces. I think it was Fred Friendly who said that doing television was like writing with an eight-hundred-pound pencil. By the way, Jerry Bellaggio called."

"What did he want?" Bellaggio was the private detective in Boston under whose license Harvey had worked for three years to qualify for his own.

"He just left a message saying he wanted to have lunch and catch up with you. Also some woman from Waban called and left a message. She wants to hire you to rescue her daughter from the clutches of some kind of cult. Here's the number."

Harvey took it down on the hotel stationery, which featured a pen-and-ink drawing of the venerable Edwards Hotel in the upper left-hand corner. "Thanks, Mick."

"You're welcome," she said, and the strange, hurt formality of it made him want to cry.

ON THURSDAY MORNING, after breakfast in the lobby coffee shop, where his cereal bowl arrived with a single-serving-size box of raisin bran reclining in it, Harvey returned to his room and left a message for the woman in Waban that he was busy on another case. Then from his wallet he removed the slip of paper Dena the waitress had given him. He tried the first name on it, Cathy Susi in Cape Elizabeth.

"Oh, my, yes, we were very happy with his work," Susi said. "He's a real craftsman. But even more importantly, he didn't drag the job out."

"Do you know him personally?" Harvey asked. "I mean, is he a friend of yours?"

"Oh, no. It's just we'd admired some built-ins we'd seen at a friend's house and he gave us Terry's name."

"May I ask who your friend is? I'd like to get as many references as possible."

"His name is Bob Steltz."

"Ah. Yes. I've already got his name on my list. Thank you."

When he called the Steltz number, a woman picked up and said, "Robert Steltz Associates. May I help you?"

"Is Mr. Steltz in?"

"He's in a meeting right now. May I ask who's calling and I'll have him get back to you?"

"Uh"—the first name that came to him was his old teammate on the Providence Jewels, Les Byers—"my name's Byers, but I won't be near a phone. I'll call back. Thanks."

Harvey tried Eunice Claherty and got a machine.

Les Byers had been through Boston a year ago and happened to mention that Charlie Manomaitis, the light-hitting shortstop on the Providence Jewels team for which Harvey had held down centerfield in his last year, had opened a restaurant near Portland, his wife's hometown, after being waived by the Orioles at the age of twenty-nine. Harvey opened the Portland white pages. There was a number for a Charles Manomaitis in South Portland.

"Hi, I'm looking for Charlie," Harvey said to the woman who answered.

"Who's this?"

"My name's Harvey Blissberg. I played ball with him. Is this his wife?"

"Oh, hi. Yeah, I'm Tracy. Charlie's mentioned you." A child was crying in the background.

"Well, I'm in the area and I thought I'd look him up."

"He's at the restaurant. Let me give you the number. As you can hear, I've got my hands full." She told him the number. "I know he'd love to hear from you."

When Harvey dialed the restaurant, a man answered "Charlie's Marshside" over the clatter of cutlery.

"Is that you, Charlie?"

"Yeah. Who's this?"

"Blissberg."

"Professor!"

Harvey hadn't heard his old nickname in years. He hadn't much liked it. There had probably been three hundred "Professors" in the history of major league baseball. To qualify for it, generally you only had to be observed reading a hardcover book. Once. The fact that his brother was a college professor conferred some extra legitimacy on it.

"Yeah, it's me."

"You here?"

"Yeah."

"What're you doing?"

"I'm on a murder case that brought me here yesterday."

"Murder? Man, you don't fool around."

Harvey laughed. "And you've got a restaurant?"

"You got to come by and try the moussaka, Professor. Where you staying?"

"The Edwards, downtown."

"Whyn't you stay with me?"

"No, no, no."

"Don't be silly, Professor."

"Forget it, Charlie. Don't be ridiculous. Anyway, you've got a baby. I heard it in the background when I just spoke to your wife."

"Yeah. Casey. Year and a half old. She throws right, bats right. She walks just like Felix. You remember how Felix walked to the mound when he wanted to pull a pitcher? All bowlegged, like he was wearing big diapers or something?"

"Yeah, he always looked like he had a load."

"Listen, I'd love it if you stayed at my place. So would Tracy. C'mon."

"Thanks, anyway." But the prospect of another night at the Edwards was rapidly losing its lustre.

"There's plenty of room, Professor. Real estate's cheap in Maine. I got two extra bedrooms. Count 'em!"

"All right, Charlie. You're on."

"Great!"

When the matter of directions had been taken care of, Charlie said. "Hey, are you still with what's-her-name?"

"Mickey?"

"Yeah, the foxy redhead. The one that did sports for one of the locals."

"We live together in Cambridge now."

"No shit. That's great. So, uh, tell me—you miss ball?"

"Of course."

"Me too." There had been enough of a pause before he said it to suggest that this wasn't small talk for him. "It all happened so fast, didn't it?"

"Yes, it did, Charlie."

"Hey, Professor, you know I've got some of my baseball stuff up on the wall here. Got the Jewels team picture from eighty-four. You got to come see it. If you come by today I've got halibut, Greek style."

"I'll call you later to let you know what my schedule is. It's a little shaky at the moment."

"What the hell kind of case are you on, anyway?"

"An unsolved one, Charlie."

"Oh, man," he laughed. "Those are the worst kind."

Harvey hung up and tried Robert Steltz's office again.

"He's free now, Mr. Byers," the receptionist said. "If you'll just hold."

"I can recommend him without reservation," Steltz said after Harvey explained his business. "He's also a fine designer."

"Have you known him a long time?"

"Is ten years long enough?" Steltz chuckled.

" 'Cause, you know, I heard Terry, uh, you know, went through a bad time there." Harvey said and held his breath. He didn't know how to make it any more general than that, and he certainly couldn't make it any more specific.

"Oh," Steltz said, "you mean that terrible thing with what's-her-name? His girlfriend."

"Yeah," Harvey said, opening his notebook. "Yeah, that's it."

"Joanie. That was her name."

Harvey wrote the name down. "Yeah. Boy. That was tough."

"Yeah, whoever would've thought she'd do something like that? They seemed pretty happy together." Steltz clucked into the phone.

"Wasn't there a guy involved?" Harvey asked.

"Well, the shrink she was seeing."

"Yeah. Yeah." Harvey's heart was racing now. "His name was, uh . . . Peplow, wasn't it? Peplow."

"Oh, I don't remember the guy's name. But you sure seem to remember a lot. Are you an old friend of Terry's?"

"Just an acquaintance."

"You seem to know a lot about him, Mr. Byers."

It's tap dance time, Harvey thought. What was this guy Steltz, a lawyer? A prosecutor? "We used to have a mutual friend. Maybe I met him once. You know, it wasn't a secret."

"Terry never talked about it much," Steltz said sternly.

"Well, enough, anyway. Not that I thought something like that would affect his work." Harvey was running out of generic conversation.

"Uh-huh." Steltz wasn't helping him out.

But he'd poached some game. Now he simply had to extricate himself from the phone call without totally tripping Steltz's alarm system. "But you're right," he said. "Terry wouldn't like some relative stranger bringing it up. If you mention this call to him, maybe you could leave that part out."

18

HARVEY CALLED HIS psychiatrist.

"Do you have a free hour?"

"Aren't you in Chicago?"

"I'm in Portland now. Portland, Maine."

"Let me see. Well, tomorrow's no good."

"How about late today? I can be down there in two hours."

"Let me see," Dr. Walker said. "No. Yes, well, I could make time for you at seven tonight."

"That's fine. That's great. I'll see you at seven. Thanks."

From his briefcase he removed the printouts listing the interviews the Garden Hills police had conducted with entries in Peplow's address book. There was no one named Joanie. No one named Terry. No nothing.

He called Charlie Manomaitis to say he was going to Boston but would be back tomorrow. By the time he was packed and ready to go it was almost four. He checked out, threw his bags into the back of the Toyota Tercel, and drove west to pick up Route 295, the spur leading back to Interstate 95. He drove south at a steady seventy miles per hour through the almost faceless green countryside, crossing the tab of New Hampshire that forced its way to the coast between Maine and Massachusetts, and picked up Route 1 north of Boston, slithered through Charlestown up onto the Tobin Bridge and into the city. He drove along the glassy Charles River on Storrow Drive, within a few hundred years of Fenway Park, where he had spent the bulk of his major league career with the Red Sox. He felt like he ought to pay this fact some sort of mental homage, but he couldn't quite turn his thoughts to that much of the past. Off at the Harvard Square exit, he wound his way along Memorial Drive, and cut up to his stucco house near Brattle Street. It was just after six.

On the kitchen table Mickey's unfinished mug of morning coffee sat next to a plate with half an English muffin on it. He stood in the doorway for a moment gazing sadly at this tableau of interrupted life. He looked at the objects in the kitchen with alarm; none of them seemed to belong to him anymore. They seemed like props left on a stage, for a play that had recently concluded its run.

Mickey had left the Arts section of *The New York Times* on the table folded back to an article about the conservative right's campaign to discredit public television and force Congress into further cutting its support. The margin was stained with a greasy thumbprint. Harvey stood over Mickey's chair and scanned a paragraph about some troglodyte who was blaming the nation's undereducated youth on "Sesame Street"'s Big Bird.

So lost was he in thought that it took him a moment to realize what was missing—the feline reception committee. He had forgotten about Duane. He found him in their bedroom upstairs, listless on top of a pillow on the bed, his joints poking through his ruffled, lustreless coat. He had dropped a couple of pounds. His nose leather was parched and cracked. Through his slack mouth he was breathing in rapid wheezes.

Duane acknowledged him with a constricted bleat but didn't move. As Harvey sat on the bed and stroked him, Bubba jumped on the comforter, sniffed his brother's face perfunctorily, and then lay across Harvey's lap, kneading his thigh. Harvey spoke quietly to Duane, getting a weak purr from him. On the nightstand was a jar of

Vaseline, a tube of nutrient paste, and a box of tissues. Harvey put a little Vaseline on the cat's nose. After reading the instructions on the tube, he squeezed some paste on his finger and scraped it off behind Duane's front teeth on the roof of his mouth. Duane jerked his head back and forth, fighting a little for breath before swallowing some of it. His expression scolded Harvey for the indignity.

"Don't check out on me, Duane," he said. He gathered Duane, ethereally light, in his arms and dialed Mickey's number at WGBH.

"I'm here, Mick."

"At the house?"

She seemed a little pleased, even, and his spirits revived. "Yeah. Can we have dinner?"

"Okay, but I'm working a little late."

"That's all right. I've got a seven o'clock appointment with Dr. Walker."

"Oh. Well, then I'll meet you at the house sometime after eight."

"Good."

"You just drove down?"

"Just this minute."

"You with Duane?"

"He looks terrible. He lost so much weight."

"Is he responding to you?"

"About the same as you do, Mick."

"And I can breathe through my nose," she said.

"Bubba's the only one who loves me anymore."

"Duane and I still respect you, though." And she laughed that little jagged laugh he hadn't heard in a while.

"I'm not ready for Duane to die, Mick."

"Try using the syringe. The more food we force down him the better."

"What do I do?"

"The syringe's in the bathroom. Mix a little canned food with water until it's soupy. And mash all the bits. Load it up and fire away.

Stick it into the inside of Duane's cheek. And you might have to wrap him in a towel. He doesn't go for it in a big way. And do it in the bathroom. You don't want to have to clean Friskies Mixed Grill off anything but tile."

AT TWO MINUTES after seven, Harvey took his seat in the upholstered bentwood armchair in Dr. Ellyn Walker's Spartan Lexington office. She lowered herself into her armchair, tugged her skirt to the edge of her knees, and proceeded to say nothing.

Harvey swallowed dryly. He was old enough to know how his own character had hardened, but it didn't stop him from nervously anticipating some forthcoming magic at the beginning of each hour with her—an insight from Dr. Walker that would illuminate years of odd behavior, a revelation that would relieve him of the burden of being himself. But the moment of silence with which Dr. Walker always greeted him told him otherwise, that there was to be no performance, no magic, no *son et lumière* of the soul. He fumbled for a beginning.

"I need some more advice on this case. If you don't mind."

"It's your hour." There was a trio of small portrait prints on the wall behind her head. Two men, one bearded and neither of them Freud, and a woman.

"You remember I told you about Frederick Walls and how he wouldn't talk but he gave me a name to call."

"Charette."

This alone sometimes seemed worth the price of admission, that so little went by her. "You have an excellent memory," he said with a smile, and she nodded in bored agreement. "I flew to Portland yesterday and paid Terry Charette a visit," he went on. "He won't talk, either. I know that he knows something. So I posed as a potential client of Charette's and phoned a guy who knows him pretty well."

Dr. Walker nodded.

"So, as a shot in the dark, I said to him, I said, 'I heard he went through a bad time.' And this fellow said, 'You mean that terrible thing with his girlfriend Joanie?' So, of course I said yes and he said, 'I never thought she would do something like that.' Now, naturally, I can't just come out and say, 'What was it she did again?' So I said, 'Wasn't there some guy involved?' And he said, 'You mean that shrink she was seeing?' And I jumped at that and said 'Peplow?' "

"The murder victim."

"Yes. But he didn't know the name. And that was pretty much it. But I've got something now, at least."

"What do you have?"

"Well, obviously, my first thought is that Charette's girlfriend Joanie had gotten involved with Peplow and left him."

Dr. Walker looked at him benignly. "And?"

"That's where my thinking's kind of stalled."

"And that would make Charette the murderer in your mind?"

"That's just it. I don't think he's a killer. He was defensive and a little aggressive when I talked to him, but that was a pretty normal reaction under the circumstances. He didn't try to lie to me. There was something almost likable about him."

"Likable people sometimes commit murder," she said.

"Maybe it was the books. I don't know. He had a lot of books in his apartment. That's a prejudice of mine, I guess. The well-read don't kill. But I know better. No, he's not a murderer. There was a touch of sadness in him. Maybe that was it. One thing I remember is, he was pissed at my showing up, but when I finally left he didn't slam the door. He closed it kind of quietly."

"As though he were a little sorry to see you go?"

"Maybe." Harvey sat up. "But, look. Charette would have to've traveled to suburban Chicago to kill Peplow. And why would he have waited all this time to do it? If his girlfriend ran off with Peplow, it happened at least four years ago. And we know that Peplow wasn't still with her. I haven't even run across anyone named Joanie so far."

"Perhaps there was a fresh insult recently."

"I hadn't thought of that."

Dr. Walker recrossed her legs and reached up to take a fugitive strand of hair and press it back into her graying bun. "Well," she said finally, "what do you think happened between this woman Joanie and Peplow."

She could be a prematurely graying forty-two, Harvey thought, or an unlined fifty-two. How strange it was to be talking out a case's problems with her instead of Mickey. So much had come between them. "I think she fell in love with him," he said.

"Yes?"

"And Peplow persuaded her to leave Terry."

"Do you think that Joanie and Peplow were sleeping together? What's your fantasy?"

"Fantasy?" Harvey laughed uncomfortably. "All right. Yes, let's say they were sleeping together. If she left Terry for Peplow, she would've been sleeping with him."

"Do you think she might've been sleeping with Peplow while she was in treatment with him?"

"Well, it happens, doesn't it?"

"Yes, it does."

"And some of these patients end up running off with their shrinks, right?"

"A few of them do, yes. Not many. Now, Mr. Blissberg, have you considered the ramifications of their sleeping together during treatment?"

"No. Not really."

"Well, you know that sexual contact of any kind between a therapist and a patient usually causes a great deal of harm. The malpractice insurance companies have a nice name for it: 'undue familiarity.' But that doesn't begin to tell the story. Patient–therapist sexual contact is explicitly forbidden by the American Psychiatric, the American Psychoanalytic, the American Psychological, and the AMA.

In fact, it's now been criminalized in several states. The American Psychiatric has declared that sex with a patient even *after* therapy is unethical. Anyway, sexual contact not only greater harms the patient, but it claims spouses, lovers, and friends as secondary victims."

"What about when it's true love?"

Now it was Dr. Walker's turn to sit up. "Mr. Blissberg, I don't pretend to know what true love is, but I have some very considered ideas about what it isn't. And one of the things it most definitely isn't is the romantic and sexual feelings that can easily arise between a therapist and the patient who is paying him or her. Even those therapists who have sexual intimacies with their patients out of what they consider 'love' are engaging in one of the most dangerous varieties of untrue love. I would not even call it love. If love means, among other things, a lasting concern for the welfare of another."

She hesitated before continuing. "And I will tell you that in that chair you're now sitting in, there have been many people who have come here to see me after spending years with previous abusive therapists with whom they have slept, and every single one of them—every single one—is much the worse for it. Often devastated."

"Do you specialize in this?" he asked.

"No. There are those who do, but there's no need to specialize in it in order to see these victims."

"And you think Peplow was one of these, uh, bad shrinks?" Why not, Harvey thought; Peplow had cheated at many other things.

"I'm just going on what you've told me. I'm just trying to clarify your thinking. Now, this Peplow was a clinical psychologist who gave up his practice voluntarily a few years ago and moved to the Midwest and became a real estate agent. Is that right?"

"Yes."

"It seems to me that something must've been terribly wrong for him to give up the considerable investment of time and energy required to get a Ph.D. and establish a practice."

Harvey jumped in. "So let's assume that Peplow slept with this

Joanie while she was in therapy with him. Let's say he ran off with her, Dr. Walker. Let's say they ran off and lived together." He stopped; he had no idea where he was going with this. "Well, in any case, I don't think this guy Terry went off to find him after four years and blew his head off in a wheat field."

"You're having trouble seeing all the possibilities, Mr. Blissberg, aren't you?" she said gently.

"Yeah. I'm a little confused."

Dr. Walker looked down in thought. When she raised her eyes again, she spoke more softly than before.

"This man you spoke to—the reference for Terry Charette—?"

"Yes. His name is Steltz."

"He said, did he not, something about 'that terrible thing with his girlfriend'?"

"Those were more or less the words he used."

"Well, your first thought, you said, was that he might be referring to the fact that she left Charette for Peplow."

"That's right."

"What makes you certain this 'terrible thing' was something she did to her boyfriend Terry?"

"Well, I'm not certain. Maybe Steltz was referring to something Peplow did to her."

"Well, look, if Peplow was violating the trust of the therapeutic relationship by having a sexual affair with this woman, that would qualify, in my mind, as a terrible thing. But I had something else in mind. Just as a possibility."

"I'm kind of drawing a blank here." The hum of the window air-conditioning unit seemed extremely loud to him.

"Mr. Blissberg, what if the 'terrible thing with the girlfriend' wasn't a reference to something she did to someone else at all?"

"You mean—" It was by no means the first time he had felt completely stupid in her office.

"That's right," Dr. Walker said. "What if he was referring to something she did to herself."

19

DUANE'S BLACK MUZZLE was stained with a gruel of watered-down cat food and thick saliva. Unable to smell it, he had not bothered to lick it off. Harvey wiped it off for him with a tissue and sat on the bed stroking his sickly fur, waiting for Mickey, trying to enter the mind of an animal starving himself because he had lost his sense of smell. He tried to explain to the cat that, to those who loved him, this was unacceptable behavior.

Next to Harvey on the nightstand were some reprints of articles about "sexual boundary violations" that Dr. Walker had handed to him after the session, saying, "You may want to take a look at this material to further your education."

Toward the end of the session that evening, he had told her, "I don't know for a fact what Peplow was guilty of, but it's strange to me that until now, until speaking with you, I was unable to consider the possibility that he was sleeping with patients."

"But you're in therapy yourself," Dr. Walker had said.

Harvey found the comment elliptical.

"Well, you didn't want to admit to yourself that such things happen. That the presumed safety of this little environment here"— she spread her hands to embrace her office and Harvey saw, for the first time, that she wore a wedding ring; it was another thing he had not wanted to see before—"that this sanctuary"—now she described with her hand a line running between the two of them—"this trust, could be violated."

He shifted in his seat, feeling that she was reading his mind. He had imagined more than once what she herself would be like under less professional circumstances . . . circumstances that ran the gamut from dinner to bed. What it would be like if she gave in to his wish not only for her admiration but for something like her love. And yet he had been unwilling to look at the ramifications of these fantasies.

"You look stricken, Mr. Blissberg."

"I do?"

"Well," she said matter-of-factly, "you can probably imagine how easily a patient develops strong feelings for a therapist. To feel she knows the therapist, to feel she even loves him. Even deserves him. And how irresistible that might be to some therapists, to be so unconditionally admired, needed, and loved. How indistinguishable such feelings might appear to be from the feeling of falling in love in the real world. How easy to act on by both parties."

"Yes. I can see that."

"You know, it's the therapist's job to examine the patient's feelings toward him or her in light of the patient's history, to allow those feelings free expression but"—her pale green eyes widened in emphasis—"to contain them within a detached analysis."

He nodded. The session had become a tutorial.

"Because once a therapist allows a patient to physically act on his or her feelings and allows himself the disastrous luxury of reciprocating, what you have is no longer therapy. What you have, Mr. Blissberg, is a *date.* And a very expensive date for the patient. And not only in financial terms, of course. Because when a patient acts out his or her physical 'love' "—she clawed the air to make quotation marks—"for a therapist, the patient is merely—although I shouldn't say 'merely' because there is nothing 'mere' about it—the patient is repeating behavior from the past. Acting on a need for gratification that takes the place of insight and understanding. The patient is seeking to recreate a situation that contributed to his or her difficulties in the first place. And it is the therapist's job—no, *duty*—to prevent it from happening. Because if a therapist becomes sexually involved with a patient, it is almost without exception out of similarly misguided motives. Sex with a therapist is not the cure by a long shot. It is the intensification of the disease. And when a therapist takes valuable money, energy, and time from that patient in order to perpetuate and exacerbate a patient's difficulties, all on the pretext of helping the patient, then that therapist is guilty of the very cruelty and injustice that the patient already may have spent a lifetime trying to overcome.

"Anyway," she said, "enough of that for now. I'm lecturing. I think you get the point."

"It's funny," he told her, "how hard it is for me to see this guy Peplow very clearly." He rummaged through the last week's events for specifics for an example. "The, uh, homicide chief, for instance, in the town where he was murdered, when he showed me Peplow's picture for the first time, he said I looked like him. Which I don't, except in some vague way." He added with a laugh that sounded forced to him, "I don't like to think we have much in common."

"But you're confused? That's why you drove down here today? You needed help in thinking about it?"

"Yes."

"Something made you feel you shared something with Peplow?"

"Maybe."

She waited, mercilessly.

"The police seemed to think he'd been sleeping with someone's wife, and that's what got him killed."

"And?"

"I, uh, I . . ." he began.

She looked at him without expression, waiting. He knew she would wait forever for him to finish the sentence he had begun.

"I, uh . . . When I was in Chicago this past week, I had a little affair myself." He detested the casualness of his confession. His eyes went to the cheap clock she kept on the bookshelf. It was five to eight. He wished he hadn't brought it up when there was no time to even relate the facts.

Dr. Walker clasped her hands in her lap and waited.

"I was unfaithful to Mickey." He didn't know what direction to go in in the few minutes left. "Uh, she was a very sexually aggressive person."

"You were helpless before her," Dr. Walker said with what Harvey felt was a very small smile. A very small, ironical smile.

"Of course not. I take full responsibility. Anyway, I mean, it's over now. It's the kind of thing that happened to me once or twice when I was playing ball, but not for years."

She nodded. Harvey wondered if it didn't surprise her, or even if she had expected something like this from him. Was she only unflappable or had she already divined the worst about him?

"I was interviewing her in connection with the case," he stumbled on. "She was a former client of Peplow's. He'd shown her and her husband some houses."

"She was married, then?" she said with unnerving equanimity.

"Well, if you could call it a marriage. She said she and her husband never slept together. They don't have children. She's very strange."

"And you believed her?"

"Believed what?"

"That she and her husband never slept together."

"Yes. Why? Shouldn't I have believed her?"

"I don't know. The point is, you've been identifying with this Peplow then. You could only imagine him doing, perhaps, what you yourself were capable of, and not more."

The words echoed for him. You could only imagine him doing what you yourself were capable of. It was true. He identified. Harvey had envied him his relationship to Norm. Peplow had been his brother's friend, saw Norm two or three times a week, had become a basketball "brother."

"It made it difficult for you to see the possibilities."

"I can see that now."

"In any case, as you know, because you keep looking at the clock, our time's up."

HARVEY LISTENED NOW as Mickey turned the key in the lock downstairs, heaved something—probably her briefcase—onto the Shaker table by the door, and trudged up the stairs. Some people wear their hearts on their sleeves; Mickey Slavin wore hers on the soles of her feet. Her heavy footsteps indicated at best a bad day at work, at worst a mounting desire to crush Harvey's head between two large rocks.

When she appeared in the doorway to the bedroom, she stopped and looked at Harvey stroking Duane and stuck out her lower lip in an expression of exaggerated pity.

"Is that for me or Duane?" he asked.

"Duane," she said, stepping out of those half cowboy boots he hated. "For you I reserve a different expression."

He got up and they kissed, then embraced. It was an embrace full of longing for things to be better. It used to be that they were on each other like teenagers the instant they were reunited after even two days apart.

"Your hair."

She reached up her hand to pat it.

"Or, rather," he said, "your absence of hair."

"I had it cut."

"I see. When the cat's away, the mouse goes right to the beauty parlor."

"What do you think?"

"Jean Seberg in *Breathless*."

"I was thinking more along the lines of Joan of Arc."

"That's a pretty skirt," he said.

"The only time I get compliments like this is when you've been away."

"Absence makes the garment grow more beautiful."

"You should stay away more often." She went to the bed, touching Bubba as she passed, took Harvey's former seat next to Duane, and kissed him several times on the top of his head. "How about some delicious dinner *à la syringe?*" she whispered to him.

"I missed you," Harvey announced, trying to establish some emotional credibility.

"I missed you too." But she said it in a way that left it unclear whether his return had alleviated the condition. "How was Dr. Walker?"

"Fine. I needed some help on the case. And she was very helpful. She—"

"Did you give him any water?"

It was all right; he didn't want to talk about the case either. "No. Just the water I mixed in with the food an hour or so ago."

She went to the bathroom and returned with the syringe, now filled with water, and an old towel. She gently forced the tip between Duane's jaws and directed some water down his throat, catching the excess in the towel. "The vet told me to tempt him with the smelliest foods I could think of. Sardines, anchovies, that canned squid he likes. I cooked some bluefish for him the other night. He barely looked at any of it. Poor little thing. But, see, he seems to have perked up a little seeing you. The vet wants me to bring him in tomorrow morning to get shot up with more fluids."

"I could take him in."

"You're staying overnight?"

"I was planning to."

It was hard to separate the gloom Mickey felt about Duane's

condition from the gloom she felt about the two of them. There was also the gloom she felt about her work to consider, and Harvey's gloom about the case. He gave up trying to sort the glooms and suggested they eat dinner at a favorite Vietnamese seafood restaurant in Allston.

"Amazing," Mickey said with surprise. "I already made a reservation there for us."

Harvey held out his hands. "See! There you go—more proof that we're destined to be together."

"Or at least to run into each other at the same restaurants."

Over dinner she didn't ask about the Peplow case and wasn't eager to discuss her documentary-in-progress, so they gossiped about their friends' relationships and marriages. This was one of the perverse consolations of growing older: There was more material to pass judgment on and you had more sophisticated tools for making those judgments. Mickey reported the breakup of a couple they had grown close to.

"But you called that one years ago," he said.

"Doesn't make me any less sad. You know, I'm looking for sheer numbers now. Success ratio. One of the things that keeps people together is other people staying together. Divorce is contagious." She picked at her plate. "I want to be with you, Bliss. But I'm so sad these days."

"Yeah."

"We need to spend some time together. You've been working so hard."

"When I'm through with this case, we'll go somewhere. Can you get away?"

"I'll make time."

"It's funny," he said. "What we're going through isn't horrible."

"It's bad enough, but, sure, it could be worse. You could be having an affair. Are you having an affair?"

"No, of course not. Anyway, it's just, you know, I have problems with the specificity of it all."

"What the hell does that mean? With the specificity of what?"

"It means I want to be with you. But, Christ, to get married, to know we'll be together forever—it's scary because it means . . . I don't know."

"Because it means you'll never be with anyone else."

"Yeah."

"It's called commitment."

"I've heard that word before."

"You don't think I have problems with that too? You think I ever saw myself as somebody's *wife*? Don't you remember what I announced to my family over dinner at Howard Johnson's when I was nine? That I was never going to get married? You think it's only men who like to be free and live forever?"

"But if we got married, Mick, then we'd be, well, *married people.* We'd grow old and wear hair nets and make wisecracks about each other to acquaintances."

"That's all happening now, except for the hair nets."

"I don't know. Some people have a knack for marriage."

"Yeah," Mickey said, "especially those who get married over and over again."

"We have a knack for not getting married, Mick. It's a much rarer talent."

She was smiling, and their romance's early charm came back to him. The brainy ballplayer and the female sportscaster. Two people who proudly defied their categories, who would refuse to grow old, who were perfectly paired in their aversion to anything as common as marriage.

"What do you want to do now?"

She called for the check and then leaned over the table. "Let's go home and screw."

· · ·

HARVEY SWITCHED ON the light next to the bed and picked up reprints of "The Lovesick Therapist" and "Psychotherapists Who Transgress Sexual Boundaries With Patients."

"What kind of postcoital behavior is this?" Mickey said. "What kind of man reads "The Lovesick Therapist" after the best sex we've had in six months?"

"It's my homework."

"I'm going to go find Duane." At some point their foreplay had forced Duane off the bed. She got out of bed, pulled on an old Providence Jewels T-shirt that left her behind exposed. Harvey watched her—and her beautifully molded butt—disappear downstairs before he began reading.

He read about lovesick therapists with their "desperate need for validation by their patients, a hunger to be loved and idealized," who "idealize patients and impulsively act on their feelings of infatuation. . . . The most common scenario is that of a middle-aged male therapist who falls in love with a much younger female patient while he is experiencing divorce, separation, disillusionment with his own marriage . . ."

He read about abusing therapists with antisocial features who "are ruthless . . . without remorse or empathy for their victims, and are the most frankly exploitative. Ethics committees have met with great frustration in attempting to rehabilitate these individuals."

He read about predatory psychopaths for whom "patients are regarded merely as objects to be used for their own sexual gratification. Because these therapists lack empathy or concern for the victim, they are incapable of feeling remorse or guilt about any harm they might have done the patient. . . . Some of these therapists have a childhood history of profound neglect or abuse, and some clinicians have understood their exploitation of others as an effort to achieve active mastery of passively experienced trauma."

He read on: "Because many therapists grew up in homes where they felt unloved, they may attempt to elicit from their patients the love they did not receive from their parents. . . . Buie observes that one of the central motivations for a career in psychotherapy is a wish to be relieved of one's sense of isolation and aloneness. . . . When the therapist feels that his loving and caring help is not curative, he may resort to sexual relations as a despairing final effort."

Mickey must have put an Allman Brothers album on downstairs because Dickey Betts's guitar riffs suddenly floated up the stairs.

"Many therapists . . . do not experience guilt because they are convinced that they are providing their patient with a better parenting experience. . . . At the most primitive level it may take the form of the clinical psychologist who felt that his semen would confer eternal salvation on the adolescent patients he was treating."

In one account, a therapist ordered his female patient to duck-walk across his office, unzip his fly without using her hands, and perform oral sex. Yet, according to one article, "Many therapists who become involved in sexual boundary violations do not appear to suffer from disturbances that are sufficiently visible to have caused alarm in their colleagues."

Therapists, said another article, "may view themselves and the patient as 'soulmates' who were destined to find each other and just happened to have done so in the context of a psychotherapy relationship. . . . One way of viewing the development of a sexual relationship . . . is that it is a recreation of an earlier incestuous situation for both persons. . . . Regardless of the nature of the sexual behavior itself, the sadistic wish to destroy is the perverse core of the lovesick therapist's relationship with his patient. . . . Studies now provide convincing evidence that at least 90 percent of patients who are victimized by therapists have serious residual harm."

Now Mickey herself floated up the stairs, cradling Duane, and announced, "I'm going to bed."

"I'll turn off the lights in a minute," he said. She climbed in beside him. Harvey picked up a newsletter of the American Psychiatric Association and read about how unlikely discovery and investigation of sexual misconduct cases were. "Unfortunately, patients who have had sexual contact with their physicians may be hindered from reporting the misconduct. There is some evidence the offenders tend to refer patients to colleagues whom they know to be sympathetic to their actions."

Mickey turned to her other side. Harvey extended an arm to stroke Duane, who hunched, gasping quietly, on the pillow between them. "Good night, Bliss," she murmured, her voice muffled by a cloud of pillows.

"Good night, babe."

The AMA, Harvey read, includes among its Principles of Medical Ethics the standard that "a physician shall . . . strive to expose those physicians deficient in character or competence, or who engaged in fraud or deception. . . . Physicians who learn of sexual misconduct by a colleague must report the misconduct. . . . Exception may be made if a physician learns of the misconduct while treating the offending physician for it, provided that the offending physician is not continuing the misconduct."

The newsletter reported a 1987 survey of 1,423 practicing psychiatrists revealing that "although 65 percent of them reported treating patients who had been sexually involved with previous therapists, and 87 percent of those . . . believed that the previous involvement was harmful to the patients, only 8 percent of them reported their colleagues' behavior to a professional organization or legal authority."

What the research implied was appalling. One survey found that the incidence of sexual abuse among prominent practitioners—tenured professors and chairmen of ethics committees—was higher than that among therapists in general. According to two national surveys, as many as 12 percent of male therapists said they'd had sexual relationships with patients.

Harvey finally set all the material on the nightstand, turned off the light, and looked out the window at the heavy, dripping foliage, eerie in the streetlight.

Mickey flopped again and drove her face deeper into the down pillow. He touched her auburn hair.

She stirred. "Welcome home."

"Thanks."

"And sweet dreams," she whispered.

But he lay in bed for more than an hour, dreamless and sleepless, torturing himself over a woman he had come to know a little too well in Chicago and another one named Joan he did not know at all.

20

BY THE TIME he reached the outskirts of Portland on Friday morning, a soft charcoal cover of storm clouds had slid overhead, leaving only a band of blue over Casco Bay. Harvey felt like he was driving inside a lobster pot whose lid had been propped open slightly. Suddenly the clouds opened, dropping hard rain everywhere. In an instant Harvey had withdrawn to the controlled environment of the Tercel's interior: windows up, headlights and dash lights on, wipers flapping, a.c. on high.

The drab shades of Munjoy Hill all ran together in the rain. Harvey parked in front of Charette's apartment building and bounded inside and up the stairs. The door of the loft was opened by the girlfriend, wearing a faded "Save the Whales" T-shirt and blue-jean cutoffs. She looked at him dully under dirty bangs. Nature had placed her eyes too close together.

"Nancy, right?"

"Yeah, that's right. Oh"—she suddenly recognized him from last night—"it's you again."

"Harvey. Is Terry around?"

"He's working."

"Where?"

"A job up in Lewiston."

"When do you think he'll be back?"

"Dinnertime. But I don't think he wants to talk to you."

"Did he say what it was he doesn't want to talk to me about?"

Nancy looked at him blankly.

"He didn't say anything to you, did he?"

She blinked. "About what?" She didn't seem to have a clue about anything. "I mean, Terry's not big on talking in general."

"You live here with him?"

She brushed her bangs with her fingertips. "For the time being. I just graduated and as soon as I find a job, I'm getting my own place."

"Have you and Terry been together long?"

"A couple weeks." The phone rang behind her in the loft.

"I see," Harvey said. So she was not much more than a stray.

"I met him at a bar a few weeks ago doing Jello-O shots and we kind of hit it off. I better get that."

"Go ahead. I'll wait here." She trotted back into the loft to pick up the phone.

When she disappeared around a corner, Harvey stepped into the apartment, went to the bookshelves closest to the door. On the endpaper of the third paperback he took down, *Dog Stories* by James Herriot, the owner's name was written in the corner in ballpoint pen: Joan Johnson. A loopy, upright script, letters like helium balloons. He closed the book quickly and slipped it back onto the shelf. He randomly chose another nearby paperback called *What Jung Really Said*. There, too, was the name Joan Johnson.

He heard Nancy hang up the phone and quickly resumed his former position outside the door.

"Anyway," she said, coming around the corner, "I'll tell Terry you came by."

"Don't bother. I'll give him a call later."

He was halfway down the stairs when she said, "What's the big fuss, anyway? Since you showed up Ter's been in such a pissy mood."

The rain had let up. From a phone booth in front of a small

grocery on Munjoy Hill, Harvey called the sports department of the *Portland Press-Herald* and reached Darren Oldfield, a veteran reporter who had covered the Red Sox for some years, and to whom Harvey was not unknown as one of the Boston players least likely to furnish usable quotes.

"I heard you were a cop now, Harvey," Oldfield said.

"I'm not a cop, but I occasionally indulge in coplike activities. Speaking of which, I need a small favor from you, Darren."

"What is it?"

"Your computer'll tell you whether someone's been mentioned in the paper, right?"

"When it feels like it."

"Well, I'm in town on business and I need to know whether three names have been in your paper in the last, say, ten years."

"Oh, all right," Oldfield sighed. "Go ahead. Hit me."

Harvey spelled the names Laurence Peplow, Frederick Walls, and Joan Johnson for him. As he waited for Oldfield to interface, Harvey smoked half of a Lucky and watched as a light green Ford Taurus passed by.

"Nothing on Laurence Peplow." Oldfield said in his ear. "There's one story about a Joanne Johnson—"

"No. Joan."

"I know, I know, Professor. I'm just saying. Let me see. No, no Joan Johnsons, and you'd think there'd be a lot of Joan Johnsons. Okay, there's one citation for Dr. Frederick Walls. An article back in eighty-nine, a feature about deinstitutionalization"—he fumbled with the word—"of the mentally ill in Maine."

"That's it?"

"That's it. I can spit out the Walls article for you, if you want to swing by later."

"That'd be good, Darren. Thank you. You're a gentleman and a scholar."

"You're too kind."

Harvey dropped another quarter in the phone and called Charlie's Marshside. "Just checking in, Charlie," Harvey told him. "I'm on Munjoy Hill, but my ship doesn't come in until dinner, so I might have to come by and kill some time with you."

"Love to have you, Professor. Now, listen, Mickey called here a couple of hours ago. You gotta call her at work immediately."

As he dialed Mickey's number, he sketched nervously with his finger on the inside of the phone booth glass. He hoped it wasn't Duane.

"It's me," he said at the sound of her voice.

"Oh my God—you all right?"

"Fine. What's up?"

"After you left this morning, I got a threatening phone call."

"Jesus. What? What did it say?"

"This guy asked me if I was Harvey Blissberg's soon-to-be widow, and when I asked who was calling, he just said, 'Think about it,' and then he hung up. It was frightening, Bliss." She began to cry.

"Mick, what kind of voice was it?"

"He was putting on a growly kind of voice. Like a witness whose voice has been electronically altered. Am I in real danger?"

"I don't know."

"Are you in danger, Bliss?"

"Mick, I don't know. But I think we ought to take some precautions."

"You don't have any idea who it is?"

"There's a guy up here who might be a candidate. In any case, you can't stay at the house. Call Jerry Bellaggio and let him know what's going on. See if you can stay at his place. If he can, ask him to go back to the house with you later to pick up the cats and your things. And don't go anywhere alone, okay? Not even to lunch." He gave her Bellaggio's beeper number.

"This sucks, Bliss."

"Whoever it is is more interested in me than you."

Mickey sighed. "And to think I could've said yes when Brian asked me to marry him in Providence. I wouldn't be dealing with shit like this now."

"Are you joking? A TV weatherman? You would've been miserable. Believe me. You went out with him for three months, remember? and all he could talk about was barometric pressure."

The levity wasn't working. He felt Mickey's terror on the other end of the line.

"Mick," he said, "you'll be in good hands with Jerry. Call me if you can't get him. I'll be at Charlie's."

"Get a fucking desk job, will you?"

"Yeah, yeah. By the way, how's Duane?"

"Happily filled with fluids, but still not eating. Now I'm not eating, either."

"I'm sorry, Mick. I was just trying to do Norm a favor."

"Watch yourself, Bliss. Oh, before I forget, Dr. Walker left a message on the machine at home this morning. She wants you to call her back."

Harvey called Dr. Walker, got her answering machine, and rather than leave the number of Charlie Manomaitis's restaurant he simply left a message that he would call back.

THE *PRESS-HERALD* ARTICLE about deinstitutionalization of the mentally ill mentioned Dr. Frederick Walls once. Described as a "prominent Portland psychoanalyst," Walls was quoted as saying: "I think we've seen by now that deinstitutionalization is by and large a failure. It deprives the mentally and psychologically impaired of helpful medication administered in a safe environment and forces them back into a world with which they are not prepared to cope. In the name of a specious liberation, we are only further imprisoning them, and holding society hostage as well."

Harvey thanked Oldfield for his work and on the way out of the

Press-Herald building crumpled up the printout and tossed it in a wastebasket. He got in the Tercel and drove out toward Charlie's place in Scarborough, south of the city. He crossed a bridge out of Portland and onto Route 1, passing motor courts and small freestanding realty offices, Chinese restaurants, and a forgotten Twin Drive-In, its massive screens rising above the trees like cheap ruins. Pampered Nails, Sparks Dating Service, the Humpty Dumpty Popcorn and Potato Chip plant. You wouldn't find postcards of this stretch of Maine.

Then suddenly the commercial district stopped, replaced by a mile of marsh, high spartina waving on both sides. Charlie's Marshside sat just beyond the marsh on half an acre of blacktop, a boxy, windowless, one-story structure covered in phony brick face. The lack of windows implied that eating was an illicit activity best conducted in dim privacy. Harvey's heart sank further. The place resembled thousands of other anonymous restaurants along America's highways. He had wanted Charlie Manomaitis's place to be charming. He wanted the whole world to be more charming than it was. But, after all, it was Charlie who on road trips had liked to spend his free time in hotel rooms watching reruns of "Gilligan's Island," impervious to Harvey's invitations to join him at rib joints or for a particularly good crab boil he had heard about in a bad part of town.

It was not a meal hour, and once Harvey's eyes adjusted to the gloom, he was greeted by a sea of empty tables. On each one's dark red vinyl tablecloth a glass globe covered in plastic netting held a sputtering candle.

"Professor!" Charlie called, dancing out of the shadows in a loud Qiana shirt.

"Hello, Charlie." Harvey took Charlie's hairy, knobby hand in his and then they embraced quickly, a kind of perfunctory postgame victory hug.

"Hey, you look great!"

Harvey squinted, laughing. "How the hell can you tell? I can barely see in here."

"You'll get used to it."

"There we go—you look great too." But Charlie looked older and sallower. After all those great fielding gems, a working man.

"Come. Sit down." He showed Harvey to a booth by the door. "Let me get you something to eat."

"No thanks, Charlie. That's okay. I don't have much of an appetite." No one in his family but Bubba seemed to be eating anymore.

"There's the picture I told you about." Charlie pointed proudly to the wall by the little alcove bar. He was talking rapidly, trying to establish a hasty connection with Harvey. "The Providence Jewels' first season." Next to the team picture was a framed photograph of Charlie shorthopping a bouncer in the hole. "It's amazing when you think about it. You know, we're part of history, man. We'll always be entries in *The Baseball Encyclopedia*."

The talk turned to former teammates and their fates, to the fortunes of their former teams, but Harvey, who had come with some vague notion of reminiscing about the good old days, found he was laboring to share Charlie's bonhomie. He could sense Charlie's disappointment. The curtain of nostalgia had parted, disclosing that they had nothing in common but the fact that they wore the same uniform for a year. In his head Harvey toted up all the new distances in his life, between him and Mickey, him and Norm, him and his former teammates, him and some earlier, sentimental version of himself.

"There's something about being on an expansion team," Charlie was saying with a look of desperation, like a lecturer who senses that his audience is looking at their watches. "You know, nothing to lose and everything to gain. I had a ball that year," Charlie continued. Quickly, his smile evaporated. "I mean, except for losing Rudy like that."

Harvey could remember little of that year *except* Rudy. That was the history he felt part of. If he had stood up and gone over to look at the team picture, he knew it would be to stare at the face of Rudy Furth, his dead roommate, and he had no desire to do that.

"What a tragedy," Charlie said, fingering the chrome rack of sugar packets on the table. "That's what got you into the whole detective thing, wasn't it?"

There was nothing he wanted less now than this invitation to recount the long and dubious story of how he gave up a fat major league salary at the age of thirty-one to sit in an office by himself and wait for people with problems to hire him. "Charlie," he said with a stiff smile, "do you mind if I make a couple of quick calls?"

"Sure, sure, Professor. Right over there. Use the phone by the register."

"I'll just be a minute."

"Sure, sure. Take as long as you like."

"It's just this damn case I'm on."

He called Mickey. "D'you get Jerry?" he asked.

"Yeah. He just dropped me off here with the cats. I've got them in the carrier under my desk. He told me to call later and he'll come by and take me home with him."

"Good."

"Yeah, I feel a little safer. Anything new with you?"

"No. I'm just sitting here with Charlie M. at his restaurant, waiting for some guy to get home from work so I can start busting his chops."

"Well, say hi to Charlie for me."

"Sure."

Harvey hung up and dialed Dr. Walker's. He got the machine again and left a message saying he could be reached at the restaurant for the next hour or so, although he did not think he could bear another hour of baseball talk. He immediately regretted leaving the message; it was presumptuous to think the elegant Dr. Walker could call him back at Charlie's Marshside. Then he tried Terry Charette's number, letting the phone ring eight or nine times before hanging up.

"So how's business?" Harvey asked, folding his frame into the booth and steering the conversation wide of the past.

"Great, great. You know, I'm something of a hero around here. Tracy grew up in South Portland—her folks live a couple miles from here—and the people have really adopted me."

"That's great. So things have really worked out."

"I can't complain, Professor. Can't complain." A cloud quickly passed over Manomaitis's face; Harvey could see it even in the dim light. "Well, sometimes I think it would've been nice to play ball a couple more years. But I couldn't hack the minors anymore. You knew Baltimore sent me down last July, didn't you? To work out of a bad slump?"

"Yeah, sure. I saw it in the sports section, Charlie."

"Well, they left me down there the whole season. Couldn't find a spot for me on the roster in September even. I think the writin' was on the wall, Professor. Besides, my knees were already tellin' me to knock it off. So, Trace and I talked it over. We thought it was time to get a life outside of baseball. And, anyway, I love having my own restaurant, and I can watch Case grow up now." His voice had the distracted, droning quality of a postgame interview. "How about you? How's your business?"

The price of not wanting to talk about the past was that Harvey now filled time by going on in far too much detail about the Peplow case. He remembered Marilyn Barger saying, "Haven't you told things to a stranger you'd never tell you closest friend?"

"And I thought I had problems," Charlie said.

At five-thirty, he got up again to call Terry Charette. Some of Charlie's tables were filling up with early birds. This time Charette answered.

"It's Harvey Blissberg."

"Now what?"

"Where the fuck do you get off threatening me and my girl-friend?"

"What're you talking about?"

"Don't give me that shit, Terry. You want to threaten me, you do it to my face."

"You got the wrong man, buddy. I don't know what you're fuckin' talking about. If somebody ruined your day, it wasn't me."

Something told Harvey it hadn't been Charette. But Harvey had no other candidates, and now he was really starting to worry. "How about you tell me you didn't do it face-to-face?" he told Charette.

"I'm telling you over the phone I didn't do it."

"No, Terry. Anyway, it's time to sit down and talk. It's time to talk about Joan Johnson."

There was a long pause on Charette's end. "How do you know about her?"

"Let's talk, Terry."

"You're going to get to the bottom of this sooner or later, aren't you?"

"That's right. But I'd rather get it from you, Terry. It's time I knew about Joan and Peplow."

"I don't know. I don't know what to do."

"Terry?"

"What?"

"Did you kill Peplow?"

"No way."

"Are you protecting someone who did?"

"No."

"Then what's the fucking problem?"

"I gotta protect myself."

"From what?"

"From the past."

"Terry, if you don't talk, I start calling up people. You don't want your past on a lot of other people's minds, do you?"

"No."

Who the hell was Harvey going to start calling? Charette wasn't even bothering to call Harvey's bluff. "Plus which," Harvey continued, "all I have to do is drop what I know on the Portland police's doorstep, and then it's going to be like a formal dance for you. You got to get dressed up and everything. With me, it's just a casual get-together."

Harvey listened to Charette breathe for a few seconds before he said, "See, Terry, the first guy they're going to suspect is you."

Charette's sigh was almost closer to a moan. "All right."

"All right what?"

"I'll meet you."

"This evening."

"All right. I'll meet you in an hour."

"Where?"

"Let me see. How about the Western Prom?"

"What's that?"

"The Western Promenade. Near the Maine Medical Center."

"Where's that?"

Charette told him. "I'll see you at the bench near the statue of Thomas Reed. You can't miss it."

When he went back to the booth, Charlie said, "Everything all right?"

"Better."

"You got an appetite yet?"

"As a matter of fact."

Charlie's angular face lit up in a gap-toothed grin. "That's what I like to hear, Professor."

"What's good tonight?"

"Professor, I don't believe you ever tasted my pasticcio."

21

THE WESTERN PROMENADE was a narrow grassy park on a high bluff overlooking South Portland and the 295 spur across the harbor and, in the middle distance, the Portland Jetport. Behind the Prom a row of grand early-twentieth-century homes lined a wide street, smugly surveying the dusky vista that, now that the clouds had lifted and dispersed, reached impressively southward in the direction of New Hampshire. Terry Charette sat alone on a slatted bench, looking out, his back to Harvey, and did not turn his head even when Harvey sat down next to him and set a paper sack between them.

"You know," Terry said, "on a clear day you can see the White Mountains fifty miles away. Some people like cities. I like places where I can see into the next state. Nice mackerel sky tonight." Along the horizon the sky was mottled and streaked with purple, gold, and rose. "What's in the bag?"

"I brought you some moussaka from a friend's restaurant over in South Portland. I thought you might be hungry."

"You fattening me up for the kill?"

"I'm really not trying to make your life—"

"That's all right, buddy. Thanks. I'll eat it later." He fell silent.

Harvey could see that the fight was out of him. "What happened to Joan?"

Terry picked up the bag and put it in his lap, where he wrapped his hands around it as if it were a purse. "She killed herself." Terry turned to Harvey. "Isn't that what you wanted to know? On March nineteenth, 1987, she killed herself."

For a moment, everything was quiet on the bluff; someone had hit the world's mute button. A toy plane made its approach to Portland in the distance. "I'm sorry," Harvey said.

"A couple of weeks after she quit her so-called therapy with that fucking asshole, she went home to Pennsylvania, put her big toe on the trigger of a neighbor's hunting rifle, and shot off the back of her head."

If only Harvey hadn't had so many questions; if only he could have just sat there with Terry and watched the sun go down.

"Let me tell you something. The only way she could tear herself away from him in the end was he didn't want to fuck her anymore. He gave her some mumbo jumbo, told her she was a bad girl. Something like that. It destroyed her world—what was left of it."

Charette groaned, as if from the sheer effort of remembrance. "The fucking sadist. Think about it. I used to think that I was helping her—you know, I did love her—but I think the only thing that was holding her together for the last two or three years was, you know, she figured, she had this fantasy, that this wonderful shrink of hers was madly in love with her."

"How long had she been having sex with Peplow?"

"Maybe three years. Almost as long as she had been going to see him. He'd been screwing her for a year before we got together."

"She lived with you?"

"She moved in a month after we started dating. I met her at a bar in the Old Port." He swallowed and cupped his palm over his mouth for a moment. "She was dead a month before I could admit it to myself, but I think she figured Peplow would just marry her someday.

I don't think I was ever the man in her life. I had no fucking connection to her happiness."

"You didn't know about it until it was over?"

"No, not until she left him. Everything I'm telling you now I learned later, after I came home one day and she was sitting on the floor with her wrists all nicked up. She'd been flicking her wrists with my linoleum knife. She said she had to tell me something horrible."

In the distance, another plane made its final approach into Portland. "For three years you didn't know it was going on?"

"Peplow told her that if she talked about it with anyone, it would ruin her chances to get well. I'm telling you, the things she brought home with her. Once she came home and told me that Peplow said that we should have sex only if she initiated it, and that to let me initiate sex would just be, you know, repeating what had happened to her as a child. She did whatever he told her. Christ, when she was shopping for a used car, he told her to buy a Honda, just like he had. And she did. And a couple of weeks after she quit seeing Peplow, she drove that Honda to Pennsylvania and killed herself."

Harvey looked down at his hands. There was a point at which other people's pain can make it hard to look at a sunset.

Terry sucked down on one end of his mustache. "She was just this sweet girl, like a broken vase or something that's been all taped together so you can see how beautiful it once was. And now she was turning to me for help because she suddenly realized her own shrink had been fucking her over for three years. Fucking her for three years. And I was supposed to make it better, even though I was the chump. No, she was the chump, I guess. I was chump number two. But think about it. I was the only one she could turn to."

"What about her family?"

Terry spat on the grass at his feet. "C'mon. If she had the kind of parents you could turn to, why would she've stuck with a guy like Peplow for three years, thinking it was a healthy thing? You understand what I'm saying? She never felt she had *anybody*. Didn't know which way was up anymore. This was a sick fuck preying on a miserable girl. I'm no hero, believe me, but I may've been the first guy who didn't completely fuck her over. And Peplow destroyed the little that we had. She'd already been abused by one father figure. She didn't need another."

"You mean her real father?"

"She remembered it happening when she was eight or nine and then when she was a teenager, and she thought it happened when she was a real little girl, too, but she'd blocked so much out. The only thing I can say for Peplow is he didn't deny it had happened to her."

Terry's hands were kneading the rolled top of the paper bag in his lap. "She was really just getting by when I met her. She'd made a suicide attempt at junior college in Pennsylvania, dropped out, and came here because she thought it was a pretty place. But it wasn't pretty enough. She got depressed again, ended up in Al-Anon, and someone recommended Peplow."

"Did she have a job here?"

"Oh, she cleaned houses, mostly. Once she waitressed for a while."

"How did she afford therapy?"

"She had a little money. I don't know, maybe from her family. Sometimes I helped her out with the bills, if you can believe it. And then Peplow didn't charge her much. Gee, I wonder why. Anyway, most of what she had went to Peplow." He sighed. "I don't know what else I can tell you. It was just really, really hard. I wanted to fucking kill him."

And he was possibly capable of it, Harvey thought, a guy like Charette, in a moment of fury. But his motive was five years old before someone shot Peplow in a field a thousand miles from here.

"Then I was too numb to think about it and too busy trying to keep Joanie in one piece to think about him. You know, I was too busy clearing the rubble to think about the bomb. Then Joanie left, and after, you know, what happened then, I went numb again. I drank a lot, I broke a few noses, shit like that."

"You didn't report Peplow to anyone?"

Terry looked at him in the last of the daylight. "Hey, what the fuck did I know? I didn't know there were people you could go to. I was just a carpenter from the Maine woods."

If Peplow's misconduct had never been reported, why had he retired and moved to the Midwest? Had one of Peplow's other patients reported him? "Did you ever do anything?" Harvey asked.

"Oh yeah."

"What?"

"About six months later I was working for some lawyer, putting in some French doors. And I told him about Peplow. And he gave me the name of a malpractice lawyer."

"And?"

"And I went to see him. I showed him the diary."

"What diary's that?"

"Joanie kept a diary during her therapy with Peplow. She sent it to me from her mother's house right before she killed herself. She must've thought I had a right to know the details of what had been going on during the time we were together."

"And in the diary she'd written down what happened with Peplow?"

The hot orange coal of the sun began to slip behind the horizon's black blade. "I couldn't read it after a while, it made me so fucking sick. When I showed it to the lawyer, he looked at it for a while and then held it up, you know, between his fingers, and said, 'You've heard of the proverbial smoking gun, haven't you?' "

"So he explained the two roads we could take. He said he could file a, you know, a tort claim saying that Peplow's actions had contributed to Joanie's death. That he might take such a case on contingency, but that Joanie's and my dirty laundry would be aired out. They'll put you and Joan under a microscope, he said, they'll try everything. They'll investigate your past relationships and hers and how you two lived together outside of marriage. They'll try to prove she seduced this shrink. It'll be horrible. It'll be in the papers. I remember what he said; he said, 'You'll be filleted like a fish.' And then he said I had another big problem. Since she didn't have a will, and since we weren't married, I couldn't get any of the damages money, anyway. It'd go to her mother or something.

"So I told him I wasn't in it for money, that I'd settle for getting the asshole out of the profession so he couldn't pull this shit with anyone else. And he said, 'Bless your heart, because the other road's a lot easier.' He said we had a strong case to get him decertified as a shrink, but that he'd have to get paid upfront for that. I told him I was just a carpenter and he smiled and said that he'd charge me carpenter's rates. And then he asked me to leave him the diary and he said he'd be in touch.

"So he called me after a few weeks to say that he'd written Peplow a letter saying he represented me and that he had Joanie's diary and, I guess, mentioned enough of what was in the diary to scare the shit out of him. And that if Peplow would agree to pack it in and everything, that we would have no interest in pursuing disciplinary hearings against him. That if Peplow supplied him with evidence he'd given up his license, the matter would be dropped." He drew a long breath.

"And?" Harvey said.

He exhaled. "And he said that Peplow's lawyer had finally called him to say that Peplow agreed to the terms."

"Just like that?"

"I guess Peplow didn't want his own laundry aired in front of anyone, especially other shrinks. And that was it. There wouldn't be any public record of what he did. I paid him his 'carpenter's rates,' he sent me back the diary and a copy of the documents showing Peplow had surrendered his license and a copy of his resignation from whatever association he belonged to, and that's the last I heard of it."

"Will you show me the diary?"

"I don't have it."

"Where is it?"

"I sent it back to her mother. I didn't want it around anymore."

"Is she still in Pennsylvania?"

"Yeah. Dead and buried in Bethlehem. Joanie's suicide finished off the job her drinking started. She died about two years ago."

"So you don't know where the diary is?"

"No."

"What about her father? Could he have it?"

"I doubt it. They'd been divorced for a few years. Not soon enough to save Joanie from him. And, anyway, I have no idea where her father is."

Nightfall had reduced the view to a quilt of hazy blues and blacks peppered with distant lights. The temperature had dropped a good fifteen degrees since they had started talking, and Harvey plunged his hands in his pockets. "Why do you think she went back to her mother's?"

"Who knows? Maybe to try one last time to get through? To get her to say, 'Yeah, you're right, your father was a sick fuck and I should've stopped him from crawling into your bed'? Who the fuck knows? Maybe she'd given up on her and she just went back to kill herself where it would hurt her mother the most." Terry crinkled the paper bag in his lap. "You know, life is really wasted on so many people."

"Yeah," Harvey said.

"I keep wondering what kind of shithead I was, three years and I couldn't see that something was really wrong. I just missed it completely."

"It's tough to see the big things."

"You know, I wasn't very good to her. That's made it harder."

"I'm sure you did your best under the circumstances."

"No, I didn't." He snorted. "But thank God for circumstances in any case. You know, without them to fall back on, we'd all feel so fucking shitty all of the time."

"So why wouldn't you talk to me for three days?"

"I don't know. I guess it took me that long to decide I could stand to hear myself tell the story."

"Well, you okay?"

"I'll survive. You'll let me know if you find out who killed him?"

"Sure."

" 'Cause you want to know something? When you called me to say Peplow had been murdered, my first thought was, Gee, I wish I had been the one to pull the trigger. And then, I almost felt like even the death of your enemies hurts."

22

AN HOUR OR so later Harvey was nursing the beginnings of his third Tanqueray martini at the bar of Di Millo's Floating Restaurant and Marina. For a while his mind was still going uphill, fighting every thought. The impossibility of relationships. The unknowability of others. The treachery people practiced on one another. Then, on the heels of a particular sip of martini, just when thinking seemed like a luxury he could no longer afford, he suddenly reached the crest after a long climb through the thorny brush. Now he stood and looked out over a peaceful, chemically altered mental landscape. Everything was tolerable. He just sat slit-eyed at the bar, watching a woman several stools down rearrange her neckline to reveal a lacy margin of camisole. Through a curtain of gin he thought he saw her smile at him. He smiled back. He was under the impression that at this moment he was the most desirable man in the world. He considered acting on a hunch that certain anonymous physical pleasures were his but for the asking tonight, but the martini might as well have been laced with curare for all the mobility he had. For ten minutes, he remained frozen at the bar with his smile affixed uncomfortably to his face.

Finally, when he felt able to move, he made his way delicately to the public phone where two days before he had induced his waitress

Dena to call Terry Charette. Things had certainly picked up in the last forty-eight hours. He hammered out his MCI access code on the face of the phone and called Norm. When Linda answered and he heard her voice, it seemed miraculous to him.

"Hey, you're my shister-in-law!" he said.

"Is that you, Harvey?"

"By the term 'you,' do you mean me?"

"Harvey, you sound like you're drunk."

"I'm laminated, Linda."

"What's going on?" she asked with genuine concern.

"It's a . . . shpecial night. I need to tell Norm . . . shumthing." He had a new feeling now: how beautifully human and humbling it was to be slurring one's words like a common drunk.

"He's out."

"Can you leave him a meshishdge?"

"A what?"

He was aware he was using more syllables than the word normally required. "A meshishdge," he repeated.

"Sure, but I don't have to leave it for him, Harvey. We live to-gether."

"Tha' helps keep a marriage together."

"I'll just give it to him personally."

"Tha's great, Linda. Now thish is what you tell him. Tell him that Peplow was a bad boy. A very, very bad boy."

"That Peplow was a very bad boy?"

"Tha's it. Tell Norm I love him, but he'sh got to pick hish friendsh better."

"Should I have him call you?"

"Can't. I don't know where I am. And by 'I' I mean me in this inshtance."

"Are you all right, Harvey?"

"Linda?"

"What?"

"You are . . ." He was too deep into the sentence to back out, so he grabbed for the first adjective that went by. ". . . grand. Just grand."

He hung up the phone, reviewed the evidence, and concluded that he was still too drunk to make his next call. He had a new feeling now: He was embarrassed to be with himself. In the men's room he slapped cold water on his face and while pissing lapsed into a fugue state from which he was aroused only by the vigorous flushing of the neighboring urinal.

After a while he was back at the pay phone, dialing Dr. Walker's number in Cambridge. He was in the middle of leaving a message when she picked up.

"Mr. Blissberg."

"Yes. Hello," he barked, shaking his head to clear it. "I got your message."

"Hello. Where are you?"

"In Portland. Listen, I just had a talk with the boyfriend, and I'm afraid your instincts were correct." His tongue was heavy, but the words seem to be forming themselves all right.

"Yes?"

"Yes, she killed herself after a three-year affair with Peplow. During therapy. All that stuff you gave me to read, it was very helpful. Almost prophetic."

After a pause she said, "I was afraid it might be."

"She left behind a diary," he said. "The boyfriend took it to a lawyer and Peplow thought better of remaining in practice. He surrendered his license without a fight."

"A diary." She paused. "Yes, I imagine he had no wish to be humiliated in front of his peers on the APA Ethics Committee for something that is the subject of casual conversation between therapists."

"What do you mean?"

"Well, the reason I called you earlier is that I made an inquiry about Frederick Walls. It seems that he has something of a reputation in psychiatric circles up there. For having sexual relationships with female patients."

"How do you know that?"

"I spoke to a colleague of mine in Maine. Apparently Walls is not above regaling his colleagues with the occasional exploit."

"And this is the guy that Peplow went to for help? The guy who headed up some ethics committee?"

Dr. Walker was silent on the other end.

He pressed his fingers against his closed eyelids. "The impaired leading the impaired. My God, it's unbelievable. Look," he said to Dr. Walker, "could you—I wonder—could you do me a further small favor?"

"What's that?"

"The name of the colleague you spoke to."

"I'd rather not."

"It's not to contact him—or her. I think it may come in handy. Indirectly. It won't come back to haunt you."

"I promised my colleague this was confidential."

"Well, it seems to me that the confidentiality of these things is a big part of the problem, but, like I said, it won't come back to haunt you."

She sighed lightly. "His name is Dr. Curtis Chamberlin."

"Thank you."

"I'll see you next week at your regular time?"

"Yes. Barring an act of God."

Two hours later, when he had fully sobered, he drove to Charlie's through the balmy night, the sweet smell of honeysuckle and wet mown grass filling the car. Every two minutes he flicked on the wipers to erase the mosquito carnage on the windshield. In South Portland, the neighborhoods were full of the sound of crickets and cicadas and the shouts of children loose in yards. Parents in T-shirts and tube tops watched them from their stoops and nylon-weave lawn chairs. Harvey caught snatches of their laughing conversation as he rode by, his tires hissing at him on the puddled pavement. What a strange place the world was, that it could tolerate so much, that it embraced Laurence Peplow and barbecues, summer evenings and suicide. When Harvey was a boy, the world was rumored to contain many bad things—madness, drugs, divorce, death natural and unnatural—but they were only dark silhouettes hovering outside childhood's translucent shell. Then, slowly, as the years passed, the world let in first one bad thing, then another, gradually exposing you to life's grim bargain. Unless you were one of the unlucky ones who were not allowed a shell, like Joanie Johnson, you learned to adjust, to participate. But Harvey wondered if almost everyone, in the end, felt the same way—unlucky, taken in, fast-talked, never quite able to read the small print, tired of the rotten deal, and ready, finally, to die.

HE WAS AWAKENED the next morning by one-and-a-half-year-old Casey Manomaitis, wearing only a disposable diaper and the remnants of her breakfast. "Howey," she repeated while tugging at the covers, "Howey. Belle pway bah." She held a soft vinyl baseball.

"She wants to play ball, show you her knuckle curve," Charlie translated from the doorway of the guest room, where he balanced a cup of coffee and saucer on his palm. "She can't get it anywhere near the plate, but she's got a lot of movement on it."

"Belle pway bah," Casey said, her face split in a big gummy smile.

"Who's Belle?"

"From *Beauty and the Beast*. She's got herself a little confused with the main character."

"I get it," he said. "She's beautiful, Charlie."

"Thanks."

"It must be great."

"There's nothing like it."

"I bet."

"You never had a day in baseball that could compare to this sweet thing."

Casey tossed the ball on the bed. Harvey retrieved it for her and cupped her head of dark hair in his hand. "What time is it?"

"Nine-thirty."

"Jesus."

"Get up, 'Howey,' " Charlie said, "and we'll chuck it around some in the backyard before I go off to work."

Harvey swung his legs over the side of the bed, yawned, and kissed Casey's forehead. "Let me wash up and make one phone call, Casey, and then you can show me your stuff."

He poured himself a mug of coffee from the Proctor Silex coffee-maker in the kitchen of Charlie and Tracy's modified ranch and looked up Dr. Frederick Walls's number in the phone book. He didn't know what to expect—it was Saturday, after all—but the same even voice answered that had called him back on his car phone five days ago.

"Yes?"

"Is this Dr. Walls?"

"Yes it is."

"I'm so glad I reached you," Harvey said, talking quickly, trying to add a note of frenzy to his voice. "My name's Lester Byers and I need to see you, Dr. Walls. Dr. Chamberlin referred me to you. Really, I wouldn't have bothered you if it weren't something of an emergency. People speak very highly of you."

"What kind of emergency?"

"It's my son. He came home from college with a gun. I found it in his bedroom. I'm afraid he's planning to use it on himself. I don't know. He seems extremely depressed but he won't talk to me. He keeps talking about something called the Sex Club, Doctor, and all these sexual acts taking place where they're not supposed to. I think he's—what's the word?—delusional. He's had emotional problems for quite a while."

"Where's the gun now?" Dr. Walls asked. Harvey had hooked

him, either with the direct appeal to his vanity or the subliminal one, to his promiscuity.

"I took the gun away and hid it and now he's going crazy. He's threatening me if I don't give it back. But I don't want to bring the police into it. I just want the best evaluation I can get."

"Is your son on any medication?"

"None that I know of."

"Has your son been hospitalized before?"

"No. But I'm beginning to think he ought to be. I just don't know. If you could just see him for a minute. The situation's getting out of control, Dr. Walls."

"All right then. Do you think you can get him in the car and bring him over to my office?"

"Oh, yes, that would be great. Really, I don't know what I'm going to do. When can you see us?"

"Can you be here by eleven?"

"Yes."

"Do you know where my office is?"

"Yes, I have the address right here."

"Good. Then I'll see you at eleven, Mr. Byers."

Harvey hung up and finished his coffee. It could not have gone better. Through the kitchen window, on the broad lawn that ran into a rolling meadow, Charlie was flipping the ball to Casey and clowning for her like a base runner caught in a rundown, trying to escape phantom pursuers coming from either direction. Harvey could hear Casey's throaty giggling. She brought her hands up to her cheeks in delight and stamped her bare feet on the grass.

When Harvey joined them in the yard, Charlie produced two of his old baseball gloves and an American League baseball streaked with grass stains. Harvey slipped on one of the gloves. While Casey amused herself with a set of plastic nesting bowls, he and Charlie silently tossed the ball back and forth, loosening their arms, slowly extending the distance between them, gradually adding zip to the throws, until they were standing a hundred feet apart, just like they used to be when they warmed up before games on the sidelines of Rankle Park in Providence. Back and forth they threw the ball, holding up their gloves to see if the one could find the target without forcing the other to move his leather. They were too old to be playing catch, and yet they were still young enough to be playing it for money. Now he and Charlie started putting everything they had into it, taking a little crow's hop to get more juice on the ball, snapping it between them in perfect rhythm.

Tracy came out of the back door, watched them for a brief moment, and called out, "Harvey, it's Mickey on the phone."

"Is everything all right?" he said into the wall phone in the kitchen.

"Everything's okay. But, listen, Bliss, Jerry and I drove back to the house this morning to check the mail—"

"Everything okay there?"

"Yeah, yeah. No sign of whoever it was."

"Good. Good. You sleep okay at Jerry's?"

"Yeah, fine. Now, look, there was a package for you at the house. It came Air Express with no return address on it."

"Did you open it?"

"No. You know I don't open your—"

"Well, don't!"

"What's the big deal? You think it's a bomb or something?"

"I just don't want to take any chances. How big is it?"

"I don't know. It's flat. About the size of a small pizza?"

"A pizza?"

"A small one."

"Can you read the postmark?"

"Rice Lake. Wisconsin."

"Wisconsin?"

"What's wrong?"

"Is Jerry there?"

"Yeah. He's downstairs."

"Put him on."

"Hold on."

A moment later, his mentor and former employer was on the line. "Greetings," he said.

"Hi, Jerry. Thanks for looking after Mickey."

"Don't mention it. She's a terrific kid." He was from that generation that used "terrific kid" and "stand-up guy."

"About this package addressed to me."

"What about it?"

"It's safe to open it?"

"You expecting a bomb?"

"It's not funny, Jerry."

"Well, damn it, we know it's not a mercury-switch bomb, 'cause if it was you'd already be out one girlfriend and one licensed detective. Were you expecting something?"

"No."

"Let me run upstairs and look at it. Hold on."

Jerry was on the line again in thirty seconds. "I've got it here. Well, it's not the *least* suspicious package I've ever seen. No return address."

"Maybe you ought to x-ray it."

"You want me to run it down to my friends at the Brookline PD and take a look?"

"I hate to make you do something like that, but it wouldn't hurt."

"Blissberg," he said, "you sound a little on edge."

"It's been a rough week."

"What inning are you in?"

"I think it's the eighth, but it still feels like the top of the third."

"Anything I can do?"

"No, I'm all right. So, anyway, maybe you could take the package down to your friends."

"All right. But I'll open it if you want."

"C'mon, you may not think your life's worth shit, but *I* can get more use out of you."

Bellaggio laughed. "All right, you pussy. I'll take it down with Mickey and call you back in an hour."

23

DR. WALLS'S OFFICE was in a large, red brick house, just a couple of hundred yards from the bench on the Western Promenade where he and Terry Charette had talked the night before. It appeared to be Walls's residence as well. He parked on the street, followed a brick path to a side door, and found himself in a small waiting room with Herman Miller chairs and a table stacked with copies of *The New Yorker* and *Yankee* magazine.

Harvey had less time than he would have liked to compose himself because almost immediately one of the three doors in the waiting room opened and a short man of about sixty stood erectly in front of him. He had a boyishly smooth face with small features and neatly barbered brown hair, threaded with gray and severely parted. He looked, in his pressed blue suit, blue shirt, and maroon-and-powder-blue striped tie, as if his mother had dressed him. There was a slightly absurd formality about him.

He looked at Harvey over his half-moon reading glasses and said, "Please come in." Harvey preceded him into a brooding office weighed down with books, dark upholstered furniture, and a memento-strewn mahogany desk. Half-drawn burgundy curtains kept out enough of the daylight to warrant the use of lamps. Walls indicated a leather armchair for Harvey and seated himself in a larger one next to his desk. His feet only barely reached the floor.

"Before we start, Mr. Byers, my fee for an initial consultation is a hundred and thirty-five dollars."

Harvey nodded. "I'm sure it will be worth it."

"Where's your son? I understood you were bringing him here."

"I'm afraid he couldn't make it."

Walls looked confused. "I see. Well, suppose you tell me what seems to be the problem."

"You," Harvey said.

"I'm sorry."

"I said, *you* seem to be the problem, Dr. Walls."

"In what way do you feel I'm the problem, Mr. Byers?"

"My name's not Byers. It's Blissberg. Harvey Blissberg."

Walls's mouth opened slightly and closed, like a fish's. "I see," he said. "You made an appointment under false pretenses."

"I'm not going to quibble with that interpretation. You wouldn't have agreed to see me otherwise."

"What is it that you came all the way here for, Mr. Blissberg? I gave you a name. I hope it was helpful."

"Terry Charette didn't kill Peplow."

"Well," Walls said, "I tried."

"Oh, listen," Harvey said, "make no mistake. Charette was very helpful. And I want to thank you for it. After all, you provided me with the name of the boyfriend of a patient of Laurence Peplow's who committed suicide. And you knew that. Peplow was your patient. You knew that Peplow had been carrying on a sexual relationship with this patient, Joan Johnson, while she was in therapy with him."

Walls held up a hand. "You're going very fast, Mr. Blissberg."

"I'm confident you can keep up with me, Dr. Walls. You told me you saw Peplow as a patient for two or three years in the mid-eighties. Is that correct?"

Walls repositioned himself with a squeak in his shiny leather wingback. "Yes."

"Well, Joan Johnson committed suicide in March of 1987. I don't know whether or not Peplow was still in treatment with you when she killed herself, but it would be difficult to believe you weren't aware that he was sleeping with a patient. After all, he was in therapy with you during some or all of the time he was carrying on an unethical sexual relationship with her. Correct?"

"I would have to review my notes on that."

"You don't have to review your notes on that. All you have to do is decide whether to tell me the truth. Now—and correct me if I'm wrong—Dr. Peplow sat in this chair, or maybe he was on that couch over there, and he told you about having sex with Joan Johnson."

In the cool gloom of his office Walls looked at Harvey without expression, except for a slight contraction of the muscles around his mouth.

"I'll take that as a yes, Doctor. And the fact is that you didn't report his unethical behavior to any of the appropriate authorities. To the American Psychological Association or the state Department of Professional and Financial Regulations."

"You have little understanding of these matters," Walls suddenly said.

"My understanding is that you had firsthand evidence of gross professional misconduct on the part of a licensed psychotherapist and you did nothing to report it."

"These things aren't quite as simple as you represent them."

"Dr. Walls, here's my feeling. My feeling is that you gave me Terry Charette's name because you feel guilty."

"Guilty?" He said it as if the emotion were beneath someone of his stature. "Is that your interpretation?"

"You must have felt a little bad for the last five years, ever since you learned that Joan Johnson killed herself. Was Peplow still seeing you when it happened?"

"No."

"Did you know about her suicide at the time?"

"No. Not until later."

"Ah. You must have learned about it when Peplow was contacted by Terry Charette's lawyer, who had Joan Johnson's diary in his possession. Here's my guess, Dr. Walls: My guess is that Peplow contacted his own lawyer when he received the letter from Charette's lawyer, and then Peplow contacted you. He was in trouble. It was natural for him to turn to you for advice. He may even have come in to see you."

Walls smoothed his tie with his palm.

"And here's my other guess. You knew he had been offered an excellent deal from Charette's lawyer. All Peplow had to do was surrender his license and go quietly and he could avoid any public humiliation or professional review. The alternative, given the existence of the diary, was for him to go loudly. And going quietly, Dr. Walls, would save your sorry ass, because you knew that if Peplow was questioned by an ethics committee, he would likely bring your name up and the fact that you did not consider his transgressions serious enough to report them. And that might jeopardize your hallowed standing in the psychiatric community. And so you strongly counseled Dr. Peplow to take the deal and get the hell out of town. For all I know," Harvey added as a bonus threat, "the diary even mentioned you."

There was silence for ten seconds. Harvey tore his gaze away from Walls's face only long enough to glance at the clock on Walls's mahogany desk, ticking between a marble-base fountain pen desk set and a small bronze elephant. He had twenty-five minutes left in the hour.

"I was not legally bound to report Dr. Peplow's conduct as a therapist to any authorities."

"You were ethically bound, Dr. Walls. Or didn't ethics enter into it for you? As a member of the AMA, you are obligated to expose incompetent colleagues who come to your attention. You didn't think that obligation extended to a licensed psychologist who had revealed to you he was sleeping with an extremely vulnerable patient?"

"Doctor-patient confidentiality was my foremost concern. It was a judgment call."

"Well, God save your patients if this is an example of your judgment. Now, I'd like you to tell me a little about your treatment of Larry Peplow."

"That's confidential, as I told you before."

Harvey clasped his hands in his lap. "Dr. Walls, nothing is preventing me from going to the Maine Board of Medical Registration or, for that matter, to the Maine Psychiatric Society or any other damn groups you belong to. Nothing's stopping me from going to them and filing charges against you for covering up practices that are now considered a felony in this state."

"You wouldn't do that."

"Feel free to try me."

In an effort to reassert his authority, Walls crossed his little legs and plucked at his pants crease. But when he spoke, it was in a voice higher and slower than the one with which he had begun the hour. "I urged him to stop."

"No doubt. Why did Peplow come to see you initially?"

Walls cleared his throat and said, "Impotence."

"Impotence?" It took Harvey a moment to take in this new information. "You mean it wasn't second thoughts over what he was doing to Joan Johnson?"

"He was, uh"—Walls tried to work up some saliva in his dry mouth—"he was experiencing some sexual dysfunction in regard to a woman he was involved with."

"Another patient of his?"

"No. Not a patient. Someone he felt strongly attracted to."

"But, at the same time, Dr. Walls, Peplow wasn't experiencing impotence with Joan Johnson?"

Walls coughed into his fist.

"Well, was he?"

"I don't believe so."

"So," Harvey said, "here we have a man who has no trouble performing with a woman who was sexually abused as a child and who is now paying him to experience still more sexual abuse, but who can't get it up with a woman he really cares about."

"That, I suppose, is one way of looking at it."

"And you chose not to use your authority to help protect Dr. Peplow's patient from his sexual abuse?"

"He promised me he would end the affair with her. But what is it that you're getting at, Mr. Blissberg? I don't know who killed him."

"Did Peplow have sexual relationships with other patients of his?"

"I can't say."

"Yes, you can. Did he?"

Walls brought his fist to his mouth again and coughed. "I don't know," he said. "But now look, I have no information about who might've murdered Peplow, so there seems to be little point in sifting these ashes. You have to understand—he acknowledged his problem, he was expressing remorse, and was making headway."

"Not enough for Joan Johnson, though, huh? Were you under the impression that Peplow had changed his unethical behavior while you were treating him?"

"Yes, I suppose I was under that impression. He led me to believe he had it under control."

" 'Under control.' " Harvey gave a little snort. "By that, do you mean that he felt he had been engaging in a little bit more of it than was good for him?"

"No, I didn't mean that."

"But, anyway, he didn't have it under control, did he?" Harvey studied Walls's blue eyes, eyes that some patient at some time or other had no doubt found "soulful." Harvey wondered: Would he have done better in Walls's shoes? The pressures to report Peplow were not insignificant, to be sure: professional guidelines, the love of justice, and a concern for the welfare of strangers. But arrayed against them were an army of inducements to silence: simple inertia; the vanity of believing he alone had the power to modify Peplow's behavior; the responsibility of taking the fate of a colleague's career into his own hands; and the belief—so easily disguised as honor—that to cast the stone one has to be without sin oneself. It was easy to see the price of Peplow's mental illness in the light of Joan Johnson's suicide; but before she killed herself, would Harvey have been able to assess the damage from a distance and take the extraordinary step of turning in a colleague?

"So I guess you wouldn't call your treament of him successful," Harvey said.

Walls separated his palms to indicate he was helpless before the intransigence of certain human behaviors.

"Would you say Peplow was just a lovesick therapist or something more?"

"I see you've done your homework."

"I try to stay abreast of the literature."

"Well, I'd say Peplow had a narcissistic character disorder."

"Yet you saw no reason to report his misconduct?"

"I believed I could help him."

Harvey paused before playing his last card. "Of course," he said slowly, "the prognosis was prejudiced further by your own conduct, wasn't it?"

"I beg your pardon." The color was already draining from Walls's face.

"When Peplow first consulted you, he must've known that you shared his tendencies. Known that he was going to get a—what?—a tolerant and understanding hearing."

"What are you saying?"

"What do you think I'm saying?"

"I asked you what you meant."

"And I answered it with a question. That should be a technique you're familiar with. What do you think I'm saying?"

"I couldn't begin to guess."

"Dr. Walls, don't you think it's funny that you get to learn so much about your patients and they get to learn so little about you? Except a colleague like Peplow, of course, who must've been acquainted with your reputation."

"What are you insinuating?"

"That you too sleep with patients."

Walls's face was now white. "You have no evidence of that."

"I don't have any of your patients' diaries, if that's what you mean."

"You should be careful. That's a very serious charge."

"Well, you should know, as someone who's served on ethics committees," Harvey said with a malevolent little wink. "Yet when you were presented with firsthand evidence of Peplow's guilt, you didn't think it was serious enough for you to report actual sexual misconduct."

"I'm certainly not going to sit here and defend myself against spurious charges from some so-called detective."

Harvey almost smiled; his target had grown too large. He stood up, saying, "I'm afraid our time is up."

"You ought to be careful with statements like that," Walls cautioned, standing up too.

Harvey looked him in the eye and said unexpressively, as if it didn't really bear mentioning, "Dr. Walls, I have reason to believe you sleep with female patients. I believe that your own unethical practices, by removing whatever motivation you might've had to report Peplow's misconduct, contributed to this young woman's death."

"You can't argue that either I or Dr. Peplow contributed to her suicide."

"Well, the two of you sure as hell didn't help prolong her life. In any case, I want to thank you for giving me Terry Charette's name. Whatever your motive in doing so, it's been extremely helpful to my investigation." Harvey opened his wallet and handed Walls a business card. "You can send me your bill at this address."

24

THE NOTE ON Charlie and Tracy's kitchen table read, "Call Jerry's house. Casey and I went grocery shopping. Help yourself to lunch. Tracy." When Harvey dialed Bellaggio's home number, Mickey answered and said, "It's a book. The X ray showed a book."

"What book?"

"I didn't open it."

"Open it now."

After a moment, she said, "No, it's not a book. It looks like a journal. No, wait. It's a diary. Let's see, there's a name on the inside cover. Joan Johnson. Does that mean any—"

"Yes."

"What?"

"Mick, I need to see it. How'd you like to get in your car with the diary and drive up here?"

"I can't."

"Why not?"

"I promised Paul I'd look at the rough cut of the first ten minutes of the show this afternoon."

"It's Saturday."

"We're on deadline."

"Please, Mick."

"All right. I'll call Paul and see if we can put it off."

"Thank you. I owe you one."

"You owe me more than one."

"How many do I owe you?"

"You owe me about thirty-eight or forty."

"That's a lot."

"I could knock it down a little for good behavior."

"Mick?"

"What?"

"Fill up the gas tank before you leave and don't stop until you get here. If you're being followed, or someone starts to harass you on the road, get off at the next exit, go to the first gas station you see, and call me. All right?"

He hung up and dialed Terry Charette's number. His girlfriend Nancy called him to the phone.

"Yeah?"

"It's Harvey, and you're not telling me everything."

"I told you everything I could stand to. C'mon, I feel like I've been hit by a truck all over again."

"Joan's diary just showed up at my house in Cambridge. Post-marked some place in Wisconsin."

There was a pause on Terry's end. "Well, it wasn't me."

"Then who was it?"

"I don't know."

"Like hell. The timing's pretty suspicious, Terry."

"Last time I saw it was five years ago."

"Don't grease me, Terry."

"I've done my duty, buddy. You're on your own now."

"You don't know how I can get hold of Joan's father?"

"No, man. Look, if you want, go to Bethlehem, Pennsylvania. That's where her mother used to live. Laura Johnson. She lived on Pole Street. That's all I know." And he hung up.

He drove to a nearby mall. If he made it quick, he could be back at Charlie's before Mickey was really on the road. It was good to be shopping with a purpose. He picked up a glazed Italian pasta bowl for Tracy, speckled blue-and-white, like the broad shallow bowls you saw all over now in delis and food stores holding the tortellini salads and the baseball-size fresh mozzarellas that had replaced the chemical-tasting macaroni salad and cole slaw of another era. In the mall's toy store he found a dwarf folding canvas chair for Casey. The aisles were congested with children noisily trying out swords and doll carriages. Everywhere in the mall families roamed in a daze, tranquilized by goods, romanced by lilting, piped-in renditions of rock 'n' roll classics. The immense effort it took, he thought, to decorate this existence of ours, to keep the carnival of life going, while somewhere in a tent in the far corner of the fairgrounds were all the gamy adult secrets, the freak show.

As he shopped, the weight of what he still didn't know pressed down on him. Frederick Walls. What if Peplow had been threatening to expose him, as part of a bid to get recertified, to clear his name? What if Peplow had simply had second thoughts about so blithely giving up his license and was trying to blackmail Walls into compensating him? Asking for money Walls didn't have to give him? What if Walls, to protect his prominent name and position, had been driven to arrange Peplow's death in a field far away, then handed Harvey the name of Terry Charette as a diversion?

In the last year Peplow had made no long-distance phone calls to his former psychiatrist. However, Peplow could have conducted his business with him by mail or by pay phone. He'd have to talk to Dombrowski about subpoenaing Walls's toll calls. But that would entail filling Dombrowski in, and he wasn't ready to do that. Not with Joan Johnson's diary on the way up from Boston. How, he wondered, could her diary have suddenly ended up in his possession?

He looked down at his left hand to discover that he had slipped a child's baseball glove onto it. It was bright blue and made of leather of so low a grade it felt like vinyl. The pocket was so stiff that nothing would ever stay in there. Harvey's first thought was, this would be a hell of a first baseball-glove experience to inflict on a kid. The kid's ball-catching self-esteem would be damaged for life with a glove like this. His kid would have a glove of top-grain cowhide.

With this thought he grew a little dizzy. The shelves of loudly packaged toys swam in front of him. He steadied himself against one of the store's pillars. This urge to procreate took him unawares these days, pressed up through all the muck and detail and fear. It shot out of nowhere like a hand in a horror movie, to seize him and drag him away to another world. No, no, he felt like screaming, I'm not ready.

Mickey arrived safely at four, and he hugged her tightly in Charlie and Tracy's driveway. She squeezed back with equal intensity.

"I tried to make a reservation at the Norumbega," he told her. On two occasions, but not for a couple of years, they had been to the stone-and-wood inn on Penobscot Bay two hours north in Camden.

"Well, Saturday night, everything'll be booked."

"So I thought we'd just drive north and take our chances."

"Fine," she said, arching her back to stretch the muscles after the two-hour drive from Cambridge.

"You're stiff. I'll drive," he said.

"Fine."

Harvey left the rented Tercel in Charlie's garage and took the wheel of Mickey's green Honda Accord. They drove north back through the city, past Back Cove at low tide, and set out north on Route 1. Mickey sat next to him in the front seat saying nothing, reading *The New York Times,* her blunt tan loafers propped against the dash. She kept snapping the Metro section into better reading position. Harvey looked over at her, pleased by the familiar scene. Car trips brought out the best in them. The uncertainty of their relationship, the feeling that they were tiptoeing across a fraying rope bridge that swayed between the past and some unreachable future—all that

seemed to belong to two other people for now. They'd be fine, he
thought, if they could just spend all their time in an automobile.

"How's Duane?" he asked.

"Oh, I forgot to tell you!"

"He's eating again?"

"No, but he's *looking* at food."

"He's *looking* at food?"

"The vet gave me a new antihistamine for him—something called
Cyproheptadine. Last night I put out some fresh turkey for him and
he sat there and watched it for fifteen seconds. And then walked away."

"Well, I guess it's progress."

"Bliss, this is an animal who only yesterday turned his back on
shrimp. It's like he's beginning to remember what food is. I think it
means he can smell a little. Anyway, Jerry's on syringe duty."

He hung his left elbow out the window and smiled to himself.
"Mick, remember the time a few years ago we got caught in a
downpour in Portland and we screwed in the car?"

"Was that you?" she said.

"Was that *me*?" Harvey whipped his head toward her. She gazed
poker-faced out the windshield. "What, are you kidding?"

Now she turned to him, grinning demonically. "Yes. Just
kidding."

His eye caught sight again of the corner of the Jiffy mailer sticking
out of her worn leather briefcase on the seat, sucking him rudely into
the present, and after five miles of pine and potato fields he asked,
"Do you mind driving for a while?"

"No. You want to do some reading?"

"Did you look at it?"

Now she carefully folded the Op-Ed page in half lengthwise and
slapped it with the back of her hand. "No. I've got enough problems
of my own."

They traded seats at a Hess gas station. Out of the Jiffy bag he pulled the diary, a cardboard-bound composition book, speckled like the bowl he had bought for Tracy. The pages, with their blue lines as faint as veins, were filled with Joan Johnson's handwriting in various pens and markers, the same round cursive hand he had last seen in the book he'd taken down from the shelf in Terry Charette's apartment.

25

MARCH 10, 1984

I haven't kept a diary for years, but something tells me this is going to be an interesting time in my short, screwed-up life, and as I haven't really made any good friends since I've been here I need someone to talk to besides Dr. Peplow, who I've been seeing now for two months, the shrink Carla (met her at Al-Anon) told me about. Like him okay. He's very good-looking and not old. I've told him about Daddy's "playtime" (teenage years, what I remember, as opposed to what I think happened when I was younger) and he didn't bat an eye. Encouraged me to talk about it, didn't seem suspicious of the memories like Dr. Yastrow in Bethlehem. Dr. P. even smiles sometimes, unlike Dr. Y. Also he's pretty informal and told me to sit anywhere I liked when I first came.

APRIL 7, 1984

Talked to mother on the phone. Kind of distant as always. It's like talking through one of those screens in prison like you see in the movies, only I don't know who's the prisoner, me or her. I guess we both are. I pretended things were going fine because I know she doesn't like to hear the truth and why begin now? (Dr. P. agrees that I should "take it up" with him now, not her or even Emmie, who hardly ever calls.) Mother said she still goes over and cooks for Daddy once a week (even tho they're now officially divorced). It's like she'll never get away. I wonder if I will???

MAY 3, 1984

Told Dr. P. sometimes I fantasized about sleeping with him (he's so easy to talk to!). He asked if I meant just "taking a nap" and I said no, also touching. He smiled and said that this was natural, that I would no doubt experience a lot of different strong feelings toward him during "our work together." Carla and I drove to Freeport on Sunday and tried not to spend all our money at the outlets. . . .

Harvey opened his notebook and wrote "Carla" on a new page.

JUNE 10, 1984

Told Dr. P. about Peter, a guy I met at Bobby's house over the weekend, that I hoped he would ask me out. I said that I always had this desire for a guy at first and then right away I would feel just hopeless, like I had missed so much already, that I was so lacking in experience that it would be humiliating to get involved, that no guy would put up with my problems, and I would talk myself out of being interested before I made any contact at all. Told Dr. P. I had gotten used to living in my block of ice. He asked me if I knew how to touch a man. I asked what he meant and he said that if I had to ask what he meant then I couldn't possibly know, but that it started with knowing how to touch a man's face. That most little girls learned how to do that with their fathers, how to caress them appropriately, without fear of being taken advantage of. He said I never got that, that I never learned not to be afraid. Then we did an "exercise" where he sat next to me on the couch in his office (I normally sit in the chair facing him, but we sat on the couch for the exercise) and I got on his lap and after a lot of awkwardness on my part I brushed the hair off his forehead and squeezed his nose and tickled his ears and he didn't touch me back or anything but just kept calling me his "little girl." And I started to shake and cry and I had the image of this block of ice again with me all huddled inside of it, but the ice was beginning to melt and puddles were forming on the carpet in his office. He asked "Does it feel okay to be this little girl?" and I said yes, but it's scary, and then he asked what I wanted my real daddy to have done in the past and I said that I wanted him to just hold me and not have liquor on his breath and not make comments about how beautiful my legs were getting or what a nice ass I had or my hair or anything. Just hold me. And Dr. P. just held me. Then I asked him if he would just say something very nice to me, like a real daddy would, and he said, "Joan, you're a very wonderful girl, did you know that? I like who you are." And for the last three days, over the weekend, I kept hearing "I like who you are" over and over in my head, sometimes in Dr. P.'s voice, sometimes in Daddy's voice, and sometimes in my own voice, which was the best voice of all. Yesterday I was cleaning the upstairs bathroom at Mrs. Moser's house and feeling like I would never get out of this horrible life of mine, ever, and then I starting hearing "I like who you are" in all these different voices, including mine, and it made me feel better, although I also felt kind of bad that I was the kind of person who needed to hear these voices saying that in order to feel better.

JUNE 17, 1984

So much is happening! The puddles of melted icewater on the floor are getting bigger and sometimes I feel like dancing around in them with an umbrella like Gene Kelly in "Singing in the Rain." Nothing happened with Peter (we went to a Corvette rally in Brunswick together, but nothing clicked) but Dr. P. has been doing more "exercises" with me. I sat on his lap again and I pretended to tell him about my day at school, like I might've when I was a kid, and he listened and he laughed at my made-up stories, and it was great. I told Dr. P. it was like having a snapshot of how my childhood could've been, and he said that when I had a lot more snapshots I could put them in an album and look at them whenever I wanted and then I could throw the old album of painful memories away.

Right before I got off his lap, I asked if I could kiss him on the cheek, and he said that I should do what I felt like doing, that spontaneous affection was real affection. He said, "Nothing happens unless you want it to."

JULY 9, 1984

I don't know where to begin! Dr. P. and I have continued our "exercises," but only on Friday. He said it's important we keep "one foot firmly in the *present.*" Anyway, this past Friday I was on his lap again, straddling his legs, and I said, "What if I ask you to rub my back?" He said, "Then I wouldn't be your daddy anymore because good fathers don't rub their daughters' backs after a certain age. It's too suggestive." So I said, "Okay. Poof! You're not my daddy anymore!" (like I was doing a magic trick). He said "Who am I now?" and I said "I don't know. I think you might just be a guy I'm interested in. Like someone I met at a party." And he said, "Do you really think you're ready to give up your daddy and have a boyfriend?" I said I thought so. He said, "Well, maybe you are and maybe you aren't. But when you're ready, it'll show you that when you have a good and loving father, then someday you are ready to leave him and be with a man of your own, but that when you have an abusive father like yours, you can never leave because you must always hang around emotionally waiting for him to be good and loving, which he never will be, but you don't accept it, because you just won't give up your right to a good father." He said, "You'll do anything to hang on to the bad father in the ridiculous hope that he will become the good one." And I said, "So if you rub my back, it won't be as my father?" And he said no. "And it won't be as my therapist?" And he said, "No. When I'm your therapist I sit in that chair" and he pointed at his usual chair. So who will you be? I asked him. And he said, "That's for you to decide. I won't rub your back today, but you think about who you want me to be and then, depending, I might rub it next week."

AUGUST 15, 1984

. . . We did an awful lot of stroking and when I asked him if I should remove some of my clothes, he said that it was up to me, that it was just his job to make new choices available to me. So I got down to my underwear and I told him I wanted to take his clothes off. He just looked at me nicely the way he often does on Tuesday when I'm in the chair and not sure what to say and he just looks and waits. So finally I unbuttoned his shirt and took that off and his pants too, and he didn't resist and it was amazing because I was never able to act on my desire like that before. I felt so confident. We caressed and then we made love and I could not believe any of it, that I wasn't afraid

or that it was really Dr. P. on top of me. During, I remember saying to him,
"So this is how it feels" and he smiled at me in a very loving way altho I
know he's holding a lot back (he is my therapist after all!) and I guess I am
too. Afterwards, I felt like the heavy curtains had parted and I could see out
for the first time in a long time. I felt very safe and warm and loving.

"By the way, I had Frank Tucci over to look at the leak," Mickey
said, "and he says we need a new hot water heater."
"You tell him to go ahead?"
"Yeah."
"Okay."
"Two-fifty or three hundred, he said."

DECEMBER 17, 1984

The holidays haven't been as gruesome as usual altho I'm indulging in
my usual seasonal enjoyment of alcohol. Dr. P. asked me to go with him to
this little cabin he has on Lake Sebago after our session two Fridays ago! So I
went and we made a fire and watched the snow and our "exercises" continued.
I don't know what's happening, but I think I enjoyed myself.

He wanted to know if I ever mentioned our "exercises" to anyone and I
said I hadn't and he made me get down on my knees and cross my heart and
promise I was telling the truth and would never mention them to anyone. He
said that if I couldn't "honor the seriousness of our work together" that I could
just leave and never come back and that it would be a shame because I would
never get well again or ever find anyone willing to take the risks he was to
make me whole again. He told me I was "damaged goods" still and that our
exercises had to proceed with the "utmost caution and discretion." I promised
and promised him and he gave me that beautiful smile of his again.

JANUARY 30, 1985

Emmie called the other night to make sure, as she put it, that I'm "doing
okay" and she asked if I needed any money. I reluctantly accepted her offer
because things are pretty tight and she's sending me a thousand. I told her I

needed it to pay for therapy, but of course I didn't tell her the other stuff about
Dr. P. and me altho I wanted to because I wanted her to know I was
overcoming so many of my fears. I remember when I was a teenager and she
came home late from a date and told me what it felt like to have a boy put his
hand inside you and it was like listening to someone from a different planet. I
was so afraid of what she was telling me and I didn't know why.

He added "Emmie" to the list.

FEBRUARY 5, 1985

It's been a little over a year since I started going to Dr. P. The block of
ice keeps melting little by little and I can begin to see the person inside more
clearly. It's me! and I can honestly say I like her! When I got dressed at the
end of the session Friday (we went over), I couldn't find my panties. They just
disappeared. Dr. P. said he'd look for them later. He said, "It's all right to
walk around once in a while without panties. Many women do."

FEBRUARY 16, 1985

Met a guy named Terry at Rainbow's in Old Port two nights ago. I was
on my third stinger, completely smashed, and I ended up necking in his car
with him for about an hour. (Well, what do you expect, it was Valentine's
Day!) He's a carpenter with a soul. A poet with a tool belt. I still wonder
whether guys can tell how inexperienced (sexually) I am (if you don't count the
stuff with you know who and you know who II). I still feel so trapped in a
block of ice. If I hadn't been so smashed I never would've ended up with Terry
in his car. He asked if I was involved with anybody. I told him no, but then
the image of Dr. P. came into my head. Terry wants to see me again, but I
had the feeling I was cheating on P. Anyway, almost passed out. I know I
shouldn't drink so much on top of the Xanax and will try to stop. Still so
confused. Dr. P. has taught me so much about feeling, but how to transfer it
over to my "real life" when the hours I spend in Dr. P.'s office are beginning
to seem like the only real life I have?

FEBRUARY 27, 1985

I told him I was still having spells while I cleaned houses and depression a lot of the rest of the time and panic attacks, and he kept saying, "It's darkest before the dawn." But things don't seem right again. I keep trying to "use" the insights from my therapy in my regular life, but I don't know what to use them on. The panic attacks make me afraid to socialize so I have less regular life to use them on anyway.

He said each act of love between us would undo the effects of my childhood abuse, that it was like slowly chipping away the bad to reveal the good beneath. He said, "Just think of me as your chisel." And we both laughed (I love his laugh), but then he got quite stern and reminded me that what went on between us had to remain just between us or the good effects of it would be "compromised." Also that most people would look down on what we do, but it's because most people, particularly other therapists, are afraid of "what works." He acknowledged that his "exercise" techniques wouldn't work in the wrong hands, but he had the ability to separate my needs from his, just as I needed in the past to learn to separate my needs from Daddy's.

I told him about Terry and he asked if I had had sex with him yet and when I said no he said "good, because you don't want to blow it and you're not ready yet." When he asked me if I was still drinking every night, I lied.

MARCH 11, 1985

Dr. P. had Dr. Walls, he's an M.D., write out a prescription for Halcion to help me sleep. I've been waking up again at 5 a.m. shaking, but Dr. P. said it was part of the treatment and not to worry, I had a lot to "process" and "no pain, no gain."

JUNE 18, 1985

Dr. P. asked me to describe the sex I have with Terry. When I said that I didn't feel right about it, he pointed out (I'm sure he's right, as usual) that my being able to discuss it in therapy, to bring myself to talk about it like an adult, would be a terrific sign that I was integrating my sexuality in a healthy way at last. Dr. P. wanted to know how long it took Terry to come and when I told him he said, "You know, when it takes that long with a man it's often a sign of boredom."

AUGUST 1, 1985

Emmie came to town (alone) for two days and Terry and I had a little dinner party for her (a seafood stew—Terry can really cook up a storm when he's in the mood). She seems great and I tried to be real cheerful tho the truth is that I've been pretty down again trying to balance things and keep T. and Dr. P. separate in my head. Sometimes it's such a strain just not to tell Terry what's going on with Dr. P., but he (P.) warned me again about how I was on probation and he would kick me out in a flash if I didn't honor the treatment.

On Saturday I felt panicky and didn't want to go out, so Terry and Emmie went out driving by themselves up to Auburn for a crafts fair. I keep thinking about enrolling in some courses in the fall, but don't know.

SEPTEMBER 24, 1985

Dr. P. said, "I had bad parents too. Very bad. That's why I can help you."

He told me for the second time last Friday that I was too smart for Terry. I got a little angry with him (brave me!) and told him I didn't know whether I wanted him to be passing judgment. And he got even angrier and said that he'd be the judge of whether to pass judgment or not. I didn't want to do any "exercises" with him because I was pissed (I hate calling them exercises now because the truth is I've never had such a deep relationship with anyone before and it deserves a better name), but he got quite stern and said that only children let negative feelings get in the way of the work that needs to be done and that anger was not a valid excuse to vary the routine. Then he did something with me during the exercise that we had never done before (too embarrassed to even write it down here) and after it he asked me if Terry had ever done it. Then, at the end, after we were dressed, he smiled and said, "You're at the top of the mountain, ready to receive the tablets."

NOVEMBER 6, 1985

I told him I had been having suicidal thoughts for the first time in over a year. He said that maybe he was pushing me too fast in the treatment, that we were doing too much too quickly, that "there were still too many old photos in the album and not enough new ones" and then he asked me what snapshots I kept seeing. . . .

FEBRUARY 20, 1986

On Friday, Dr. P. told me he had been discussing my case with Dr. Walls, who may be the only person as qualified as he is to deal with my kind of case and that Dr. Walls' opinion was that we should cut back on the exercises from every Friday to every other Friday. . . . But instead of not doing an exercise he wanted to try something new. . . .

APRIL 28, 1986

Since P. and I cut back to every other Friday I've had reason to wonder what his feelings really are about me. I mean, if he can just do that, cut our love in half (I know it's therapy and not real life) then I must be fooling myself about him, but the whole purpose of therapy is to unfool me about things, especially Daddy, and if I'm being fooled in a different way, I don't know, it makes me feel like I'm going crazy, but P. keeps assuring me that it's all going as planned and that he told me at the beginning over two years ago that all surgery has its side effects and that I would have to "travel back through the pain to get to the here and now."

JUNE 15, 1986

More fights with Terry, which I don't need. Started to cry at dinner with his parents and I could tell that they've been trying to poison Terry's feelings about me and get him to split up with me. Panicky because if it turns out that he's my real life and P. isn't (which I know he isn't), then boy do I need things to be cool with T., altho how can they be cool when I'm still not leveling with him about P.? My God, what have I done?

JULY 5, 1986

Fireworks all right, but the wrong kind. P. and I went back to our weekly schedule again, but then he told me on Friday that he "didn't like my attitude" and we were going back to every other week, and he wouldn't tell me what I had done. I told him that reminded me of how Daddy would never explain what I had done wrong to cause him to be angry or drunk or want to have "playtime." P. said he was tired of hearing about Daddy, that he had tried to "rectify my situation in the past" and that I was just using the past to sabotage myself. "Are you saying I've failed here?" I screamed. "Maybe you weren't ready for really effective treatment like mine," he yelled back. He said maybe what you need is just some sort of maintenance program. It made me feel like a tiny pebble back in my block of ice and I cried and cried and he kept saying, "Think for yourself! Think for yourself!" and I screamed "What the hell does that mean?" and then all he said was that he would continue my treatment only under certain conditions. . . .

OCTOBER 19, 1986

I'm feeling torn apart like you wouldn't believe. Terry says that Dr. P. sounds like my father and Dr. P. says that Terry is nothing but a "transitional object" and that the idea that objects have opinions at all is ludicrous. I felt like spilling everything to E. when she called last night but at the last moment I realized that I would have to confess it to P. and that would be the end. Slept, thanks to three Xanax.

NOVEMBER 13, 1986

I told P. I wanted to die and he got very gentle with me and said that these were just the old feelings again. I'm in a world of hurt.

JANUARY 9, 1987

A new year but old frozen feelings. I begged P. to help me thaw out again, that I never thought I'd have to go through this again, and all he said was that there must be events in my past that I've been keeping from him and I said that it wasn't fair to make it seem like my fault because I was doing everything he asked me to and that I even bought the car that he thought I should have and he said, "What's the damn car have to do with it?"

JANUARY 27, 1987

Mother called to say that Daddy's not doing well and I got so balled up with my feelings that I couldn't even comfort her, which a grown-up would surely be able to do. All I wanted to do was scream at her, "Why did you ever marry him in the first place?"

FEBRUARY 1, 1987

Terry and I haven't had sex in three months. P. and I have, that's for sure, but it seems like the only thing we do that has any meaning.

FEBRUARY 10, 1987

Overwhelmed, most of all by guilt. I feel this has been so unfair to Terry.

MARCH 2, 1987

P. told me that there would be no more exercises. I said, "You got me into this and you better get me out" and he said that even Freud didn't bat a thousand or even close to it and I started screaming and he came over and put his hand over my mouth until he thought I had calmed down a little and when he took his hand away I bit it and he said "That's not a very nice thing to do when you consider that I've been undercharging you for your therapy for three years." I said, "You call this therapy? I feel like killing myself!" and he said he'd be glad to continue seeing me without the exercises for a while but that he might want to refer me now to Dr. Walls and all I could think of was that I had to tell Terry. I've got to tell him.

And that was the last entry, and all the pages after it were empty, blank, blindingly white.

26

NORTH OF CAMDEN, near Belfast, they found a blazing white
Victorian inn in a residential neighborhood. It stood on high ground
with green candy-striped awnings and wisteria like huge dollops of ice
cream all over the front yard. Between the gables of the two houses
across the street, the bay window in their second-story room provided
a pie-slice view of the shimmering water. When Harvey opened the
sticky old windows, the white eyelet curtains flew up in the breeze.

They dozed and read and walked. On the way to dinner Saturday
night, Harvey had the curious urge to hold Mickey's arm on the
street, and when she felt his hand she patted it, like one of those little
gestures of gratitude that pass between elderly spouses surprised to
find themselves still together, and alive. On Sunday they awoke at
eight but fell back asleep for two more hours in each other's arms,
something they had not done for years. Harvey felt like they were
floating through a white-and-green dream in silence, broken only at
breakfast by the garrulous innkeeper with his pious stories of a city
life left behind and later by the rustling of the Sunday papers and the
veranda's wind chimes.

Only on Monday morning did he wake up again to his real life.
His eye went immediately to the composition book on the table next

to the Depression glass vase of dried wildflowers and lingered there until, it seemed, he had summoned again all of its dreary contents.

When he rose out of the billowy bed, Mickey, still sleeping soundly, acknowledged his departure with a mumbling moan. He dressed, had breakfast downstairs in the sunroom, and at the phone at the foot of the stairs made a credit-card call to the Edwards Hotel in Portland to see if anyone had left him a message.

"Yes sir," the clerk said after putting Harvey on hold for two minutes, "there's one message for you. From a Lieutenant Dombrow-ski on Saturday. His message was: 'EPA says nothing in soil but soil.' "

"Thank you."

"You're welcome, sir."

Mickey was still sleeping when he came back to the room, and he watched her breathe. They had crossed a line; well, anyway, *he* had crossed it. He wondered if this silence of the last two days was not in fact the calm before a domestic storm but was itself the next stage in their life together, the one he had always feared when he saw it in other couples, the look of resignation, like inmates staring out through the bars of life's prison. Even the best marriages dried out over time, like a piece of fruit shrunk to a more durable state. Had he and Mickey somehow achieved this without the benefit of marriage? He missed the days when they kept nothing from each other, when there was so much less to keep to themselves.

He sat in the chair by the window and fanned through Joan Johnson's diary. He thought of biographies, which he read avidly but always with the illicit feeling of having trespassed on time: How dare relive someone's entire life in a few hours? In biographies everything was so compressed, so anticipated; there was no sense of a life lived, blindly, fumblingly, from day to day. He dreaded that last chapter, with its inevitable death and final appraisal. He felt like an execu-tioner, with each turned page bringing the subject closer to oblivion.

Joan Johnson had decided her life would end at a certain moment, like you would decide to plunge into a cold lake or buy a dress you couldn't afford or screw up your nerve and talk to an attractive stranger. He wondered what it was like to decide that nothing was better than nothing at all. He shuddered at the thought. He would have to send the diary to Dombrowski soon. Otherwise he'd be a liar too. Lies made the world go around. It was the truth that stopped it cold. He would have to send Dombrowski the diary and tell him what he'd been doing with his time and leave the whole thing in his lap and call his brother, Norm, and tell him what kind of guy his friend Peplow had been but that he never had been able to figure out who killed him.

The message left by Dombrowski only confirmed what he had suspected. There was no toxic waste buried under Rimwood Estates. If Vaultt had killed Peplow, it was for another reason. Had Peplow nonetheless told Marilyn Barger that there was toxic waste? But what reason would he have for making up such a story? Why would Peplow wish to create the false impression that he was in a position to blackmail Jim Vaultt? He wouldn't. It wasn't Peplow who had lied about Rimwood Estates. It was Marilyn who had lied about Peplow.

Harvey took out his notebook and studied the list of names he'd made while reading the diary on Saturday. Carla. Peter. Bobby. Emmie.

He raised his head as Mickey turned to her other side and flattened a pillow over her head with her forearm.

Emmie. Strange spelling. Not Emily or Emmy, but Emmie.

Emmie.

Mickey stirred. How could he have toyed with her trust? What was wrong with him?

Em. Mie.

Em. Oh.

M. O.

As in M. O. Givens, the man who succeeded him in center field for the Providence Jewels.

Em. Mie.

M. E.

He felt suddenly queasy, his body already knowing what his brain was just putting together.

The hand towels.

The monogrammed hand towels in the Bargers' powder room in Dancedale, Illinois. Harvey had been drying his hands on one after escaping from Scott in the kitchen, and he had studied the monogram for a moment to make sense of it. And the initials on it had read "M. E. S. B."

Marilyn E. Samuels Barger. She had included her middle initial, so much a part of her childhood nickname. Emmie.

Harvey opened the diary again and quickly scanned for the mentions of Emmie. He had passed right by it the first two times he had read it.

*(Dr. P. agrees that I should "take it up" with him now, not her—*Joan's mother—*or even Emmie, who hardly ever calls.)* And later: *Emmie called the other night to make sure, as she put it, that I'm "doing okay" and she asked if I needed any money. I reluctantly accepted her offer because things are pretty tight and she's sending me a thousand. . . . I remember when I was a teenager and she came home late from a date and told me what it felt like to have a boy put his hand inside you and it was like listening to someone from a different planet.*

"Morning, Blissberg," Mickey said, yawning, from the bed.

"Morning."

"What's wrong?" she asked. "You look pale."

"Oh, it's nothing," he said, turning to the window. And the name Samuels, rather than Johnson. He had a pretty good idea where that came from.

27

"MA'AM," HARVEY WAS saying into the inn's phone, "you understand that I don't need a copy of the certificate itself? I just need a name that's on it? I'll still send you the fifteen-dollar check for your trouble. But I need the information *now*."

"It's not our policy to give out information over the phone," said the woman with the brittle voice at the town clerk's office in Bethlehem, Pennsylvania.

Mickey stood at the front door with their bags, looking peeved at the prospect of a four-hour drive back to Boston.

"Ma'am," Harvey said, "it was not this country's policy to sell arms to Iran and funnel the proceeds to the Nicaraguan contras, but people do make mistakes. I'm just asking you to slip up for a moment. For a good cause. Pretty please."

"You'll write a check today?"

"My checkbook's out. My pen is poised. The name again is Joan Johnson and she died a suicide on March nineteenth, 1987."

"One moment."

After a minute she came back on the line. "I have it in front of me."

"I really appreciate this."

"Just send the check. What is it you want to know?"

"The mother's birth name, please."

After a slight pause she said in a beleaguered voice, "Samuels. The mother's maiden name was Laura Samuels."

Bingo. Of course. Marilyn had changed her name, had taken her mother's birth name before college. She had not wanted to take her father's name out of the house with her.

"Thank you," Harvey said.

"Just send the check. Town Clerk's Office, Bethlehem. Here, let me give you the zip code again."

On the drive down Harvey needed silence, and Mickey, whether out of general irritability or intuitive courtesy, gave it to him. It was unusual for him not to share a case's discoveries with her, but this was not a case he would have relished discussing with her under any circumstances. He drove in an anxious trance, reading Marilyn's guilt back into everything that had happened between them. Terry must have phoned Marilyn right after first hearing from Harvey last week, called his dead girlfriend's sister to say that some private detective had just told him Peplow had been murdered in suburban Chicago and that he'd somehow gotten Terry's name. Because it was only an hour or two later that Marilyn had come to Harvey's hotel room again in one last bid to fog his glasses. He knew now why she hadn't bothered to ask him where he was going the next day—because Terry had as much as told her. Harvey wondered now whether Terry had come right out and asked Marilyn on the phone if she had killed Peplow. In any case, Harvey knew now why Terry had stonewalled him in Portland, stonewalled and protected Marilyn and then lied about sending the diary to Joan's mother.

In Portland he picked up the Toyota at Charlie's and returned it to National while Mickey followed in her car. Together they continued on to Boston in preoccupied silence, Mickey annotating transcripts for her documentary, Harvey still behind the wheel, figuring out how to mop up the case as well as cleanse his own soul. For beginners he would have to call Dombrowski when he got home and let him and his men handle the rest of the legwork.

In Cambridge he dropped Mickey off at WGBH and watched her disappear through the heavy glass door on Western Avenue. He went home to call the lieutenant.

"Where are you, son?"

"I'm back home in Cambridge."

"I left you a message in Portland."

"I got it this morning. Vaultt must really be sore the EPA did all that digging."

"Your friend Marilyn Barger's a liar."

"I know that."

"I'm trying to haul her in here for some questioning, but I can't find her, son. I'd really like to stick her with this. But she and her husband haven't been seen since last Wednesday."

"Doesn't surprise me, Lieutenant."

"Perhaps you would happen to know where they are?"

"No."

"I was hoping you would, seeing as you saw her last Tuesday night in your North Shore Suites Hotel room." His tone darkened. "Where you put your pecker's your own business, son, except when it's my business too. Where'd she say she was going?"

"She didn't."

"I'll can your ass, son, if you're withholding evidence or obstructing justice."

"Lieutenant, I don't know why you'd want to can the ass of the guy who's about to save your ass."

"What're you saying, son?"

"I'm saying I'm about to tell you why Marilyn E. Samuels Barger did Larry Peplow."

There was a silence on the other end of the phone that Harvey wanted to think of as respectful.

"I'm waiting, son," Dombrowski said.

"When Peplow was a shrink in Portland, he had a patient named Joan Johnson, a young woman whom he sexually abused over a period of three years while she was in treatment with him. When he told her he didn't want to have sex with her any longer she killed herself. She left behind a diary that leaves little doubt as to what happened. When Johnson's boyfriend finally went to a lawyer and Peplow was threatened with an investigation, he simply pulled up stakes and started over in Coleridge, Illinois, as a real estate agent. But as his bad luck would have it, he moved a few miles from Johnson's older sister and only sibling, Marilyn Barger."

After a moment's pause, Dombrowski said, "You sneaky son of a bitch."

"I have the diary. I'll Express Mail it to you today."

"You're sure she pulled the trigger?"

"If you'd read the diary, you'd be capable of it too."

"How'd you get it?"

"It was sent to me anonymously, postmarked Rice Lake, Wisconsin. I'm sure it was Marilyn."

"Just kind of fell in your lap then, son?"

"Hey, don't get snippy, Lieutenant. I never claimed to be good."

"Don't be so damn sensitive, son."

"Anyway, for your information, one of the numbers in Peplow's address book that you guys couldn't track down was the Portland number of Peplow's former shrink. He coughed up the name of the suicide's boyfriend, Terry Charette. I think he thought the boyfriend had done it. Charette coughed up the tragic past for me. But it took the diary for me to make the connection to Marilyn."

"You think she wants to come in from the cold?"

"Who knows? Maybe the diary was just her farewell gift to me and the woman could be deep into Canada by now. What I think is, Charette must've told her I knew too much to be stopped, that it was only a matter of time before I figured out it was her. Though the fact is I was too dumb to get it without the diary. Which Marilyn probably sent me just to fill me in on the mitigating factors. You know, just for the record. I don't think she's going to gift wrap herself and show up at the station with a big bow on her ass."

"Thanks for the advice, but I've already entered a warrant for her arrest in NCIC and I'm about to ask the local feds to issue a UFAP."

"Good luck."

"I take back all the things I said about you, son."

"What things?"

"When you weren't around."

"Well, you're welcome, Lieutenant. Now listen. Call this guy Charette first. I'm sure he's been in touch with her all along. But don't sweat him too hard. He's been a pretty good scout."

"Son, there's some things you haven't told me."

"I've pretty much laid it out there for you, Walter."

"No, sir. According to my records here, you had one lunch with Marilyn Barger and she came to see you twice at your hotel and God knows how many other times you saw her and you haven't had the courtesy, the common decency, to tell me if the wiggly was any good."

"Lieutenant," he said, "I'm surprised your desk isn't covered by now with tasty surveillance photos."

"Fat chance. Anyway, son, I'm sure if the wiggly was any good you'll be hearing from her, in which case I'll be hearing from you. Is that clear?"

Afterward Harvey sat in his leather chair, staring at a wall of built-in bookshelves on which his and Mickey's libraries were hopelessly mingled. Then he went out to pick up the mail. In the kitchen he put the unopened mail aside and unscrewed a glass jar of anchovies. Only a jar in which the anchovies had been packed upright would do. You could never trust those cheap tinned anchovies. He pulled out eight or ten fillets and coarsely chopped them. He diced a small Vidalia onion and scraped it all onto a plate. He sliced a lemon and squeezed both halves of it through a strainer over the mixture. His mouth was already watering. He broke up a sheet of matzo into smaller pieces and fanned them out on the edge of the plate and took it back to his study with a glass of Juicy Juice cut with seltzer. Anchovy and onions. The recipe had come from his mother's Estonian side, a dark and salty family secret that trickled down from one generation to the next. With a fork he carefully placed some on a piece of matzo, leaned back in his chair, and chewed contemplatively. As Norm liked to say, "Anchovy and onions! What could be better?"

After phoning Jerry Bellaggio to arrange to pick up Duane and Bubba later, he called his mother in Natick.

"Mom, I just thought you'd like to know, I'm sitting here eating anchovies and onions."

"Oh, honey, all that salt's no good for you." She seemed to have forgotten all about the dish's sentimental value.

"But, Mom, it's kind of a tradition."

"Traditions can give you heart disease as good as anything else."

Harvey tacked. "I just saw Norm in Chicago."

"How's his weight?"

"His weight's fine, Mom."

"How's Mickey, honey?"

"She's great."

"Did she fit into that blouse I sent her? She can always take it back and exchange it if she doesn't like it. I won't be hurt. What were you doing in Chicago?"

"Norm asked me to help him out with something."

"What?"

"A friend of his was in trouble. No big deal."

"That's all you're telling me?"

"I helped him straighten something out. That's all."

"You know, when you boys were little you used to go out and come back giggling and covered with mud and you'd never tell me where you'd been. And you're still not telling me."

"Boys will be boys."

"I'm an old woman, Harvey. I'd like to know what it is that boys do when they're being boys."

"Use your imagination, Mom. Listen, you want to come into Cambridge for dinner with Mickey and me on Saturday? We haven't seen you for a few weeks."

"I thought you'd never ask."

"So we'll see you then."

"No, you won't. A couple of the girls from the temple and I are going to see *Forbidden Broadway* in town on Saturday night."

"How about Sunday night?"

"If you insist."

Harvey put the mail in his lap and separated out the envelopes of junk mail. That left a handful of bills and a single square envelope, addressed to him in hand-lettered Chancery script. What a quaint artifact in this day and age a handwritten letter was, he thought, holding it by a corner. It had no return address. If Michele Slavin's name had been on the envelope as well, he would have suspected one of those art-opening or film-screening invitations that came Mickey's way as a perk of the media professions. Perhaps some distant cousin of his was getting hitched. He sliced open one end. Inside was a single white vellum card and on it, written in the same mellifluous Chancery, was the following:

Come to a Surprise Party!

A Very Special Get-Together
And You're Invited!

June 18th at 11 p.m. Sharp
1635 Tander Avenue
Coleridge, Illinois

No RSVP Necessary   *Come As You Are — And Alone*

Suburban Chicago

28

THE CLAPBOARD COTTAGE at 1635 Tander was still unrented. Harvey, standing in the shadows on its wraparound porch, peered through the gaping windows, as if hoping to catch a last glimpse of Laurence Peplow. In Dot and Abe Chernoff's tall Victorian next door, a single light burned in a second-story bedroom window, shielded by a maple bough.

He had taken the last flight out of Logan to O'Hare, picked up a car—a bulbous Ford Taurus—and driven straight to the address on the invitation. Two weeks ago, when he had first stood on this porch, knowing nothing, chatting with Dot Chernoff, the house had seemed so rich with mystery. Coleridge, Garden Hills, Dancedale, Wahatan— when they all had been hiding something, it seemed they existed for his benefit. But the geography had been reduced by what he now knew to be little more than places he had once been. It seemed to him that Larry Peplow's murder, now virtually solved, had been absorbed back into the routine workings of the world.

A Plymouth Voyager passed on Tander, going east toward the lake. He tilted his wrist and saw that it was now after eleven. He lit a Lucky, dragged, extended his lower lip, and fired a geyser of smoke straight over his head. Why had he come back? To finish the job? He *had* finished it. But Marilyn Barger had something more to tell him.

It was the promise of new information he couldn't resist. Then a new thought occurred; not new, actually, but he had managed to suppress it for a few days. What if it hadn't been Marilyn who squeezed the trigger, but Scott, whom she was protecting? No, she simply wasn't the type. Harvey remembered now the logic he had used yesterday: that, of the two acts—taking a second to fire a gun or spending a lifetime passively protecting a man she didn't really love—Marilyn Barger would find it far easier to commit the former.

Where was she? The possibility that he was being stood up occurred to him for the first time. Stood up . . . or set up? Suddenly, he felt injected with fear. There was a cool, swarming sensation in his veins. His eyes shot left and right, scanning the silent street. Then, as he moved deeper into the shadows of the porch, feeling a few soft planks underfoot, he saw what he had obviously been intended to see right away—another white envelope, just like the first one, stuck like a hankie in the mailbox mounted by the front door. He opened it and inclined the card toward the milky streetlight.

Welcome! So glad you could make it!
Let's party hearty or at least try to fake it!
Three blocks west, then south for one block,
I'll see you under the library clock.

One long block west of the cottage the business district began and Harvey walked along the Tudor storefronts, past the crackling neon in the optometrist's window, past the dress shop's headless vamping mannequins. He turned at the drugstore and headed south past the record store, the delicatessen where hard salamis hung like stalactites over the giant jars of sour tomatoes, the gift shop with its lazy Susan of Precious Moments figurines. Suddenly, an Isuzu Trooper loaded with teens peeled around a corner on the other side of the Chicago and Northwestern train tracks and screeched off, yelps fading into the night.

The Coleridge Public Library was a buff sandstone building surrounded by topiary. A glass-enclosed sign on the lawn advertised in movable black letters a July lecture series on Shakespeare's tragedies by a Barat College professor. Above the entrance a round Longines clock shone like a pale moon. As Harvey looked up, its long black hand trembled, then jerked silently and stiffly forward a minute. He sat on the top step, feeling his little Smith & Wesson in its clip holster press into his side just above the belt. At eleven-twenty a northbound train of double-decker cars, full of bright yellow windows like a miniature city, rumbled into the restored Victorian train station a block away. When it clattered away, it left a single man in a suit on the platform.

When Harvey returned his glance to the street that ran in front of the library, he was startled to find a dark red Subaru sedan idling by the curb. A woman with corn-colored hair cropped as short as a boy's rested her elbow on the edge of the car window and said in a stage whisper, "Get in."

He came down the stone steps, climbed in the passenger side, and looked at Marilyn. The effect was confusing. Lightened and plucked eyebrows, heavy eyeliner, and frosted yellow lipstick that almost matched her new hair color had given her a hard, tarty look. She wore a simple sleeveless white blouse and blue-jean cutoffs. The dashboard lights cast a greenish glow on her flawless thighs, which held an open can of Meister Bräu between them.

A buzzing sensation danced through him, which he thought was fear. "I hardly recognize you," he said.

"You never recognized me."

"Well, you didn't want me to. You lied about everything."

"Oh, come on, Harvey, not everything."

"You even lied about where you went to high school."

"You still didn't want to know me." Her voice was different, too; it had lost its suburban lilt. It was as if she didn't have to pretend anymore. Harvey wondered if all of this—even the yellow hair—might be the original Marilyn Johnson of Bethlehem, Pennsylvania.

"Maybe," he said.

"But now you would." She put the car in drive. "Why else would you travel a thousand miles for a party?"

That's right, he thought ruefully. A thousand miles, and for what? Even now, she was getting him to do what she wanted. She drove under the viaduct and through the sleeping suburban business district.

"So this is how it happened," he said. "You had him meet you at the library."

"Well, I sure as hell wasn't going to chance the neighbors. It's funny, he was sitting on the steps waiting for me, just like you. Beer?" She yanked a can of Meister Bräu from the six-pack next to her on the seat and held it toward him.

"No thanks. Where we going?"

"Anyway, after all that time I wasn't about to blow it. I'd been like toying with him forever." She drove west, past the camera store with the big Kodak families in the window. "But he didn't mind. It takes one to know one."

"It takes one what?"

"People who use people. I mean really use them. We're like a secret fraternity. Don't bother to apply, Harvey. I called him and said, 'My husband's out of town, it's a nice night out, let's go for a drive. Let's go look at Rimwood again. Get a feel for it at night.' "

The buzzing sensation went through him again, and this time he knew what it was. Not fear, but longing. He wanted her to pull off the road and stop so he could smell her, taste her. The urge that had bypassed every other consideration, had crashed through every moral roadblock, and headed straight for his pants. Is this why he had come back? He waited till the sensation subsided, like a chill.

"And you knew he'd say yes?" he asked her.

She shot a glance at him. "Are you kidding? By then he was dying for me. He'd been dying for me since that first time we met, when he showed us the houses. When Scott was in another room, I remember I asked him if he was single, but I asked him in a certain way. So that he like knew. I had it written all over my walk. Guys fall for all sorts of shit."

They had left Coleridge's business district. It was remarkable how little life was left in a suburb at night. It was as quiet as a prairie again. She drove at an easy thirty miles an hour, sipping Meister Bräu. "It was the most incredible few weeks of my life. I had so much power, Harvey. I knew every detail, 'cause that's what Joanie left me. She like left me the knowledge. And he had no idea. He just thought I wanted to play grab-ass with him."

They were on Route 40 now, under a dense dark cloudy sky perforated here and there to let the stars through. "I did run into him at the mall," she said. "I just want you to know I wasn't lying about that part. Only he didn't mention toxic waste. Sorry about that—it was the best I could do under the circumstances. Would you like to know what really happened at the mall? You know what I told him?"

Harvey glanced in the sideview mirror and saw no cars behind them. "Tell me."

"I told him I'd once made love with a guy in a fitting room. I swear to God, he was actually licking his lips. He was like doing a fast idle." Then her voice dropped low. "But I never touched him. Not once. You must understand that. I never put so much as a finger on the guy. Will you tell me you believe that?"

"Yes, I believe it."

"I never touched him. The thought of what he'd done to my little sister was never out of my mind for a second. You don't think I touched him, do you?"

"No, I don't think you did."

"Okay. So, anyway, by April seventeenth, he was ready for anything and everything with me."

"You haven't told me how you found him in the first place."

"Oh, that. I didn't. He found me. That's the incredible part. Sometime this past February the *Coleridge Weekly* ran a picture of him as the North Shore's 'Real Estate Agent of the Month' or some shit. The guy *was* a born salesman, wasn't he? I'm sitting there at the beauty salon waiting for my toenail polish to dry and suddenly I'm looking at Joanie's murderer. That's how I'd always thought of him. He'd slowly poisoned her. He removed the life from her, a little bit at a time, until she was dead. Suddenly I'm looking at the guy. It's like he'd been delivered to me for justice. I couldn't believe my luck. For a couple of months I just thought about it, letting it grow inside." She pulled on the beer.

"When my hate was big enough," she said, "I called him and said I was looking for a house." She turned left onto Sky View Road. "A happy house."

"Quite a coincidence, you two ending up within a few miles of each other."

"God must've been cutting me a little slack."

"Right in your own backyard."

"Well, you know what they say about real estate: location, location, and location." She blurted another hollow laugh. "Still, you have to remember we were in neighboring towns for four years and didn't know it."

"Do you think Peplow might've gravitated here—you know, unconsciously? He must've known Joan had a sister in Chicago. You think he came here to, you know, get what was coming, in a manner of—"

She waved away the hypothesis. "I had to listen to all his lies, Harvey, all his phony stories. But I loved it. I truly, truly loved it. One of the best times I've ever had. Because I knew the ending."

On Sky View they passed under some trees, strangled by bittersweet. "And this is the route you took."

"He was sitting right where you are in his nice ironed alligator shirt."

"By now you'd told him who you were?"

She glared at him. "What, are you out of your mind? You think I'd be crazy enough to blow the suspense? No way. We were just talking. I said something like, 'I bet you think I'm a little forward, don't you, taking you for a drive?' And he said, 'I can handle it,' and I say, 'I'll bet a shrink learns how to handle all sorts of tricky situations.' And he looked a little stunned and he said, 'How'd you know I was once a shrink?' And I'm like, 'I like to know things about people I like.' I said, 'I'll bet you know how to handle all sorts of situations, like when patients fall in love with you and shit like that.' And when I said that, he kind of looked at me. He was starting to get the message. But that old dick of his was saying, 'Full speed ahead.' "

"Did she look like you?" he asked after a moment.

After another moment, and without looking over: "She was prettier."

She slowed at the gate to Rimwood Estates, cut her headlights down to the parking lights, and turned up the drive. Harry took another look in the sideview. No cars. He touched the butt of his Smith & Wesson through his shirt. He looked at her in the green interior light of the car and didn't think she could have a weapon concealed on her person. Ahead, the houses were dark. He could just barely make out the ink stains the trees made against the sky.

"Some party," he said.

"I've gone to a lot of trouble, Harvey. So have you."

"You knew I'd come?"

"Oh, c'mon, I knew you couldn't resist," she said, letting Harvey know that she knew she'd scored by the way she left the remark dangling in the dark. She eased the Subaru to a stop just off the drive about fifty feet in front of Rimwood Estates' gate. She killed the engine and the parking lights, plunging them into near blackness.

Harvey looked around. Even if Vaultt was home he was at the far end of the development, well out of earshot.

"I figured you'd want to put the last piece in place," she said.

"What piece is that?" With the engine off, the night started to pulse with crickets.

"The piece I'm going to show you. I think of you as a guy who likes to get to the finish line. Like, I thought you'd appreciate the scavenger-hunt angle tonight. You're a scavenger. Did you appreciate it?"

"Very much."

"You want the prize. That's one reason I thought you'd come."

He could barely make out her silhouette. "There's another reason?"

"I knew you'd want to hand me over yourself. Show Dombrowski who's boss."

"I've got nothing against him."

"But it'd still be nice to finish the job, wouldn't it?"

"Is that what you're going to let me do tonight, Marilyn? Take you in peacefully?"

"I don't know. Maybe I'd like you to help me escape."

"Couldn't do that, Marilyn."

"Teach me how to disappear, Harvey. I couldn't stand prison."

"But you sent me the diary, Marilyn."

"Yeah, and I also told Terry he might as well talk to you. I wanted you to know the truth, Harvey. But that's different from wanting to pay the price."

"But you killed a man, Marilyn."

"And it was easier than I thought." She leaned her head back against the seat. "Oh, I don't know. Sometimes I feel like I could just check out of my life, like Joanie. But, of course, you know, that's not really my style. I fight back."

Now she twisted her face to Harvey. "See, Joanie and I were like the same hurt girl. You know, I've had years to think about this. *I* saw shrinks too." She exhaled audibly. "Only I despised my pain more. That's what saved me. Joanie was too sweet for all that. She kept it inside. That was her nature. Me, I just turned it back on the

world. You ever wonder about that—how one kid can go through
something like this and turn out one way, and another kid in the same
family goes through it and turns out the opposite?"

"Maybe."

"Daddy fucked both of us, but I learned to fuck back. Joanie kept
getting screwed. But don't get me wrong, I didn't escape. I've always
struck out with that little thing people like to refer to as 'normal,
healthy human relationships.' You know, my marriage to Scott . . .
Let's just say he's as damaged in his own way as I am. Anyway, sex is
the only way I ever knew to make things better, make the pain go
away. It's how I tried to make the pain go away with you."

"Well, I admit it slowed me down."

"Yeah, well, it has its limits." She drained her can of Meister
Bräu, dropped it at her feet, and opened a fresh one. "Tell me,
Harvey: Isn't it touching I plan parties for a living? So *other* people
can have a good time? But at least I'm here, rather than there"—
Harvey could just make out that she was gesturing toward the
sky—"or wherever we all go when it's over."

Then he heard her take a hard swallow of beer and say, "I love
you, Joanie."

He could hear her tears in the darkness, and now he felt ashamed,
deeply ashamed. He had thought her trivial until now, a troubled
housewife, a sexual curiosity, as if those judgments would put some
valuable distance between him and his desire for her, as if there were
people with whom things didn't quite count. To preserve Mickey's
place, he had had to devalue Marilyn. But she had become real, and
what he had wanted to see as peculiarity was actually damage. Who
among us could point a gun at an unarmed human being—whatever
his offense—and pull the trigger? He looked at Marilyn's form in the
dark and considered how gravely mistaken he had been about her.
Was this why he had come, to be punished for his illusions?

"You never know what people look like on the inside," he
said, feebly.

She sucked back some beer, not hearing him. "I had a blanket in the backseat."

"You what?"

"I had a blanket in the backseat and I said to him, 'Real estate makes me horny. Let's go out in the field.' "

"Where'd you get the gun, Marilyn?"

"Scott. He was Special Forces once. A Green Beret. You didn't know that, did you? Just used it for target practice. Over at a range in Dancedale."

"So he knew?"

"No, he didn't know anything until a week after I killed him. I mean, I never even told Scott who the guy was until he came into the kitchen one night a week after I did it and he asked me if I had been using his gun. And then I told him what I had done, and he exploded. He completely unloaded on me. And you know something? I think that's the first time I realized he actually loved me. And let me tell you, *that* scared me. You know, he couldn't believe I would do what I did and put our marriage in any real danger. Because I don't think he can bear the thought of being without me."

"So that afternoon when he invited me in for a beer, he was just sizing me up?"

"Yeah."

"But he couldn't do better than a threatening phone call to my girlfriend?"

"Well, yeah, you know, he didn't want to do anything rash and run the risk of getting put away without me."

"Where's Scott right now?"

"I left him up in—where we're staying now. I told him I had to come back here to pick up some stuff."

"So you intend to go back?"

"I have to be free, Harvey."

"I can't let you go, Marilyn."

"Yes, you can. I know you can. You know what he said?"

"Who?"

"He said, 'Real estate makes me horny too.' "

"Oh. You mean Peplow."

"Yeah. Him." Then she said, "Let's go."

"Marilyn, I've already seen where you did him."

"I want to make it real for you."

"It's pretty damn real already."

She left the beer on the dash and opened the car door. "Not real enough."

29

HE MADE MARILYN walk in front of him out into the black field, the beam from her nine-volt flashlight bouncing ahead in the dry grass. After thirty feet she stopped, and Harvey stopped with her. Her words came in a hard monotone, like something made by a machine. "I asked him if he remembered Joan Johnson. And he looked real confused. And said did I know her? And I said real well, we grew up together. As a matter of fact in the same family. And then he swallowed real hard. And he said now that you mention it I see a resemblance. And he said with that polish of his, you know I wish I could have done more to help her.

"And I looked at him and said like what—screw her twice a week instead of once? And he said, 'You don't know what you're talking about.'"

It sounds just like something Frederick Walls would say, Harvey thought.

"And I said, 'Aren't you forgetting about the diary? You're a very sick man. You need to be put out of your misery.' Then I showed him the gun. And he started sweating and said, 'Hey, look, I'm sorry. I've made amends. I left the profession. I didn't come here and hang out a new shingle as some sort of therapist.' And I said, 'You think you're supposed to get credit for that?' He could've been Mother Teresa's fiancé and I still would've shot him. He said, 'You're not going to shoot me, are you?' And I said, 'Hey, if I had the time to kill you slowly over three years, just like you killed Joanie, I'd do it. But, you know, I've got to get on with my life.'

"He's like, 'Let me explain about the diary.' And I said, 'Don't tell me—you're going to say she made it up, she was hallucinating. I'm not interested. Listen, you motherfucker,' I said, 'you killed the sanest person in my family.' And he was saying, 'I'll do anything, just don't hurt me, okay, I'll do anything.' He was already pissing down his leg. 'You didn't think you could get away with it, did you?' I said and he's like, 'It was a mistake, a horrible mistake, I'll do anything to make it up, blah blah blah.' "

Marilyn started walking again, and Harvey followed, the grass crushing quietly with each footstep.

"Yes?" he said.

"What?"

"Then what happened?"

Marilyn stopped again and pivoted. "And then I went bang," she said calmly.

"Marilyn—" Harvey started to say.

"And now it's time to meet the other guest," she said, raising the flashlight.

"Guest?" His stomach contracted. Why had he come? "Marilyn, what's going on?" Norm must be right, he thought; he liked to feel the lion's breath.

The narrow beam moved forward slowly across the black grass until it found a pair of cheap running shoes twenty feet away, and then the beam moved up a pair of jiggling legs in chinos, and finally it shone in the empty, blinking face of an old man he had never seen before, strapped into a wheelchair in the middle of the field, wearing a blue Ban-Lon shirt buttoned up under his chin. He stared at them with watery, startled eyes. On his head, ridiculously, there was a silver conical paper party hat secured under his badly shaven chin with an elastic string.

"Is that you, Laura?" the man said, hunched in his aluminum crate.

"Now, now, Daddy, you know Mom's dead," she said and then turned to Harvey. "Alzheimer's. Later stages."

He remembered. She and Scott had gone to visit him two weekends ago. My dad has Alzheimer's, she'd told him on the phone, that always puts me in a foul mood. It was one of the few times she had told him the truth. On Sky View Road he heard a couple of cars pass, murmuring on the asphalt.

"I'm scared," Marilyn's father said as she teased his face with the flashlight's beam.

"Don't be," Marilyn said, leading Harvey closer. "Here, I just wanted to introduce you to a friend of mine, Daddy."

"How're my Phillies doing?" her father said in an agitated tone. "What's Richie Ashburn batting?" If there was a family resemblance, Harvey could only pretend to detect it in the same short nose and high cheekbones.

"He thinks it's the 1950s," she said to Harvey. "Him and his damn Philadelphia Phillies. He can't remember that he fucked his own daughters, but he remembers some guy named Ashburn. Daddy, say hello to Harvey. He wants to arrest me."

"You just left him here?" Harvey said. It was madness, leaving the man in the middle of a field at night.

"You think that's cruel?" she said, shining the beam directly in her father's eyes. "Daddy, why don't you tell Harvey something about cruelty?"

"Where's Laura?" said the old man.

"Laura's dead, Daddy. And so's Joanie. It's just you and me now."

"Who?" her father croaked.

"What's the point of this?" Harvey said. He thought he heard a car slow on Sky View near the Rimwood Estates entrance.

Marilyn ignored him, saying: "There was a moment in college when I thought I ought to do something to help her. She was thirteen when I went away, more than old enough to replace me, you know, and I assumed. . . . You know, Joanie had written me, in a kind of code, we never talked about it, really, there's like always this totally insane conspiracy of silence with these things. So I thought I ought to save her, but, you know, it was exam period, I had a boyfriend now, and, you know, I like left her at his mercy. . . ."

"Get the damn light out of my face," the old man said.

"Shut up, Daddy," she said over her shoulder. "You know, I chose to believe whenever possible that he wasn't doing to her what he had done to me." Now she walked over, stood by the wheelchair, and put her hand on the back of her father's neck. "But you were, Daddy, weren't you?" she said. "You little piece of shit."

"How're my Phillies doing?"

"I remember him crawling into my bed with his stinking feet. Remember what it was like to stumble through school like a zombie with my horrible secret. You can't know what it's like to go through your life carrying a thing like him around in your head. What he had done, what he was going to do next. Why you were always separated from others. Look at him now. Harvey, what kind of God is it who gives this man Alzheimer's while I have to keep remembering?"

"Why don't we get him out of here and back to wherever he belongs?" Harvey said. The night was full of little noises now, crickets and rustling breezes and cars passing on Sky View and what he thought might be footsteps crackling in the grass.

"But that's not the worst part. I did more for Daddy than I ever did for Joanie," she said. "That's the worst part, Harvey. After Mom died and Daddy couldn't put his own pants on and there was no one to look after him, when he didn't even know anymore that you're supposed to wear pants when you go outside, I brought him here from Bethlehem, the little piece of shit. I brought him here and Scott and I broke our piggy banks and put him in a place in Wahatan where they take terrific care of him. What kind of person looks after a father who fucked her and fucked her sister and I never, ever, not for a fucking moment, Harvey, did I ever step in to protect her, not for an instant, and say, 'You may've fucked me, Daddy, but you're not going to touch her'? I could've called the cops! I could've called the social services people! I could've brought her to Champagne–Urbana to live with me on a mat in my dorm! I could've done anything, but I didn't. But as soon as Daddy starts walking around his neighborhood in his boxer shorts, I'm on the case! Marilyn to the rescue! I could scream! How am I supposed to live with myself?"

"I don't like it here," the old man whined.

"Shut the fuck up, Daddy," she said, squeezing hard on the back of his neck.

"Ouch!" he cried.

"I could've called some agency. I used to bathe Joanie when she was a baby! I taught her to read! What insanity made me take *him* over *her*?"

"Let's go," Harvey said. "Let's get him out of here."

"I did something horrible to Joanie."

"Stop blaming yourself."

"I'm talking about something else. I'm talking about Terry." She sobbed deeply, hoarsely sucking in air.

"Don't cry," the man in the wheelchair said.

"Charette?" Harvey said. She said nothing, and in the silence he remembered the passage in Joan's diary. It was amazing what your brain could produce in a pinch. The day Joan stayed home and Marilyn, who was visiting, went to some fair in New Brunswick with Terry. "You slept with him?" Harvey asked.

"Just once," she said, running her hand through her cropped yellow hair. "Just once. I had to kill him!" she said through clenched teeth. "I had to kill him because, as you can see, Daddy's already dead! Aren't you, Daddy? Harvey! I had to do something! I had to protect Joanie, just once! You remember Joanie, don't you, Daddy?

No, of course not. You don't remember anything. Even so, Daddy, you don't want your oldest girl to go to prison, do you?"

"Take me home," the old man said. "Please take me home."

"It's time to go, Marilyn." Harvey felt that Dombrowski was near now.

She was standing behind her father with both hands on his shoulders near his neck, and for an instant Harvey thought she might be about to strangle him, but instead she dropped to her knees next to the wheelchair and cried, "Daddy." Her flashlight lay at her side on the grass, its beam pointed meaninglessly into the night. "Daddy!" she cried, "what did you do to your little babies?"

Harvey went to Marilyn and tried to pull her up.

She swung her elbow, striking Harvey sharply in the chest. "Get your hands off me!" she sobbed.

Harvey rubbed his stinging sternum. "Marilyn," Harvey said, "please let's get him out of here. This is crazy."

At that precise moment, Harvey was silenced by the cool touch of metal against his skin behind his right ear.

A voice said, "Don't talk, don't scream, don't move. That's a Colt forty-five you feel against your skull. Please just follow my directions. Put your hands on your head."

"Scott!" Marilyn said with alarm. "What're you doing?"

"Hate to be a party pooper, hon."

"Scottie, please!"

"You wouldn't listen, hon."

Scott moved directly behind Harvey; now he felt the gun's touch at the center of the base of his neck. Scott frisked his upper body with his free hand, quickly finding Harvey's Smith & Wesson under his shirt and removing it from the clip holster, saying, "I don't think you'll be needing this." Harvey could smell his beery breath. Then Scott Barger knelt and frisked Harvey's legs.

How could he be so stupid? He tried to make sense of Scott's arrival. It was hard to believe that Marilyn had set him up—drawn him back to Chicago first with the diary, her token of good faith, then with the cute invitation—in order to have him killed. There was no profit in it. She hadn't wanted him dead, just well informed. She must have assumed he had already figured out that she was Peplow's killer before sending him the diary to fill in the gaps in the story. And now she wanted him to see this, her father, so she would feel acquitted in his eyes. But why had she told Scott where she'd be? Why had she risked this scene?

It now occurred to Harvey that Scott might want to kill him because Marilyn had told her husband about the two of them. Perhaps Scott thought she loved Harvey, and it was a thought he couldn't tolerate.

"Don't hurt him, Scottie," he heard Marilyn say.

The prospect of his extinction was like a terrible, cheesy taste in his mouth. His heart thumped in its cage. He felt weak, as though his bones were gradually dissolving and soon would no longer support him. Maybe Scott had acquired the knack of killing in Vietnam, and this execution would be relatively easy for him, over in a minute. On the perimeter of Harvey's vision, Scott's arm seemed to quaver. Harvey tried to rise above the fear to weigh his options. Reason first.

"It makes no sense, Scott," he said. "You're not thinking."

"Put the gun away, Scottie," Marilyn said. "Harvey didn't do anything."

He stepped back from Harvey, swiveled, and now the gun was aimed at his father-in-law's head. "Then maybe I'll just put *this* shithead out of his misery." He rotated like a turret and covered Harvey again. "Don't get any ideas." He spun back to Marilyn's father. "Say your prayers, Pop."

"Don't!" Marilyn shouted.

"Shut up, hon," he yelled.

Marilyn placed herself between the gun and her bewildered father. Scott Barger turned again, his Colt .45 trained once again on Harvey, who had turned and now looked down its barrel.

"Put the gun down, Scott," Marilyn said.

Scott looked from one to the other, stymied. It was as if he had forgotten his lines.

Harvey thought that in his confusion Scott might actually lay down his piece, but instead he ordered Harvey down on his knees. "And keep your hands on your head," he said.

"It won't work, Scott," Harvey said, lowering himself to the grass.

"Of course it'll work," Scott Barger said. "Because I've got a gun."

"If you use it, you'll be dead yourself within seconds. You may be dead even before."

"What's that supposed to mean?"

"You don't really think I'd show up tonight all alone?"

"I don't know what you're talking about."

"C'mon, Scott. I called the Coleridge police from Boston. I called Lieutenant Dombrowski again from O'Hare tonight. I told him where I'd be and he's been tailing me all night. They're here."

"You're lying."

"They'll shoot you through the head if you don't drop the gun." Where was Dombrowski when he needed him? Why had he thought that a rinky-dink suburban police force could protect him?

"Bullshit. They don't even know you're here."

"If you don't believe they're here, why don't you just take Marilyn and her father and go? I can't stop you now."

"No."

"I'm telling you the truth, Scott. Go. I'm not in your way. Just fucking go."

"I'm hungry, Laura," the old man at Harvey's side said. Marilyn was sobbing.

"It's bullshit. You're lying," Scott said. "If the cops were here, they'd *be* here."

"The dumb money's on you. If you hurt me, you go away, Scott. Is that what you want?"

"I want Marilyn."

"Then take her and go." However, Harvey heard sounds in the grass and he knew it was too late. "But drop the damn gun, Scott."

"No."

"Drop it."

"Forget it."

"Scott, no one wants to see anything bad happen to you. Drop the gun."

And suddenly they all lit up in a police floodlight, bright as day, and a voice boomed through a bullhorn:

"Drop the gun! This is the police. Drop the gun now! Drop the gun and get down on your stomach! Put your hands behind your back! Now! Now! You have three seconds and we're firing." It was Dombrowski's amplified voice.

"Drop it," Harvey said to Scott.

Scott lowered the gun, but hesitated, and suddenly a shot rang out and Harvey's bowels twisted, but everyone remained where they were. It had been a warning shot, but it got Scott to finally drop the gun and lie down on his stomach next to Harvey in the deep grass with his hands clasped behind him.

"That's better," said Dombrowski's amplified voice.

Dombrowski and six uniformed Garden Hills officers converged on Barger out of the darkness from several directions and covered him with their service revolvers while Dombrowski cuffed his hands behind his back. Scott was burbling now, his ashen face pressed against the earth.

Harvey got to his feet and said, "Jesus, Lieutenant, what's the big hurry? Whyn't you just let him hold the fucking gun to my head for another hour or two? I was just starting to like it."

"Don't complain, son. You're still breathing." Dombrowski said. "Besides, only the good die young." He turned to address a geeky-looking officer with long, hickish sideburns: "Read him his rights, Tommy." Tommy read Scott his rights, and then another two officers helped him up and led him away to a squad car concealed by the night.

"I'll be right back," Dombrowski said to Harvey now and handed him back his Smith & Wesson. He indicated Marilyn ten feet away. "Watch her. She's in your custody till I come back." Then he hiked up his pants and followed Scott to the car.

Harvey, still trembling, went over to Marilyn, who stood with her hands on the handles of her father's wheelchair.

"I couldn't run," Marilyn said with a fresh sob. "I'm all he's got left."

It took Harvey an instant to realize she was talking about her father.

"By the way, thanks for inviting Scott to the party," Harvey said. "Thanks for almost getting me killed."

"I didn't invite him. He must've followed us. Oh, well." She laughed, and the laugh became a sob. "My God. People fuck you up. They fuck you up for your whole life, but in the end all you can think of is what *you* did wrong."

Dombrowski was now lumbering toward them.

"Marilyn, Marilyn," Harvey said.

"Emmie," she whispered.

"What's the E. for?"

"Eve. Marilyn Eve Johnson. Who's all alone."

Dombrowski was standing in front of them in a dark blue western-style shirt, a flashlight dangling at his side.

"Ma'am," Dombrowski said with an oddly chivalrous nod.

Marilyn wiped her eyes with a forefinger. "Please don't handcuff me."

"I don't think that'll be necessary."

And while he recited her Miranda rights to her, Harvey felt her cold hand reach for his at his side and hold it tight until Dombrowski was through and led her away gently by the arm. Harvey followed, pushing the old man through the grass.

30

"I'M SORRY," NORM was saying to him from Chicago. "I couldn't've known."

"Every time I've talked to you in the last few weeks," Harvey said, "you apologize."

"What do you want? I almost got you killed."

"To die for you would've been an honor."

"Fuck you, Harv. At least send me your expenses. It'll relieve some of the guilt."

"All right. I'll shove my receipts in an envelope. I promise."

"Don't you think there's some way to throw another light on it?"

"Like what?" Harvey was pacing in his Cambridge study. It was mid-July.

"Okay. First, he was a bad therapist. Granted." Norm did not want to let it go.

"He wasn't a bad therapist," Harvey explained. "A bad therapist is someone you go to for years and at the end of that time you're still dating inappropriate women. Peplow destroyed Joan Johnson."

"But let's say he fell in love with this young woman. It took him by surprise. It elicited all his worst tendencies, this latent need to control and manipulate. Then he panicked. He started sinking in the quicksand."

"Norm, the guy was predatory. He violated this woman's trust, a professional code of ethics, every rule of common human decency, and he persisted in doing this for three years. Did you read the copy of the diary I sent you?"

"I looked at it."

"Read it, then talk to me."

"But, Harv, I knew this guy."

"This is not true. You did not know this guy. You played basketball with him. Which was different."

"He snapped, Harv. People snap. He made a terrible mistake. That doesn't indict his whole character."

"You don't get it, do you, Norm?"

"Harv, I'm not defending the guy, but I think your job has blinded you to some of the ambiguities of human nature."

"Has it? Norm, this is pissing me off. What the guy did was evil."

"Evil? You mean in the Hannah Arendt sense?"

Poor Norm. He wanted so badly to reconcile the Peplow who fed him the basketball on fast breaks with the Peplow who had mesmerized Joan Johnson. But Harvey, too, wanted to square the details of the case with a compassionate view of human nature. In retrospect, it was easy to impute malicious intent to Peplow's actions. But, in reality, one went step-by-step into the dark. You just lied to yourself. It took so little effort. When you lied to others, you had to keep your story straight, you had to keep a straight face.

"I saw her again on CNN last night," Norm was saying. "*Superb-looking woman. The *Trib* says she's going to go away for a long time."

Marilyn Barger had been booked and released on $750,000 bail. The requisite 10 percent had been raised among their friends by Scott, against whom Harvey had seen no good reason to press charges. Marilyn's case had gone to a Lake County grand jury in late June without a preliminary examination. The grand jury returned an indictment against her for first-degree murder. The key evidence consisted of her husband's Colt .45 semiautomatic, which matched the hollow-point bullet fragment retrieved by the Garden Hills Homicide Unit, and a sworn deposition signed by Harvey Blissberg and read to the grand jury by Lieutenant Walter Dombrowski. In it, Harvey had reconstructed the chief elements of his investigation and reported the defendant's voluntary confession to him on the night of her arrest. Following the grand jury indictment, Marilyn Barger's lawyer entered a not-guilty plea and then settled in to begin the process of plea-bargaining with the prosecuting attorney.

"No, she'll plea down to second-degree homicide, no sweat," Harvey told his brother. "In Illinois, that's four-to-fifteen. And let me tell you, after the judge reads her sister's diary, I'd be surprised if she gets more than six. She may even get the minimum and be out in two for good behavior."

"Hey, Harv."

"What?"

"I'm really grateful to you, man. I'm really proud of you, too."

"Thanks, Norm."

"Harv?"

"What, Norm?"

"To change the subject for a minute."

"Yes, Norm?"

"Can you name the four major league pitchers who have one hundred victories in *both* the American and National Leagues?"

"Norm, I've got a lot on my mind these days."

"All right. But, look, you think about it and let me know if you can come up with all four."

"Maybe when things ease up here. My mind's not on trivia at the moment."

"Hey, fine. Don't worry about it."

"Norm?"

"What?"

"Let me just say something to you. Nolan Ryan, Gaylord Perry, Jim Bunning, and Cy Young."

After a moment of silence, Norm said, "You're such a schmuck."

Harvey devoted most of July to helping Jerry Bellaggio with some routine "frequent flier" cases, people who didn't work but made a living going from one slip-and-fall workers' comp case to another. For one of them Harvey documented with his Nikon that a man claiming a disabling lower-back injury was nonetheless able to play a vigorous game of singles. It was plain-vanilla stuff, and Harvey threw himself into it, hoping to shield himself from the complex feelings he carried away from Chicago. He had even thought of calling the Maine branch of the American Psychiatric and the Maine Medical Board of Registration to inform them of Frederick Walls's role, but the urge passed. He needed to begin detaching. And, like Norm, he was trying to throw the best light on it. So he chose to conclude that Walls had failed to expose Peplow because he honestly believed it would have jeopardized the success of his treatment. Harvey had yet to receive a bill from him.

Harvey was surprised by how emotional Duane's recovery made him. In public he might scoff at a man's attachment to his pet, on the faulty premise that a man's capacity for loving animals was somehow deducted from his capacity for loving other humans. In private, though, with Duane purring on his chest, Harvey sensed the deepest and most quizzical exchange of sympathies. As soon as Duane was eating normally again, he adopted the touching habit of draping himself over Harvey's head in bed at night. Harvey would fall asleep with one arm over Mickey's flank and the sound of Duane's tiny, tireless heart beating gratefully against his ear.

Harvey gave Mickey a sanitized version of the facts of the Peplow case. In her face he saw a mixture of pride in his competence and distaste for the danger his work put her in. Moments of kindness passed between them, but they were still a little like courtesies extended from one diplomat to another while waiting for the official negotiations to begin.

By the end of the month, though, their evasions had finally

become too great a burden. In early August they drove north to spend a week in a rented house on a secluded island near Bar Harbor, Maine. Half an hour south of Portland, on 95, Mickey interrupted a silence that had prevailed literally since Portsmouth and figuratively for well over a month.

"Bliss? I have to tell you something."

Harvey tensed at the wheel, wondering if she had been quietly summoning the courage to leave him. But why do it at the beginning of a week away? His responsibilities at the wheel gave him an excuse not to look at her. "What is it?" he asked.

"While you were away on that case, I had a little thing with Paul. You know, Paul Sarnes. My executive producer."

He watched the heavy summer traffic on the highway. Why was it that he always felt a little humbled by her forthrightness? But thank God she'd fallen from grace too in recent weeks. It evened out the playing field. "How little a thing?" he asked.

"Relatively little."

"You slept with him?"

"Not really."

"Not really? C'mon, Mick, I'm looking for a yes or no."

"No, I didn't sleep with him, but we fooled around. We sort of—well, we sort of made out. He started coming on to me, very sweetly. It was so—it was like—" She sighed, and Harvey hoped it was from nervousness and not remembered joy.

"Like what?"

"Like he adored me."

Harvey didn't bother to comment. In the adoration department, he would have to concede victory to a colleague with a crush.

"We're talking about heavy petting?" he asked.

"Light to moderate."

"What is this, a traffic report? I'm asking you how far you went."

"It's immaterial, Bliss. I'm not going to give you a blow-by-blow. I don't adore this guy back. I let him caress me for a reason."

"Like what?"

"Like because I knew you were cheating on me in Chicago and I figured that the only way I could live with that and still be with you, which I want to be, was to go out and indulge myself a little."

"You mean a preemptive strike?"

"Not preemptive, because I sensed you had already struck. You had already struck, hadn't you? I've told you the truth, so it's your turn."

"There was a little something in Chicago."

"I knew it. How little?"

"Petting. Moderate to heavy."

"Ha! Please! C'mon, Bliss. I know guys. Tell me the truth. Saying you stopped at heavy petting is like Orson Welles saying he stopped after the soup course."

"I'm serious. We just fooled around."

"Once?"

"Twice."

"Who was she?"

"A woman."

"Yeah, I already figured that part out, Bliss. Tell me who she was."

"No one, really."

She backed off. They rode along in silence, trying to find a place for these events in the mythology of their relationship. Near Portland, when Harvey turned off onto Route 302 and headed west, Mickey said, "Where the hell you going? You stay on this to go to Bar Harbor."

"I need to scratch an itch."

"What're you talking about?"

"Peplow had a summer house on Sebago Lake. I want to see what it's like."

"C'mon, Bliss."

"Just for a minute."

"The case is over. Done. It's Miller Time."

"I didn't plan this, Mick. Really. It's just it occurred to me a few miles back that in his case file it said he had a place up here. I'd like to see how the guy lived. His rental in Coleridge had been cleaned out by the time I arrived on the scene."

"We're on vacation."

"Indulge me."

"Okay, you're the one driving," she said with a sigh, taking *The New York Times* Metro section off the seat and snapping it open.

After a mile or two he said, "Are we okay?"

She didn't bother to look up from the paper. "About what?"

"You know."

"You mean, have we had our little fun?"

"Something like that," he said.

"Well, are you okay with it?"

"I think so."

"There isn't any more that you want to tell me about it?"

"Naw. I don't think so. You want to tell me any more about Paul Sarnes?"

"No. It was what it was," she said. "It was just a little thing out of time."

After another mile he said, "So we'll call it a draw?"

She smiled. "Yeah, all right. Sure. If we have to call it something."

"But we're okay?"

"Yeah, I guess we're going to be okay," she said.

Harvey felt a surge of sadness. They had traded confessions, but its effect was as if they had agreed, from now on, to keep secrets, to rope off an area. His guess was that her executive producer had touched her feelings in ways she had no desire to comment on, any more than he could convey to Mickey the strange, lost excitement that Marilyn Barger represented. But if they were no longer completely and passionately sufficient for each other, he could tell, just by the way

Mickey was now briskly pulling an emery board across her fingernails and the pleasure it gave him to have her there doing it, that for each other they remained necessary.

In the lakeside town of Raymond, Harvey went into a store that sold a little bit of everything, and the woman behind the counter handed him the thin local phone book and he looked up Laurence Peplow. Sure enough, there was a listing for him on Long Needle Road. Ten minutes later they pulled onto a dirt road that ran down under crowded pines to an inlet. In front of the last cabin on the left, a For Sale sign with the name and phone number of a local Realtor on it was stuck into the ground. Harvey drove the car up close to the house and turned off the engine. Nailed to the shingled cottage was a wood plaque with the name Peplow burned into it.

"What're you going to do?" Mickey said.

Harvey opened the car door. "Look around."

"You're trespassing, you know."

Harvey started to get out.

"Come here," Mickey said.

"What?"

She pulled him toward her by the arm and gave him a big kiss on the mouth.

"I could start to like you again," he said.

"Don't be long," she replied, and for the first time in months he felt that he was part of something that would always be there.

The front door was locked, but the screen door to the porch, warped from moisture, yielded to a soft kick, and soon he stood on a rag rug in the cabin's living area. The musty smell lodged in his nostrils. The room was filled with a jumble of yard-sale furniture. On the painted pine dining table was a yellowing Portland paper from the previous September. Fishing rods and bamboo poles leaned against the wall in a corner. A tackle box sat on the spindle-legged table next to the window over which a makeshift curtain of plain brown material had been tacked directly onto the wall.

Harvey walked across the room, past the alcove kitchen with its sagging shelves of mismatched coffee mugs, and looked into one of the bedrooms, then the other. The first was empty except for two single beds covered in pale green chenille and a nightstand between them. The other bedroom had touches of homeyness, a feel of former occupancy. It contained a double bed with a white wicker headboard and an Adirondack chair over which a red Hudson Bay blanket was carefully folded. On the wall next to the bed, in flimsy dimestore frames, were two photographs of outdoor scenes and a cheap reproduction of a Winslow Homer watercolor.

Only when Harvey came into the room and turned around did he see the photograph on the wall opposite the bed, of Peplow and another man posed side-by-side on a dock, both of them holding huge pikes aloft. Peplow, bareheaded, smiled heartily into the camera. The other man had turned his head slightly to admire his catch. Beneath the floppy fishing hat, it was indisputably Walls. Shrinks on vacation. He thought of something Bellaggio had once told him: *The design is always larger than you think.*

Beneath the photograph stood a narrow oak dresser with a bad varnish job. He tugged open a middle drawer to find half a dozen chamois and flannel men's shirts in solid colors and two pairs of worn corduroy trousers. Peplow's. He couldn't bring himself to touch them. In the drawer below was a folded electric blanket. In the one above, four heavy pullovers and a torn Bowdoin College hooded sweatshirt, its silkscreened letters cracked with age.

Harvey opened the top drawer and saw a neat pile of boxer shorts, a collection of balled-up woolen socks, and a fishing license. When Harvey picked up the fishing license to examine it, he glimpsed an assortment of clear plastic bags at the back of the drawer, each filled with what looked like a rag or a handkerchief. He reached in and pulled the bags out of the drawer's shadows and into the light.

In each of the plastic sandwich bags was a pair of women's panties, most of them white and off-white, with a few pale yellows and blues, and one tiger print. More than a couple were trimmed with lace. And each of them was identified like a specimen with a small adhesive label stuck to the upper left-hand corner of the bag. But the labels bore not the names of the specimens within, but the names of their owners.

"Phelps, E." read one bag. Another, "Steinmetz, S." "Chenier, R." read the third.

And here was a pair of simple cotton panties, of the palest blue, labeled "Johnson, J."

He cleaned off the bags with the tail of his shirt and carefully replaced them in the dresser drawer behind the expired fishing license, and then he dusted all the places in the room that he had touched. He wanted everything to look undisturbed when he called Dombrowski and Dombrowski called the local sheriff to say he had a tip that in a dresser drawer in a Sebago Lake cabin there was some evidence pertaining to a murder case in his jurisdiction in Illinois, evidence that might also criminally implicate a prominent Portland psychiatrist.

A discreet honk of the Honda's horn brought Harvey to the bedroom window. Through the pine trees he saw Mickey look impatiently in his direction before getting out of the Honda and arching her back in the dappled sunlight. She walked around in front of the car, reached down, and picked up a handful of small pinecones. Then she began firing them one after another toward the lake with that fluid, mechanically correct throwing motion her father had taught her as a little girl.

When she saw Harvey coming toward her, she turned without a word and threw him a perfect strike.